Sight
UNSEEN

Sight UNSEEN

Kasha Thompson

WEBSTER AVENUE PUBLISHING
LINCOLN, CA

CONTENT NOTES

Please note Sight Unseen discusses topics which could potentially trigger certain audiences. Some readers may consider the following as spoilers.

- Moderate coarse language
- Sexually explicit scenes
- Foster care
- Domestic Violence, NOT depicted in page.
- Anxiety/panic attacks

CHAPTER 1

QUINCY

Assessing myself in the mirror, my mouth turned into a sour line. "Maybe I should've worn the navy suit. What if she hates hunter green?"

"Quincy, you look great. She'll probably be too nervous to care about your suit color." Walter Kemp, my best friend, reassured me.

"Fuck, what's taking so long?" I glanced at the clock on the wall, then to my watch to confirm the time hadn't changed since the last time I checked twenty seconds ago. "I just wanna get this over with and get to the drinking and dancing part. Emphasis on the drinking." Absentmindedly, I fidgeted with the bow of my tie, re-adjusting the edges to ensure symmetry.

Walt clapped my back giving my shoulder a quick kneading. "Thirty minutes until showtime, buddy."

Turning away from the mirror, I stared Walt dead in the face. "Am I crazy? This is crazy."

Walt bobbed his shoulders. "Oh yeah, marrying someone you've never met is deranged."

Taking inventory of the scene before me, I feared Walt was right. The suite was spacious but with my three groomsmen, the production team consisting of the, camera operator, audio support tech, producer, production assistant and a bunch of other crew members, there was hardly room to turn around let alone have a mini freakout with hyperventilating and hand-wringing.

"Try not to look at the camera." The production assistant instructed.

Two months ago, I'd gone to a casting call for a reality show on a whim. AJ, my college roommate, thought it would be fun to try out for a relationship reality show that, if picked, came with a walk down the aisle. That was my first mistake, because AJ often had bad ideas that got me in trouble. To my surprise, I was selected and was now standing in a hotel suite in downtown Chicago waiting to meet my future wife.

"I think I'm gonna throw up," I said, placing my hand over my stomach, bending at the waist. My brow was beaded with sweat and the burrito I'd scarfed down at lunch was pressing on the walls of my abdomen looking for a way out. *Who eats a cheese and bean burrito on their wedding day?*

"No, you're not, you're good." With a stiff pat on the back, Walt helped me straighten up.

I paced the small patch of carpet that wasn't occupied by furniture or filming equipment. "What if I don't like her? What kind of pathetic loser goes on a reality show looking for love?"

Walt spun me around so I was once again facing the mirror.

"I went as a joke. I never expected to get picked."

"But you didn't say no." AJ chimed in.

He was right I didn't decline. Don't get me wrong, I thought about it, weighing the pros and cons. Ultimately, I was tired of playing it safe. I never took risks. I was the guy who hung back when all of my friends jumped off a cliff into the murky waters below on our guys' trip to Bali. They teased me mercilessly and when I think back on that vacation, all I remember is I was a bitch baby too scared to take a chance.

"I was curious. Someone says they've found your soulmate, wouldn't your interest be piqued?"

The show was called *Why Knot*, a name I made fun of every chance I got during the audition process. After a series of interviews and questionnaires longer than my bar exam, I received a visit from one of the four experts informing me they'd found a match. Truth be told, I was 95 percent sure this was all total bullshit. But that 5 percent and the comprehensive pros and cons list I'd drafted convinced me otherwise.

There was a light knock on the hotel door followed by the appearance of a petite, mousy brunette who couldn't have been two years out of high school. "Happy wedding day, this gift is from your future bride to be." The brunette thrust forward an expertly wrapped box.

Thanking the woman, I set the gift on the square dining table. My groomsmen gathered round in excited anticipation. Pulling out his camera. Walt started taking pictures.

"What are you doing?" I asked.

"Memorializing the moment. This is your first gift ever from the future Mrs. Parrish."

I wrinkled my nose in doubt, the shows tagline was From Hello to Happily Ever After. Every time I heard the words *happily ever after* it made me want to gag, I didn't believe in that kind of shit. People who claimed to be in love never got what they wanted, they didn't even get what they deserved. Nine times out of ten, someone who says they're in love is with a person they settled for, Mrs. Good Enough, Mr. Right For Now.

"Well, are you gonna open it or what?" AJ asked.

Tearing away at the wrapping paper with shaky hands, I removed the lid from the box. Inside was a leather-bound flask engraved with my initials and a bottle of Maker's Mark.

My friends let out *oohs* and *ahhs*, like women at a baby shower when the expectant mother is opening gifts.

"Shit she ain't even met you and she already has your number," Walt said with a laugh.

"Don't forget to read the card." Carol, the production assistant reminded me.

Opening the card, it read:

Dear Future Husband,
Not gonna lie, it feels hella weird writing those words. I decided on the flask and liquor because if you're anything like me, your hands are probably shaking and your knees are weak. A little hair of the dog should fix you right up. Can't wait to meet you. Hope

you don't regret it. Your ride or die. And by "die," I mean of laughter or sexual exhaustion. Or both.

XOXO

Wifey McWiferton

"Oh, I like her," Riley, my final groomsmen shouted with a thunderous hand clap.

"Shall we?" I broke the seal on the bottle of bourbon whiskey.

Her note had my attention. This mystery woman seemed funny and easygoing. This helped to lower my shoulders, which were hovering near my ears. The gift itself was thoughtful and something I could use for years to come. We could bring the flask to concerts or sporting events and sneak sips during innings.

In the past few weeks, I'd found myself playing out fake scenarios with the future Mrs. Parrish. What it would be like to shop for groceries or go on a date night. And don't get me started on sex. I'd had sex with this imaginary woman in every conceivable position.

I was barely able to focus this past week, bracing myself for the worst possible outcome. As long as she wasn't one of those overly cheerful types, we should be fine. Please don't let her be one of those women who wore shirts that said "Sips Getting Real" or "I Tend to Wine a Lot." Hopefully the comprehensive screening indicated I wasn't compatible with the live, laugh, love type.

Pouring a bit of liquor in each man's cup, Walt made a

toast. "To our friend Quincy, the man who ran through practically every woman in Chicago and the surrounding areas, so he had to turn to a reality show to find someone who was willing to jump the broom with him."

"To Q," my two other groomsmen said in unison.

"Very funny," I said, tossing back my glass.

OUTSIDE THE HOTEL ballroom where the ceremony would take place, I paced back and forth. Pulling up my vows on my phone, I read them through for the millionth time. Wifey McWiferton was right, while I was still nervous the alcohol helped to level me out a bit. There was a hum of activity all around me with multiple cameras and bright lights blinding my view. Crew members with earpieces power walked through my holding area before disappearing behind closed doors.

The *Why Knot* stylist accosted me mid stride, giving me a final once-over, retying my shoes and fussing with the hem of my pants. I normally shied away from the spotlight, perfectly content with keeping a low profile. All that changed when I signed on to this show. In a few short months, millions of people would watch me take the biggest risk of my life.

"Alright Quincy, it's time to make your entrance," Carol informed me.

Straightening my bow tie, I squared my shoulders and smoothed down my beard. Walt and the others lined up outside of the door leading to the ceremony site, with me bringing up the rear.

"Spit." Walt instructed.

My face contorted into a scowl.

"Your gum, spit."

Spitting the minty fresh gum into the napkin Walt was holding, I gave my friend a good-looking-out nod.

"You ready?"

"Nope." A nervous chuckle sputtered its way out.

"Well fix your mug, cause it's time to woo the family," Walt said, before facing forward.

The double doors to the ballroom opened and I took a long, deep breath, muttering obscenities as we moved forward. Entering the room, I found my family and friends on the right side smiling at me. Across the aisle were another group of people, their eyes wide and necks craning as they attempted to get a good look. The bride's family was filled with mostly Black faces, so it was safe to assume my bride was also Black.

During the interview process I'd said I was open to marrying any race, but in this moment I took comfort in the fact my bride and I would have shared experiences. It made being strangers a little less strange. I was an equal-opportunity lover but it did get a little old having to explain my blackness, the definition of what made me who I was, to others outside of my race.

After making my way to the front of the intimate ballroom, filled with mostly guests of the bride, I gazed up at the ceiling decorated with dangling, rustic lanterns and sent up a quick prayer to the big guy. What was I praying for? Everything ... all the things. *God, I know I only call on you when I'm in a pinch. And that's crappy of me. I promise to work on that. That being said, if you could do me a solid and sprinkle a blessing over this union that would be great. Amen. Oh, and please don't let her be a buttaface. Good looking out. Amen.*

With that out of the way, I was able to take in the ceremony space. Like most men, the look and feel of my wedding day wasn't something I'd considered. If you'd asked me a month ago what my dream wedding entailed, I would have mentioned the open bar and bomb ass DJ. But this space made the minimalist in me smile. Flowers in clear vases lined the aisle, that was the extent of the decorations because the ballroom itself was doing the heavy lifting in the ambiance department.

Behind me were a bank of floor-to-ceiling windows with sheer-white curtains. On opposite sides of the room were asymmetrical features made of real grass, which the hotel magazine in the suite called a living-green space. The same detail adorned the altar and a floral arrangement of bright flowers was the final touch.

A teary-eyed face in the front row caught my attention. Advancing forward I bent down, grabbing her hands. "Are you crying?" I asked my foster mother, Naomi.

"No," she lied, running a crumpled Kleenex across her nose.

"We promised no crying."

"I'm allowed, it's your wedding day."

"Happy tears?" I asked, with a tilt of my head. I needed Naomi to be on board because as the clock ticked closer to my I do's, my feet were screaming I don't, ready to move to the nearest exit.

"Mostly." Leaning in, she whispered, "When she walks down the aisle, if you're not feeling it don't do it."

"I'm kind of contractually obligated," I whispered back, giving her hand a reassuring squeeze.

The *Why Knot* legal team presented me tons of paperwork to sign. As a lawyer, I advise my clients to never sign anything they hadn't read. After a thorough review, I determined the contract and liability waivers were comprehensive with one overarching theme, covering the network and producers' asses. One of the documents I signed stated I agreed to enter into a legally binding union with a complete stranger. If I broke that agreement and turned into a runaway groom, the show could come after me financially for breach of contract.

Standing, I glanced over at the bride's side of the room, many who were pointing in my direction while speaking in hushed tones. What was the protocol when the family of the stranger you were about to marry were a stone's throw away? Rounding my shoulders, I walked over to the front row and addressed the group.

"Hello, my name's Quincy and if you haven't guessed by now I'm the groom. Just wanted to introduce myself since we're all about to be family."

"How tall are you?" a freckle-faced woman asked.

"Um, I'm six foot two."

The woman pointed at me. "OK we can work with that."

The attendees in the room chuckled.

"Is the mother of the bride in attendance?" I asked.

Hands pointed to a regal woman sitting cross legged directly in front of me.

"It's really nice to meet you ma'am." I found myself bending at the waist as if I was addressing the queen. But the woman seated before me elicited that type of response. When people talked about matriarchs of families this is what they meant.

"Let me ask you something ... Quincy, is it?" Her voice was dripping with a British accent, and I couldn't decide whether it was real or an affect.

"Yes ma'am."

"Do you understand how serious marriage is?"

"Yes ma'am, I do." Her tone made it clear that she wasn't at all impressed by this joyous occasion.

"Marriage isn't a joke. And it would appear you and my daughter are looking to make a mockery out of the institution." She pursed her lips, her almond-shaped eyes scanning my tapered fade and landing on my brown leather dress shoes.

"Not my intention at all. Just looking for my soulmate." I almost choked on the last word. But I couldn't very well tell my soon to be mother-in-law I didn't know what the fuck I was doing and strongly doubted this little experiment would work.

"Momma, please don't. It's a special day."

My eyes traveled to the woman who'd spoken up; she had to be in her early twenties. She was attractive, so if her sister, the bride looked anything like her I was in good shape. Truthfully my future mother-in-law was also kind of hot in a Mrs. Robertson type of way. *Did I just admit I was attracted to my mother-in-law?* I shook my head trying to release the thought.

"I hope to meet you all at the reception." Plastering a huge smile on my face, I retreated to the altar.

Whispering to Walt, I said, "I think that went well."

"It did not," Walt whispered back.

The doors of the ballroom swung open causing my heart to dry up in my chest, but it was just Carol, one of the production assistants for the show. With a raised voice that silenced the murmurs in the room she called out, "OK, it's showtime people, the bride is on her way down."

Walt placed his hand on my shoulder. "Any last words?"

"None I can share in mixed company."

CHAPTER 2

EVELYN

In the elevator on the way to the ballroom, my knees grew hollow and I feared my legs wouldn't support my weight. I clutched my father's arm which, aside for the boning in the champagne-hued wedding dress, was the only thing holding me up. With my free hand, I fondled the heart-shaped necklace my fiancé gifted me. *Am I allowed to use that term when I don't even know the guy?* The necklace was classic and simple, two hearts entwined, the bigger heart covered in diamonds, it was the perfect gift. It also didn't hurt it came in a light blue box which made my bridesmaids shout out "Okaaay" and shimmy with excitement. One point for the hubby to be.

The elevator stopped on the first floor and my bridal party and the ever-present camera crew filed out.

"OK, we're just going to hang out here for a bit." Jared, my assigned handler, informed me.

With a nod, I turned to the wall sconces in an attempt to distract myself from the mind soup swirling around in my head. Three months ago, I was just a regular shmegular girl living off the kindness of strangers. And by strangers I meant the patrons who valued my art work enough to put their money where their mouth was. My art and the small accompanying gallery were hip and edgy enough that the thirty somethings in Wicker Park took notice, but still authentic which kept the attention of my real audience, my Black and Brown brothers and sisters.

"Are you breathing?" Meryl Goode, my maid of honor, asked.

"Yes, barely but yes."

"This is the hard part. Once the I dos are over you can unclench that jaw."

"This is true, unless my husband is ugly, or rude, or a total wet blanket."

"Which is worse?" Meryl laughed.

"Ugly I can handle. I think we can both agree I've dated an eclectic group of men."

"Oh, is that what we're calling them." She wrinkled her nose.

I ignored her playful jab. "If this dude doesn't have any personality it's gonna be a hard no from me dawg."

"OK I'm gonna need less Randy Jackson and more Paula Abdul. You promised you'd be optimistic."

Meryl was correct, and I'd been super optimistic up until this moment. I'd always been a bit of a free spirit and believed in the possibility of loving someone over a span of many lifetimes. Love was complex and even when you knew someone for years you were still learning new facts about them with growth and evolution. That's why love sight unseen wasn't a difficult sell for me.

I was more than OK with learning to love a stranger because honestly that's what all relationships were about. Everyone you've ever met was a stranger at one point until they weren't. But I was gonna love out loud, deeply, and fully no matter the origin story. Tomorrow was never promised, so why let fear stop you from embracing all life had to offer even if that something was for a limited time only?

Even with my just-do-it attitude I was still spinning like a top. "What if he has bad breath, or hated reading books preferring to wait for the movie? Or pronounces salmon as sal-men—"

"What if he's perfect?" Meryl countered.

"Perfect doesn't exist," I cautioned her. *But what if he's perfect for me?* This thought was more concerning than all the others.

"Any guy who gifts a diamond necklace with a cute note has to be a winner." Meryl tapped me on the arm walking away.

My hand brushed the new piece of jewelry around my neck. Pulling his note from the pocket in my dress, I read it again.

Wifey To Be:
What the fuck are you doing? Who marries a complete stranger? I don't know if I should be relieved or concerned they found someone as crazy as I am. I hope you like the necklace. It's a little cliche I know, but it represents

us giving our hearts to one another. Are you laughing at me? Because I'm laughing at me. The sappy shit isn't exactly my forte. I'm more of the strong, silent type. Anyway, meet you at the altar. I'll be the one smiling like an idiot.

PS You look fucking beautiful.

The man, the myth, the legend.

Seeing his words on the notecard made my heart race, just like in the hotel suite the first time I read it through. If he was half the man in this note, this could work.

Jared clapped his hands. "It's time to head to the ceremony site. Let's hustle people."

Hooking my arm into my father's, my mini entourage lined up in front of the double doors leading to the ballroom. Behind those doors was my husband to be and my new family. *What if his mother didn't like me? What if I didn't like her?* This just wasn't about me and a mystery dude. We were merging our lives. I just prayed his family was the cookout, uncles in leather sandals at the grill, Frankie Beverly and Maze line dancing type, and not the bougie dinner, showboating type who barely tapped their foot when my namesake, Evelyn Champagne came on.

"Well, looks like we are at the endgame pumpkin," my father said.

"Looks like it."

"Remember, you're the prize. This knucklehead behind

these doors better understand that or I'll slap some sense into him."

"Let's try not to threaten the groom before you meet him." I patted my father's arm.

"You just say the word and we will hightail it out of here. I'll text your mother and have her meet us at Morton's for a nice steak dinner."

"Tempting but no."

Jared fussed with the train of my dress and adjusted my veil. "You sure you don't want to cover your face to add to the element of surprise?" he suggested.

"No, I'm surprise enough."

I hummed "Chapel of Love" by The Dixie Cups under my breath, which was stuck in my head because Meryl added the song to the wedding-day playlist, and I'd listened to the tune at least four times over the course of the past few hours. At that one part my bridesmaids all yelled "Gonna get married." Causing all the ladies to laugh uncontrollably which helped to calm my nerves.

"It's go time." An unfamiliar voice said over Jared's walkie talkie.

That voice acting like a windup key because Jared flared his arms screaming. "It's go time people. This is not a drill. Let's get these two married."

The makeup lady dabbed at the sweat dotting my fore-head and upper lip. Jared made his way toward the doors leading to the ceremony site. His shrewd eye inspecting the bridal party one last time. He positioned himself opposite another fellow who was already standing at the ready on the other side of the double doors.

"Good luck Evelyn." Jared called loudly.

As the doors slowly swung open, I hoisted my neck hoping to get a glimpse at the groom. But I couldn't see anything past the bridesmaids, just a shit ton of hair and flower arrangements.

With a steadying breath, I accepted that this was finally happening. Since the *Why Knot* crew informed me I'd been selected for the show all I could think about was this moment, finding it hard to think of anything else.

I was doing my best to keep my expectations low. Butterflies weren't required, it was perfectly normal if there wasn't an immediate attraction. Love at first sight was overrated. You can't truly love someone you don't know, no matter how fast your pulse raced, or your lady parts throbbed. I wasn't looking for insta-love. If this guy had good energy we could work toward the rest. He didn't have to look like Daniel Kaluuya, although if he did it would greatly help.

As Norine, the first bridesmaid started to walk, my father yelled out. "Is he ugly?"

"Daddy please." I said, swatting at him in disapproval.

The guest inside roared with laughter.

CHAPTER 3

QUINCY

I rubbed my palms together as each bridesmaid made her way down the aisle, each one prettier than the next.

"That's a good sign, she rolls with a crew of bad bitches." Walt said.

"Maybe, it could also mean she's the ugly friend." I whispered back.

As the bridesmaids caught sight of me their faces lit up one by one. Each scanning the length of my body, sizing me up. When the last bridesmaid entered the room, the doors closed abruptly behind her. This woman must be the maid of honor, which meant she was the bride's best friend. I straightened my back flashing a smile, it was important I made a good first impression.

The petite woman stopped at the center of the altar, turning to the crowd and said loudly. "I'm not mad at it."

Another one of the bridesmaids called out, "That's the one right there."

Holding out her hand, the maid of honor introduced herself. "I'm Meryl, the bride's best friend."

"Nice to meet you. I'm Quincy."

"Prepare to be sick of me because I don't play when it comes to my friend."

"Noted."

Meryl took her place in front of the other women.

Carol's voice croaked. "Please stand for the bride."

The crowd rustled to their feet as the doors opened one last time. My eyes tightened at the corners, I could see a woman at the entrance with a man I assumed was her father. Unfortunately, she was still too far away to make out any of her features. The bride and her escort walked slowly down the aisle, at about the halfway mark she finally came into focus.

When I caught sight of her I did a double take, certain this was another one of the many dreams I'd had since being selected. My dreams always varied, sometimes the bride was drop dead gorgeous like today. Other times she was, fugly, or a WWE wrestler, or the curvy female rapper with the colorful hair. I'd enjoyed that particular dream.

Back in the present, my heart was an offbeat rhythm of pitter patters as it sunk in that this beautiful goddess was here for me. This had to be a prank thrown in for dramatic effect by the *Why Knot* crew, there was no way this woman had agreed to marry a total stranger. Women like this did not need a dating show to land a husband. She was breathtaking, surely she could pull any brother with the snap of her fingers making them her willing concubine for life.

A wide smile pulled at the corners of her mouth, exposing a rack of perfectly aligned teeth. Her skin was flawless and rich. It reminded me of the deep-red rock structures in Sedona, Arizona where my law firm had an office. When I'd visited four months ago, I went for a hike and marveled at the vibrant colors and beauty all around me. Any future visits would now remind me of her majestic beauty.

My eyes worked overtime trying to take her all in, pinging from one interesting feature to the next. This woman was solid; she had to be five foot seven or five foot eight, the muscles in her arms were well defined. Because her dress was puffy, I couldn't make out much else, but I liked what I could see. She seemed like the type of woman who could take a back shot and not crumble. *Was it wrong for me to think about having sex with my future wife before the ceremony even started?* When she stopped in front of me at the altar, I was still in disbelief, smiling like an idiot just like my note had predicted.

The man who was still holding her arm started talking which forced me to reluctantly pull my eyes from the most beautiful woman I'd ever laid eyes on.

"This is my daughter. She is very loved and important to us. I was born and raised in Chicago. Don't let this suit fool you. If you play games with my daughter or break her heart in any way, I'ma be all over ya ass."

My eyes took up my whole face, having no doubt her father was a man of his word.

"Dad, we talked about the threats ... remember?"

"Not a threat, it's a promise."

She flashed an apologetic expression in my direction. Releasing her hand, her father went to join her mother in the front row.

Fixing my attention back on the bride, I smiled bright.

"Please be seated," the officiant said. With black book in hand, the officiant began the unconventional ceremony. "Quincy Parrish meet Evelyn Townsend."

"Hi Evelyn, it's nice to finally meet you."

"You too, Quincy." Evelyn let out a nervous chuckle before biting her lip.

I rolled her name around in my head in an attempt to lock it in. Evelyn was a good name; I could call her "E" or Lyn for short. Extending my hand so we could shake, I waited with an anxious smile for my stunning bride to return the gesture. When her soft hand touched mine, I felt a spark. An actual spark from static that most likely collected in her body as she walked down the aisle. Pulling her hand away, she gasped.

"The sparks are already flying." Naomi joked aloud.

As the guests laughed, I leaned in and said, "You look amazing. Like ten outta ten, pinching myself gorgeous, oh my God amazing."

Once again, a smile pulled at her full lips exposing her pearly whites and in that moment, I made the decision to become the next Kevin Hart so I could witness that smile on her face every single day.

"You don't look too bad yourself." Her eyes dropped from my face to my suit. "Hunter green is a bold choice."

Screwing up my face I asked, "Do you hate it?"

"No, I love it. You look dapper. I like a man not afraid to make bold choices." She placed a hand on my arm giving it a squeeze.

Was my future wife flirting with me? I could see a mischievous slant in her big, mink eyes.

The officiant addressed the crowd. "Today is about faith

Believing in something you cannot see. Trusting in someone you do not know."

"Do you wanna hold hands?" I whispered, immediately wondering what was wrong with me.

This woman was intoxicating, and I wanted to feel her skin against mine. Right now, holding hands was the only option. Stepping back, she handed her bouquet of flowers to her maid of honor before slipping her hands into mine. As the officiant spoke to the crowd, all I could focus on was Evelyn's thumb stroking my left hand. Her hands were soft and fit perfectly into mine. I suppressed a laugh when I remembered how nervous I'd been the past few days. If I knew this was who would be meeting me at the end of the aisle, I wouldn't have lost a wink of sleep.

"Quincy and Evelyn have written their own vows. At this time they will share those vows with one another." The officiant rested his eyes on Evelyn.

"Oh, am I up first? OK."

She dropped my hands causing my lower lip to bend into a pout. Reaching into her ample bosom, she pulled out a slip of paper unfolding it with her perfectly manicured fingers.

"This is funny because my notes say 'Insert name here,' obviously when I wrote these vows I had no clue who you were but I had hopes. So ... Quincy I hope ..." Pausing she inhaled a shuddery breath.

"It's OK, take your time baby." A woman with a round, painted face called from the left side of the aisle.

Clearing her throat Evelyn continued, "I hope we laugh with each other. I hope you can dance so we can speak without words. I hope you teach me new things and hopefully I can also show you a thing or two." Dropping her eyes from her notes she added, "I hope you continue to look at me the exact same way you're looking at me right now." Back on script she continued, "I hope the days are short, but the nights are long. I hope you know I have no ulterior motives. There is no plan B just this, just us."

This time when she smiled it seemed cautious. Like the fact she was entrusting me with her heart was just sinking in.

"And now Quincy will share his vows."

Scratching the back of my neck, I reached for my cell phone. I'd written my vows in iNotes. "I wrote some vows but now standing in front of you I don't wanna say any of that." Dropping my phone back in my pocket, I continued, "These vows were written to some imaginary dream girl. But now that you're here standing in front of me, I've realized two things. I need to dream bigger, because you're just ..." I blew out a breath of air pointing my hands in her direction. "And two I probably should have taken this a little more seriously. I will never underestimate you again. I'm a fast learner and you won't ever have to tell me stuff twice.

"So I guess what I want to say is thank you. Thank you for taking a chance on me. Thank you for entering this union with an open heart and mind. I'm excited to get to know you and to share myself with you." Letting out a nervous chuckle I observed the crowd. "Maybe I should have just stuck to the script and read my vows." I felt like a novice act at the Apollo who was about to be escorted off the stage by the Sandman.

"No, you're doing fine." She reached for my hand, giving it a reassuring squeeze. I appreciated the gesture but her touch was causing heat to pump into my muscles.

"I vow that I'm gonna try. Even when it's hard, even

when I'm scared." That last part I whispered so only she could hear.

The way this woman's doe-like eyes danced across my face, I struggled to decipher what lied behind her gaze. As I reached for her other hand, the officiant continued talking about the sanctity of marriage. Which made me snicker behind closed lips. At a ceremony in which two strangers are getting hitched, it was probably best to leave out the parts about sacred bonds and the fact that marriage should not be entered into lightly.

"Now we will exchange the rings."

Walt wasted no time pulling the skinny, diamond band from his breast pocket. I didn't know Evelyn's style aesthetic, but felt safe in picking a simple, diamond band.

"Quincy, please repeat after me ..."

As the words passed from the officiant's lips, pebbles of sweat coasted down my spine. Yes, I was on a television show but this ... what I was about to do was very real and legally binding. I wasn't hard up for women, at thirty-five, with no kids, a rewarding career, and a home, I was a fucking catch. *So why did I suffer through weeks of probing personal questions, psych evaluations and background checks?* I'd experienced several, long-term relationships with one actually lasting close to four years. Finding a woman wasn't the problem. Keeping the woman once I found her had always proven more difficult. Even my longest relationship teetered on the edge of collapse most days.

Inhaling a big dollop of courage, I repeated the officiant's words while sliding the band on Evelyn's naked ring finger. "Let this ring serve as a reminder that I will love, encourage, and uplift you, in all times, in all places, and in all ways, for all my days."

Evelyn's eyes grew wide, as if she was shocked I'd actually gone through with it. *Was she having doubts?* Were all the hopes she spoke about earlier looking less like a possibility now, standing in front of me under these hot, blinding lights?

She was directed to repeat the same words. Fidgeting with the matte-black band, she positioned the ring between her fingers reaching for my hand. "Let this ring serve as a reminder that I will love, encourage, and uplift you, in all times, in all places, and in all ways, for all my days."

While the officiant closed out the ceremony with some final words, I leaned in asking my wife. "Are we gonna kiss? Give each other daps, crip walk it out? What do you wanna do?"

She didn't hesitate to give my words any consideration. "Let's kiss. All in, right?"

"All in," I echoed, sizing up her mouth.

"It is with great happiness I introduce you all to Mr. and Mrs. Parrish."

Air escaped my lungs hearing my last name in association with hers. One day ago I had no obligations, only answering to myself. Shit one hour ago I was free to do what the fuck I wanted, whenever the fuck I wanted. In the span of fifteen minutes my entire life changed. This woman standing across from me with expectant eyes was now under my umbrella of responsibility. Her happiness, security, and well-being all dependent on me.

"Quincy you may kiss your bride."

All eyes were on us, the newly married pair, as I angled for the first kiss. In one swift motion I placed one hand respectfully on her waist with the other hand cupping the left side of her face. Her skin underneath the palm of my hand sent a tingling sensation shooting down my spine. Leaning in closer, her breast rose and fell in anticipation. Her lips seemed magnetic pulling me to her with invisible sparks firing within the almost nonexistent space between our lips. When my mouth touched down onto hers, goosebumps pebbled the back of my neck. My thumb absentmindedly caressed her cheek. Evelyn moved closer, parting her lips inviting me inside.

Our tongues danced against one another, a distant cough reminding me we were not alone, I abruptly pulled away. I took a step back, fearful my hands would reverse the decision my head just made. Evelyn had not taken her eyes off of me since our lips parted. *Was she disappointed? Was she ranking our kiss among the all-time worst kisses?* Because I couldn't fairly be judged based on that one kiss alone, in front of a room in which half of the people were strangers to me including her. And don't get me started about the presence of the production crew.

A broom was placed in front of our feet. "That's right, it ain't official until they jump the broom." Someone in the crowd yelled.

Evelyn interlaced her fingers with mine, assuaging most of my fears. With a big smile, we took the leap.

Chapter 4

EVELYN

Jared led us to a private holding room, as private as one could get with an entire production crew in tow. I twisted the diamond wedding band on my finger. *What the fuck did I just do?*

"Do you want some champagne?" Quincy pointed to a table with champagne and a charcuterie board of assorted meats, fruits, and cheeses.

"Yes." I dropped my shoulders, willing myself to relax. At the table my new husband expertly opened the champagne bottle. "Wow, where did you learn to do that?"

"Open a champagne bottle?"

"Yeah, every time I try the cork ends up ricocheting off surfaces. Including somebody's face one time." I cringed, remembering him screaming in pain. Wanna talk about a mood killer.

"Note to self, don't let my wife open bottles with corks."

Heat whooshed up my neck at the sound of the word "wife" from the lips of this very attractive man.

Handing me a glass, he said, "Shall we toast?"

"Sure."

"Umm ... OK ... here's to hoping this works." He looked down at me, his face serious.

"Cheers." Note to self, my groom sucked at making toast. Clinking my flute into his, I tossed back the entire glass of bubbly.

His eyes shot wide open. "Damn, do you want another one?"

"Just a little bit more. That's good." I stopped him when my glass was halfway full. This time I took small sips for fear he'd think I had a drinking problem. As hard as I tried, I couldn't pull my eyes away from him. He had big, curious eyes and that beautiful, distinct wide nose. His bottom lip was full and suckable and I already liked the feel of his strong hand holding mine. Then there was his full beard. A beard I couldn't wait to get sticky and wet.

"I'm not gonna lie this is awkward as fuck," he said, nicking a piece of cheese from the board.

"It doesn't have to be if we don't make it," I said, hoping my words would release some of my nervous energy along with his.

"You know what you're right. We should do what any other newly married couple would do." His face lit up, grabbing a grape, he said. "Open your mouth."

"What?"

"I was gonna feed you a grape."

"Negro ... awkward." I scrunched my face tilting my head to the side.

Tossing the grape in his mouth, he nodded his head in agreement. Quincy wrung his hands, he seemed painfully aware of the cameras just a stone's throw away. "You're wearing the fuck out of that dress."

"Thank you." I struck a few poses like I was an inmate in lock up.

"Don't forget the side pose with your arms crossed." Quincy directed.

"No, I don't wanna forget that." I crossed my arms over my chest hoisting my chin high. "I just gotta do this little bid. Five to ten and then I'll be out." Dropping my voice several octaves, I curled my lip.

"Don't worry dawg. We'll hold you down on the outside. Take care of your kids and old lady."

"Don't forget to put money on my books, cuz."

"I got you E.T." Quincy clasped his hands.

The smile faded from my face. "Did you just call me E.T.?"

"Yeah, for Evelyn Townsend."

"OK, let's not make that a thing." A sharp no swept my head left and right.

"Fine, what do your people call you then?"

"Evie, my friends call me Evie."

Nodding thoughtfully, he tried my name on for size. "Hey Evie, where you at? Yes, Evie of course I'll make your favorite meal ... no need to beg."

My eyebrows inched upward as I pondered on the things I was willing to beg him to do. When it came to physical appearance Quincy wasn't exactly my type. Truthfully, he was better than my type. My type was bohemian, a brother who was free thinking, spiritual and smelled carefree like daily showering was optional. Don't fucking judge me. Have you ever made love to a slightly funky man? I guarantee you the sex is different ... raw.

Unfortunately, most of those men were rolling stones who stimulated my body and mind but offered little to no stability. Quincy on the other hand was a man that probably showered twice a day. He was well groomed and smelled like sage and bergamot. He was classic all-American fine, a man that everyone could universally agree was handsome. It was also very probable that he had a job that paid him consistently on the first and fifteenth.

"I'm assuming your nickname is Q?"

"Yeah, pretty much. Sometimes people call me Quin." I couldn't explain why but my insides trembled from the low bass in his voice and the way his nose would wrinkle when he spoke. During the course of our conversation, his hand found mine and I didn't hate it, allowing him to fondle my hand, occasionally interlocking his fingers with mine.

Jared entered the room, introducing himself to Quincy. "Hey, I'm Jared and I'm going to be your handler for the rest of the night."

"So what's the plan?" Quincy asked beating me to it.

"Up next, we have wedding photos." Jared motioned for us to follow him. In my wedding dress I struggled to keep up with Jared's determined steps. Reaching for my hand, Quincy matched my stride so I wouldn't get left behind. Over his shoulder Jared called, "You two got all dressed up and we want to memorialize the moment. We want to capture this special day so years from now you two can look back and remember it fondly."

Quincy blew a laugh from his nose.

"What?" I asked wanting to be let in on the joke.

"Nothing really, it's just that as things stand right now statistically, we have a fifty-fifty chance of remembering this day fondly. I mean it's just as likely that we'll remember this day with disdain."

His words did not elicit a laugh, instead I puckered my lips. "That should've been in your vows. Everybody needs a hearty dose of cynicism."

"It actually was in my vows but I just cut it for time." He gave my hand a soft squeeze.

"What a shame." A smile tickled the corners of my mouth.

"No one wants to hear that most marriages end in divorce right before jumping the broom."

"That's actually a myth. The divorce rate has never topped fifty percent," I said.

"So you're saying we have a fifty-forty chance at divorce?"

"Yeah, that's not bad." I flung my shoulder upward.

If you'd asked me years ago what I thought me and my husband would discuss minutes after exchanging I do, I would have guessed our all-consuming love of one another, not the survivability rates of marriage. I guess when you marry a stranger the conversation hits different.

"It's still pretty abysmal odds ..." Quincy's eyes slid over me like silk with a hint of come-hither. "But I think I'm holding a royal flush."

During the wedding photo session, the photographer encouraged me to move closer into Quincy's personal space. Directions which I eagerly followed, our faces inches apart, I tried not to burst into laughter.

"I'm so happy I popped a mint before this started," Quincy said through a cracked smile.

"Evelyn why don't you toss your arms across his shoulders," the photographer called.

Complying, I let my arms rest on his shoulders, my hands instinctually rubbed the back of his head and neck. With a mischievous grin, my gaze bounced from his eyes to his mouth.

"What?" he asked.

"Just admiring the view."

"Well take your time, I'm a lot to take in."

"Let's hope so."

His eyebrows climbed up his forehead. Leaning in as close as he could without touching my lips, he said, "Don't flirt with me Mrs. Parrish or you'll fuck around and find out."

Tingles frolicked across my skin at his words. Damn this man was sexy. I knew he was handsome the minute I'd laid eyes on him but the sexy part took a little bit longer to figure out. I just hoped he wasn't all talk and no action.

The photographer barked out instructions, interrupting the racy thoughts that had taken up residence in my head. "Why don't we try one with a kiss?"

My face lit up before I was able to hide it. I was eager to kiss him again.

"No, I think we're good." Quincy backed up, vigorously shaking his head.

His body language was even harsher than his words making it clear kissing me was not on his to do list. *Did I already say too much?* If that had him clutching his pearls then maybe we weren't as compatible as I hoped. This wouldn't be the first time my sexually aggressive personality had scared a man off. But life was far too short for mincing words. I said what I felt and let the chips fall where they may.

Once again I had to remind myself I didn't know this man from a can of paint. I was notorious for spinning elaborate stories based on very little facts. Reading between the lines, often times incorrectly was a pastime for me. If he was turned off, he didn't show it, reaching for my hand for one last picture. With the group photographs out of the way, we had a few minutes to spare before joining the reception.

"I want to introduce you to my best man." My hand still securely tucked in his, Quincy led me to a stocky brother with Clark Kent glasses. "This is Walt Kemp." Quincy tagged his friend's arm.

"Oh snap it's the bride. Hello, nice to officially meet you." He bowed at the waist like I was a member of royalty. "My condolences for being yoked with this guy, but welcome to the family."

"Thank you, it's so nice to meet one of Q's friends. Do you know we've been married all of an hour and you're the first friend I've ever met?" I gave Quincy's chest a playful swat.

"I have three questions for you." Walt said, his face turning gravely serious.

I anticipated questions. I'd hoped we could at least get past the first dance but it was fine. "OK."

"I want your honest answers, first thing that comes to mind."

"Yep, got it." I nodded.

"Waffles or pancakes?"

"Waffles, are you kidding me all those nooks and crannies for the syrup to hide in." I released a slurping sound.

"Team Captain America or Team Iron Man."

"Team Cap because he was right and Tony was wrong." I wagged an index finger in Walt's direction. I was loving these questions and the possibility my new husband was a nerd. "And because Cap is fine as fuck and I would like to do all types of ungodly things to him."

"You're a married woman." Quincy reminded me. "So, if you're doing ungodly things with anyone it better be me."

Meeting his gaze, I whispered. "Don't threaten me with a good time."

My response caused his eyes to grow wide.

Walt coughed. "I'm still here. Clearing his throat he continued, "Ok last question. What's your stance on brunch?"

My head lolled back. "I love it. Bottomless mimosas with various fried pig parts while Roy Ayers plays in the background. Yes please."

"Wow, you passed the test with flying colors." Walt smiled.

Quincy's expression had morphed from surprised, to impressed, to full out admiration. He planted a quick kiss on my cheek catching me by surprise. I don't know how he did it, but that one kiss was wreaking havoc on my normal heartbeat pattern.

Jared clapped his hands, announcing it was time for the bridal party to join the reception. We lined up, as the doors to the reception hall opened, the sounds of a Beyoncé and Jay-Z collab filled the air.

"I love this song." Quincy and I said in the same breath.

"You too?" His face lit up at the shared commonality. With a quick squeeze of my hand, Quincy and I danced our way into the party.

～

QUINCY

THE GUESTS CHEERED and whooped at our entrance. As we made our way to the center of the dance floor, the upbeat tune morphed into a mellow-jazz vibe for our first dance as man and wife. The piano chords were my cue to sweep her up in my arms. With one hand on Evelyn's waist, we swayed side to side.

"I know this song, I just can't place it," I said.

"It's My One and Only Love by John Coltrane."

Of course, I should have known that. "Did you pick this song?"

"Yes, I've never given much thought to my wedding day but one thing I always knew was that I wanted my first dance with my husband to be to this song."

No pressure. If this didn't work out she would hate this song for the rest of her life. Before entering the reception hall, Evelyn had shed the bottom half of her dress. Converting her puffy ball gown into a sleek, form-fitting number that placed her best assets on full display. When the saxophone rang out, she closed her eyes and I dared to examine her face.

If she had a flaw, I was hard pressed to find it. Her skin glowed and shimmered under the lights of the crystal chandeliers. Her full lips were painted a blood red, which made her pearly, white smile that much brighter. My hand rested on the small of her back and the raised mound of her firm and ample backside, which was the icing on an already magnificently crafted work of art.

As the music faded, she pulled away. *Who gave her permission to do that?*

"Can you get me a drink," she asked, fussing with the skirt of her dress.

"Sure, what do you want?"

"I'll take some red wine. Thanks."

At the bar I ordered our drinks, taking in the crowd while I waited. Evelyn had a big turnout of family and friends for our special day. In comparison, I think my guests took up two tables. Everyone else was here for Evelyn. When you grow up in foster care you get used to people not showing up for you. Also, I'd only told a handful of friends about this experiment. How do you tell your coworkers you're taking vacation for two weeks because you're marrying someone you never met? You don't … that's how.

A tall brother, that looked like the male version of Evelyn if she had a beard and was built like a linebacker, stopped directly in front of me boxing me in. "What's good?" he asked.

"You know just out here marrying strangers."

"Evie's my sister."

"Ahh, so we're family now." Wiping my hand on my trousers I extended my hand.

"Like you said we're family now." Before I could protest, this man scooped me into a bear hug applying aggressive pats to the back. "I'm Evan."

"Evan and Evelyn?" My face lit up appreciating what Momma Townsend did there.

"We're twins."

"Damn twins, that's hella cool." I'd never dated a twin, at least I could say without a doubt I'd landed the prettier twin.

"So, Quincy, do you have a job?"

Let the interrogation begin. "Yeah, I'm a lawyer."

"Oh, so you got a *job* job." He let out a boisterous laugh. Any attempt at playing bad cop fading with each of my responses.

I let out a two-note laugh. The question got me wondering what Evelyn did. Swallowing down a dry patch in my throat, the fact I knew nothing about this woman, except that she may like Marvel movies and had an ass you could sit a cup on, was sinking in.

"Where'd you go to college?" Evan asked.

"The University of Arkansas for undergrad."

"Oh yeah, I went to LSU, our football teams are rivals."

Evan towered over me, he had to clock in at close to two hundred and fifty pounds so I had to ask. "Did you play?"

"Football? Hell nah. I was way too wasted for sports."

"Probably for the best since your football program sucks."

Evan's head flinched backward. "Sucks? Remind me when's the last time your team won against LSU?"

"I can't call it but I do know we're ranked in the thirties. Where do the Tigers rank?"

The smile completely vanished from Evan's face with the tendons in his neck flexing as he narrowed his eyes. Walt often warned me I talked too much trash and that one day someone was going to sort me out for it. I took a step back, bracing my feet on the carpet. *Was I gonna have to punch my new brother-in-law in the face?* I'm sure that would make for a *Why Knot* ratings bonanza.

A smile etched away at the stone-like expression on his face. "Ahh, I like this guy," Evan said to no one in particular, slapping me playfully on the cheek. "Let me buy you a drink."

"It's an open bar ... but OK."

EVELYN

AFTER FIFTEEN MINUTES OF WAITING, I went in search of my drink and my man. I found Quincy next to the bar laughing with Evan.

"Hi." Quincy's laughter turned into a warm smile. "I met your brother."

"I can see that. Don't believe anything he says."

"He said you're bossy."

I flashed my twin an irritated look. I'd known Quincy for two hours and my brother was already sharing my character flaws. "I repeat, don't trust anything he says."

"I said some good things too." Evan protested.

"Like?"

"Like the fact that you love to cook and entertain and you stay with a book in your hand."

Quincy handed me a glass of wine with a kiss to my shoulder that made my insides seize up.

"Thank you." My gaze moved from his eyes to his lips and back again.

Even though my brother had deprived me of the pleasure of staring at this man for the last twenty minutes, I was happy the two were getting along. Evan was skeptical when I told him I'd been matched and was set to marry a man I'd never met in less than a week. He even offered to hook me up with one of his friends, like I was a charity case. But here he was yucking it up with the man he'd called pathetic and a psycho killer just last night ... I chose to take it as a good sign.

Dinner was followed by a pee break which took much longer than intended because of my skin-tight dress and declining Meryl's offer to help me. At the sink basin I was greeted by my mother who was touching up her makeup.

"Are you having a good time?" I asked.

Dropping her hands to her side, she turned to face me. "You know when I woke up this morning something in my spirit told me to stay home. But I said, 'Shereè, your eldest daughter is getting married and you need to support her.'" My mother pursed her lips, the church lady hat on top of her head shaking as she bobbed her head in a no. "But watching you throw yourself at that man you don't even know—"

"He's my husband."

"That doesn't negate the fact that you wouldn't be able to pick his dick out of a line up." My mother's fake ass accent was gone. "Evelyn, you don't know anything about this man and now you've hitched your rickety ass wagon to his star."

"Have you even talked to him? He's actually really nice. Evan loves him."

"Evan, who's dating that gold digging hoochie? Yeah, he's a great judge of character." My mother rolled her eyes.

"Cam is not a gold digger. If she was, she wouldn't be with Evan." My brother managed a car dealership and while he made good money, he wasn't exactly Miles Graves.

"I just don't know where I went wrong with you. I tried, Lord knows I tried. But what do I get, four years of college down the drain, so you could do what? Hmm? So, you could play in paint."

This conversation was nothing new. My mother just had more fuel to add to the "Evelyn is a huge disappointment" bond fire. We used to be best friends. I remember wanting to be just like my elegant mother when I grew up. Of course, that was before I realized what a bitch she was. When I graduated college and informed my parents I was going to pursue more creative lines of work, that's when the deep chasm between us formed. The cracks were already there but that news was like a seismic shift pushing us further apart.

Drying my hands, I inhaled a calming breath. This was my wedding day and the last thing I wanted was to get into another one of our screaming matches. I was happy and I wasn't going to let her Debbie Downer attitude ruin this day. "I'm heading back."

"What are you going to do when this doesn't work?"

"What I always do. Figure it out," I said, before exiting the bathroom.

QUINCY

Evelyn's friends and family were acting like they were at Disney World and I was Space Mountain, each lined up to meet me. *Step right up ladies and gentlemen, I can guarantee you have never in your life seen anything like this. You've witnessed the world's strongest man, and the bearded lady, but have you seen the bravest man in the world? Marrying a woman sight unseen. Will this be a love connection or will this relationship crash and burn like all the rest?* After meeting her Grammy, her college roommate, and Uncle Chester I went in search of the bride, who had been MIA for the last thirty minutes, eventually finding her in a private courtyard. Like me she had managed to slip away from the cameras and crew.

"Everything OK?" I asked.

Evelyn turned to greet me, wiping under her eyes. "Yeah, I was just having a mini panic attack. It's just a lot." She twisted the pearl bangle on her wrist.

"No, I get it, right before the ceremony I thought I was gonna puke." I slid my hands in my trouser pockets, inching closer. Her eyes were a bit red but I didn't know if that was from too much alcohol or tears.

"Ewww."

"Yeah, this is crazy. No shame in being overwhelmed." Reaching for her I played with the digits on her hand. "Hopefully you're not having second thoughts."

"Nope. Maybe I'm weird but I don't have any of those." Her smile faltered. "Why, are you having second thoughts?" Her mink eyes searched my face.

"No, I'm having *thoughts* but not second thoughts."

"Oh yeah, what kinda thoughts?" she asked, a faint eager glint in her eyes.

"Like I think I kinda wanna kiss you." I gingerly moved closer, my breath shackled inside my chest as I anticipated her response.

"I kinda wanna let you." There was an intensity in her silky voice.

I didn't need to be told twice. My mouth latched onto hers with greedy determination. Our lips clung to one another's softly at first, but as she angled her body so it pressed against mine, the kisses became more urgent. She threw her arms over my shoulders running her hands over the base of my neck. Taking my bottom lip between hers, she sucked loudly leaving me no choice but to moan against her lips.

As I walked my fingertips up her forearm, a trail of goosebumps pricked my flesh, Evelyn's skin was cold at first touch, which made sense. It was October in Chicago and while this courtyard shielded us from the wind, it was still in the low double digits outside. Cupping her face in my hands, I backed her up against a wall covered in creeping figs, accidentally hitting her head against it.

"I'm sorry." I winced, rubbing the back of her head hoping to soothe any pain.

"It's OK. I'm not fragile," she whispered breathlessly.

With a quick nod, my lips found hers again. Her mouth was sweet and warm; I didn't know if it was from the wine or some other fruity drink she'd consumed. Soft indistinguishable love sounds escaped her mouth, her hands tugging at my suit jacket. Heat rose from my core warming my chest, I couldn't remember the last time a kiss had made me feel dizzy and excited. Pulling her waist against me, my hands traveled to her ass and then immediately froze. I didn't want to cross the line, yes she was my wife but the fact remained we'd known each other for less than four hours.

As if she could read my mind my new bride taunted me. "Don't be chickenshit." She instructed before latching onto my earlobe with her teeth.

It seemed she was confusing my apprehension with me being timid. I was far from it and if she was down, I had every intention of breaking her back like a glow stick. With her verbal green light giving me permission to proceed, I squeezed her ample backside the best I could through her form-fitting, bedazzled dress. The sequin and beads making it difficult to latch on like I wanted. I inhaled a stuttered breath as Evelyn concentrated on planting kisses along my neck and jawline. Sinking my face into her chest, I kissed and sucked at her décolletage which peeked through the top of her sweetheart neckline.

It was just a matter of time before the crew found us and cameras would be shoved in our faces. The fact that we both were able to escape their watchful eye was like witnessing a double rainbow. This much-needed alone time helped to confirm what I already knew ... Evelyn was my type. When it came to women, I'd dated them all but my preference was a woman who knew exactly what she wanted. And in this moment, with her hand dangerously close to my dick it was clear we wanted the same thing.

My ears perked up when I heard commotion just on the other side of the wooden slider doors. Reluctantly, I pulled away crossing the pebbled courtyard right before the door swung open.

Jared walked in, his hair raked through. "What are you two doing?"

I wiped at my mouth. "We were just getting to know one another."

Evelyn's eyes shrouded in wantonness, landed on me. "There's just so much to learn."

"We'll just have to cram it all in." I added.

"It's a tight squeeze, but we can make it fit."

Jared's eyes bounced from Evelyn to me. "What the fuck are you two talking about? It's time for the toast. Let's go." He waved his hand brushing away our secret communication.

CHAPTER 5

EVELYN

"I met Quincy our freshman year of high school and we've been tight ever since. A few things you should know about Q is he's a hard worker, he's fiercely protective of the people he loves, and family is important to him. When he told me he was fittin' to marry someone he had never met I was a bit concerned but having known you for … what … four hours now it's pretty apparent that he's hit the jackpot. Congratulations bro." Walt lifted his glass.

It was nice to hear people say kind things about Quincy. Since I had no memories of my own to pull from, I listened intently as funny stories, and heartfelt moments were recounted.

Up next was my best friend Meryl. "Evie is the kind of woman your parents warn you about. That friend who jumps off of bridges and dares you to come with her. Evie is fearless and she has been jumping from bridges for as long as I can remember. Truthfully, I could never muster up the courage to jump. Today, we're at yet another bridge that Evie has chosen to jump from but this time she's not alone because Quincy took the leap with her. Quincy, one thing I can guarantee is there will never be a dull moment with this one so I hope you packed a parachute."

What Meryl called jumping off of bridges, I saw as living. If Quincy was open to free falling at least 50 percent of the time, this could be something special. My stomach dropped as my mother rose from her chair and took hold of the microphone.

"Hello, my name is Shereè Townsend and I'm Evelyn's mother. This is not how I pictured her wedding day. My first born, marrying a man I don't know. A man she doesn't know. She has always been stubborn, up was down, left was right ..."

My fingers tightened against Quincy's hand. Of course, my mother would want to take center stage to continue our argument when she knew I couldn't interrupt. Grabbing my half empty glass of champagne, I poured the rest of the liquid down my throat, I wasn't going to tip my glass to my mother's venting session.

"You can raise a child and teach them the way to go but at some point you just have to wash your hands. I hope you two know what you're doing." She lifted her glass before downing her champagne.

Quincy leaned in saying, "I don't think your mother likes me."

Rolling my eyes I said. "It's OK, she doesn't like me either."

Eventually I would have to explain my complicated rela-tionship with my mother. But I was sure he could sense the connection was strained. For the longest time I thought the friction between us was my fault. I now knew that it boiled down to expectations. My mother's expectations of a daughter who followed in her footsteps. And my expectations of having a mother whose love and support were unconditional.

Standing, Quincy straightened the legs of his trousers before placing a hand on the back of my neck. "Thank you all for coming out. I know some of you just came to see the shit show and that's fine."

Was that a dig at my mother? If it was, I could add one more thing I liked about this man.

He turned to me and continued, "I was just hoping my match wasn't shy and that she actually talked to me. And then you came walking down the aisle. And now I'm desperately hoping I don't mess this all up."

His thumb stroked the back of my neck sending shivers trilling down my spine. A brief flash of our first real kiss in the courtyard caused other parts of my body to shiver as well.

"I just wanna say in front of the people closest to us ... I am fully invested. And I just ask that you do the same. Invest in this relationship, getting to know me and trying to make it work. It's gonna be scary and there's gonna be tears, mostly from me." He said, that last part through a laugh. "But if we're committed, hopefully we can make it through the other side." He raised his glass in my direction.

If he couldn't tell by now, I was all in. Like I'd said in my vows I didn't have a plan B. This was the only plan, audition for a reality dating television show, get selected, be matched with my forever person and live happily ever after. Essentially this was an arranged marriage. A colleague, Maira, was arranged by her parents and was about to celebrate her seventh wedding anniversary. Love was love no matter how you found it.

I lifted my empty glass.

"To the happy couple." The crowd cheered.

QUINCY

AT THE ELEVEN O'CLOCK HOUR, the older family members started making their exit leaving friends and the younger generation of the Townsend clan. After walking my foster mother to her car, I returned to the ballroom and was immediately accosted by Evan.

"What are we drinking?" Throwing his arm over my shoulder, Evan walked me over to the bar.

"Uhm?" I didn't want to overindulge. It was my wedding night and the last thing I wanted to do was get shit-faced drunk. Not the kind of impression I wanted to imprint on my new wife.

"Mom, Dad, Grammy, and dem are gone and it's time to loosen that tie. My sister doesn't like prim and proper." Handing me a shot of Patròn, we tipped back our glasses.

The satisfying sting as the alcohol tumbled down my throat had the intended effect. I'd been on my P's and Q's all night but this was my wedding day and I should be allowed to let loose.

"Where's my wife?" My eyes panned the room looking for the curvy beauty in a white dress.

"Dance floor. She loves to dance."

Ordering two more shots, I headed in her direction. On

the dance floor she shimmied her shoulders and moved her hips modestly as she whispered with her best friend, Meryl. With a nudge of my elbow I interrupted. "I brought drinks."

"I like the way you think," Meryl said, ping ponging her eyes from me to Evelyn and then back again. "I'm gonna hit up the bar." She exited the dance floor leaving us alone like a seasoned wing woman.

Taking the shot glass, Evelyn passed it under her nose to confirm the contents. "Are you gonna dance with me?

"Yeah, sure." Any excuse to be close to her.

Downing our shots, I discarded the glasses on a nearby table. When I turned around Evelyn was swaying side to side, her arms outstretched inviting me to bridge the distance between us. Now that the older folks were gone, the music selection changed. When the reggae-infused percussion began to play, Evelyn's hips started to whine. With her hips in my hands, I moved in time with her. She danced with reckless abandon while still moving in sync with the music, arms over head. Spinning around, she pressed her ass into my lap grinding against me, dropping my hands to my side I watched as her backside aggressively brushed the front of my pants.

I did not have getting a chubby at my wedding reception on the itinerary but here we were. The fact that Evelyn leaned into my nearly erect penis not backing away spoke volumes. If I didn't know better it seemed like she was enjoying getting me hot and bothered. The DJ transitioned to another popular hip-hop song and Evelyn followed the directions in the lyrics dropping her hands to her knees while twerking against me. Bracing my hands on the sides of her waist, I let her go to work. Her backside bouncing and gyrating against my lap.

Much of the next two hours went just like this, if we weren't freak dancing then we were singing the words to a classic Busta Rhymes song to one another. Her brother eventually joined us and the three of us milly rocked, stanky legged, and crip walked all over the dance floor. Evelyn could damn well be the perfect woman. She could turn me on with the rotation of her hips and felt like one of the boys when she hit the dougie.

After Evan left to order up another round of shots, I pulled her into my arms brushing hair from her sticky face. "Are you having a good time?"

"Yes." Her hand taking its now familiar position, rubbing the back of my neck.

Our bodies swayed slowly on the dance floor even though the song playing was full of bass and snares.

"Where have you been hiding?" Licking my lips, I didn't give her a chance to answer, kissing her with a sigh.

The vibration of the music rattled in my chest, or maybe that was just the effect she had on me. When my lips touched hers, my body did strange things. My heart stuttered and stammered. My pulse became thready and my knees threatened to buckle. If I mentioned these symptoms to a doctor I would probably be admitted for inpatient care.

Breaking the hold her plump lips had on me, I stepped back. Space was needed if I wanted the erratic beating of my heart to slow. With a quick glance at my watch, I was surprised to see the small hand past two.

"It's late," I shouted over the music. "Maybe we should say our good nights and head up?"

Her eyes glimmered at my suggestion.

After protracted goodbyes which included a line dance to "Candy" by Cameo, farewell shots, and a telephone number exchange with Evan, my new best friend, we finally made it out of the ballroom and into the elevator. Just me, Evelyn, Jared, the cameraman and Carol, the production assistant all going to the twelfth floor. I glanced at my bride who was smelling her fall bouquet of blue thistles with orange and red blooms.

I knew reality television was invasive but this seemed like overkill. The cameraman panned from my face to Evelyn capturing images for the will they or won't they, that was part of the wedding night episodes of *Why Knot*. If we were alone, we'd be out of breath by the time the elevator doors opened from all the frantic kissing. My body sagged and my neck sank, all I wanted to do was grab Evelyn's hand and run far away from the lights and inquisitive eyes. As the doors opened on our floor, I took a deep breath bracing myself for what the rest of the night had in store.

∼

EVELYN

"Do you want me to carry you over the threshold?" Quincy asked, rubbing the back of his neck, uncertainty clouding his eyes.

"So your drunk ass can drop me and bump my head, no thank you." I teased.

We'd both had way too much to drink trying to live our best lives at the reception. My head was spinning and I needed my feet planted firmly on the ground if I was going to make it through the night without careening to the floor. Opening the door to our hotel suite, he stepped aside letting me pass through.

Once I was safely inside, he let the door crash in the cameraman's face. No doubt he was just as tired of all the attention as I was. How did the saying go, be careful what you wish for cause you just might get it and regret you ever made the fucking wish in the first place? But if finding my dream husband meant the whole world got to watch us fall in love, it was a price I would gladly pay.

Immediately I removed my sparkly heels; my feet had been killing me but I wanted to look cute so I'd powered through. With the torture devices off, I let out a long swoosh of air.

"There's champagne and chocolate-covered strawberries do you want me to pour—"

"Yes, to the strawberries, no to champagne." I picked a berry decorated like a groom's tux and wrapped my mouth around it, taking a bite.

Quincy's eyes traveled to my lips with rapt attention, inching closer, I extended my hand enticing him to have a taste. He opened his mouth letting me feed him, devouring the rest of the strawberry in one bite before licking melted chocolate from my fingertip.

I wouldn't be mad if he threw me on the bed, ripped the bodice of my dress and just had his way with me. Like in one of those movies where the couple can't keep their hands off one another so that not even an expensive garment could stop them. Just buttons flying, frayed fabrics, and desire. The thought made me giggle or maybe it was the wine, champagne, tequila, and beer swimming in my belly that was making me giddy.

"What's so funny?"

"Nothing, and absolutely everything. This is so awkward." I surrendered my hand into the air.

I thought alcohol was supposed to make you forget. Right now, standing semi alone with a total stranger who was also legally my husband, all I could think about were the decisions that brought me here. The *Why Knot* casting ad that showed up in my feed one night when I was absent-mindedly scrolling. Me clicking on said ad and entering my email address out of curiosity. The next afternoon when I checked my email there was an intake form with an invitation to the open casting call.

I didn't tell anyone I was going, not even Meryl and when I made it past the first round I was positive I'd be cut the next round. When that didn't happen and I advanced again I was certain I'd get the "Thank you for your interest but regretfully" email. But that email never came, instead they wanted to see my apartment. Two weeks later one of the experts turned up at my door excitedly proclaiming they'd found me a match. This man, who stood hazy eyed smelling of top shelf liquor, sage, and me.

"It's only awkward if we make it." A smile pulled at the corners of his mouth. "A wise woman once told me that."

"Don't use the words I said when I was sober to persuade drunk me. Drunk me cannot be reasoned with. Drunk me is in desperate need of some greasy burgers and fries to soak all this alcohol up."

Quincy considered my face in reflective silence for a moment, one which only lasted a few seconds but to my drunk and slightly vulnerable ass it felt like an eternity. Pulling out his cellphone, he clicked with rapid fingers across the screen. *Was I already boring him?* We'd been married for nine hours and he was already losing interest.

Setting his phone on the coffee table he said, "Why don't we get out of these clothes and just chill. You look beautiful in that dress but I have a sneaking suspicion you would look good in anything."

"Wow wee that would be *very nice,*" I said in my best Borat impression.

"What the hell was that?" Quincy blinked.

"Borat, that weird dude who pranks people he uses a thick fake accent."

Quincy stared at me in silence.

"Very Nice." I repeated hoping he would get the joke if he heard it again.

He winced inhaling a sharp breath. "Wow, I don't know why ... MY WIIIFFFE ... would do that." Sticking out his tongue he exaggerated the words just like that Borat guy.

My hands went to my chest as I doubled over in laughter collapsing to the ground. Quincy snorted a laugh which made the tears fall from my eyes as I tried to regain my composure. *They say perfect men don't exist but Quincy ... Quincy? Shit, what was this dude's last name.* Drying my tears, *Just Quincy* helped me to my feet.

Wrapping my arms around him, I pulled him close and whispered, "What's your last name again?"

Leaning back so he could see my face he said, "*Our* last name is Parrish."

The ownership and inclusion made my nipples pebble

and my nether regions throb. "Can you help me out of this dress?"

"Yep."

I turned my back to him so he could access the zipper. He swept my long, black hair over my shoulder. After undoing the clasp, he pulled the zipper all the way to the waistband of my thong. His fingertips took liberties running gently down my naked spine. With his hand securely under my breast plate, he planted a series of kisses along my neck and shoulders. The cameras in the room dampened my reaction. I wanted to release a deep moan but was forced to swallow it. Pulling away with one hand holding my dress in place, I collected my things and headed to the bathroom fearful this was moving from R-rated to triple X.

Removing my dress, I was tempted to unstrap the mic affixed to my torso. The novelty of being on a reality show was quickly wearing off. After a long pee that drained all the fluids from my body I pulled my hair into a high, messy bun. Washing my face, I scrubbed away at the pound of makeup that had been packed on to withstand the intense heat from the spotlights used for filming.

"Quincy Parrish." I let his name dance across my tongue. "Quincy and Evelyn Parrish" I wrinkled my nose, I wasn't sure about taking his name.

I knew one thing for certain: this little experiment was slated for ninety days any potential name change decisions could wait until I figured out where the two of us really stood. This day had been a dream, but in the dawning of a new one would I feel as enamored as I did in this moment? Only time would tell.

~

QUINCY

"What's that smell?" Evelyn asked, walking over to the couch.

I couldn't help but scan her body in a tank top and booty shorts, sans bra nipples semi erect. My eyes finally landed on her face, without makeup she looked much younger. Her mahogany skin was smooth and her high cheekbones made her look regal.

"You said you were hungry so I got us some food."

"What?" Her face lit up and her jaw went slack.

"You mentioned you could go for a greasy burger so I shot Walt a text and asked him to do me a solid."

"Good old Walt. God love him." Her eyes danced over the double cheeseburgers and fries.

"Wait a second, those tattoos were not there twenty minutes ago." Evelyn had a small cross tattooed on the side of her neck and words I couldn't make out on her collarbone.

"Yeah, I covered them for the ceremony." She shrugged apologetically.

Jumping from the couch, I moved closer running my hand over the script across her collar which I could now read clearly, *These Violent Delights*. "Why would you cover them up?"

"I wanted to make a good impression on the parents. Dumb I know but I got into my head and obsessed about it."

I hoped she wasn't disappointed I didn't have any parents to impress. Just Naomi.

Making our way back to the coffee table piled high with food, we both settled in on the carpet digging into the cheesy, juicy, salty goodness. We ate in silence for several minutes, the only sound from food wrappers and the smacking of lips as we devoured our meal. I didn't realize how hungry I was until the first bite. At the reception I was far too nervous and self-conscious and barely touched my meal.

"Do you have any tattoos?" she asked, pulling back the paper covering her burger so she could take another bite.

I slid down the collar of my T-shirt to reveal a tattoo on my chest. Evelyn nodded her head in approval. I chased my burger with a few sips of the chocolate milkshake.

"So, what's the deal with you and your mom?" I asked, shoveling a few fries into my mouth.

"What?" Her eyes tightened at the corners.

"You said she hates you."

"Oh, it's nothing really, just years of being a disappointment. The Townsend family has a long lineage of impressive career paths … doctors, lawyers, a fucking paleontologist. And I'm an artist. She hates it. Never mind that I make a decent living. It's not a real job to her." She dropped her half-eaten burger on the paper bag it came in.

"Navigating the parent, adult child relationship can be difficult."

"She's never even been to one of my shows, or seen the pieces I create." Evelyn shook her head as if trying to evict the negative thoughts. "I think it's too early in the getting to know you stage to lay my mommy issues on you."

"Trust me I got mommy issues too." I playfully reached for her, tugging on her ear.

"Oh yeah?" She yawned.

"That conversation we'll save for another day when we have something stronger than milkshakes."

Evelyn tilted her head in a yes. "So, what do you do for money?"

"Lawyer."

She laughed, "No seriously."

"Seriously."

"Fancy." She pulled her features into an impressed expression.

Her hand landed on my leg as she scooted closer. I resisted the strong urge to pull her onto my lap, but Evelyn … Evelyn's urge control switch was faulty. Without a warning she leaned in and licked my neck before nibbling on my earlobe. A seepage of breath helped to regulate my breathing.

I wanted to have sex with my wife but I was drunk and exhausted from all the day's activities and emotional roller coaster of the unknown. That combination made it impossible to guarantee the sex would end in a happy ending. The last thing I wanted was for our first time to leave her questioning her life choices and looking for the receipt so she could return my dusty ass.

My shoulders squared as my spine locked into place. "I just want to throw this out there straight away. I don't wanna have sex tonight," I said.

Evelyn's once pliable body grew tense. As she pulled away, confusion and disappointment were written all over her face.

"It's a lot of pressure and I just want us to chill and get to know each other."

"Yeah, great. I think that's a good plan." Pushing back the loose hairs from her bun, she pulled her knees up to her chest.

Hoping to soften the blow I added, "I just don't want you trying to take advantage of me on the first night."

"Oh, that was definitely my intention. I was hoping to corrupt you." She licked at the corners of her lips.

Her words caused me to smirk. It was cute she thought she could corrupt me. "They'll be time enough for that. I'm very impressionable."

After clearing away the trash, brushing my teeth and washing my face I returned to the living area of the suite to find Evelyn out cold.

"Evelyn?"

The soft sounds of her breath confirmed she was still alive. Scooping her up into my arms, I carried her to the king-sized bed. I performed a bit of a balancing act trying to pull back the bed linens that were tucked so tight I feared I might drop her. Once freed, I set her down surprised that despite all the movement she was still asleep.

With a click of my tongue I said, "And you wanted to have sex. Can't even keep your eyes open, you would have fallen asleep mid stroke. My ego could not take that kind of hit." Pulling the covers over her, I noticed her hair piled on her head. "Shit, hey do you have a bonnet or scarf? Evelyn?" I tried shaking her awake but she was dead to the world. "If you go to sleep like that your hair is gonna be fucked up when you wake up."

In the bathroom I searched for silk fabric, but no luck.

Returning to the bedroom, I sifted through her luggage finding a pair of purple-lace, crotchless-thong panties that held my attention for longer than they should have before locating a bonnet in one of the side pockets. After securing the bonnet over her hair, I turned off the lights and climbed into the bed next to her.

"Good night, Evelyn. Can't wait to do it all again tomorrow."

Chapter 6

EVELYN

The sound of profanity in the distance pulled me from my sleep.

"Fuck," Quincy muttered "My baby toe." This was followed by softer groans from the other room.

My eyes fluttered open and I immediately closed them trying to block out the brightness that filled the room. It took me a minute to process that I wasn't at home in my bed. *What time is it?* By my guess we made it to bed well after four in the morning. I didn't even remember going to bed, just a slow burger coma.

The last thing I distinctly remembered was Quincy rejecting my advances. And the warmth of embarrassment that washed over me immediately following. Usually when I suggested sex my offer was met with a resounding yes. Making it ten times worse was the fact that Quincy's hard pass on my Choco Taco was memorialized for the entire world to see.

The thought of his words sending me further under

the covers. Yes, I'd just met this guy last night, but if we're being honest I've had my fair share of one-night stands. Having sex with the stranger you married did not classify as a one-night stand, the sacred bond of matrimony negated all that. Who turns down the chance to have sloppy, drunk sex? I gasped, maybe he has a micro penis and that's why he's single. The perfect guy minus a few inches.

Slow footsteps approached, pushing the covers from over my head I yelled, "Do you have a micro penis?"

"Good morning to you too."

"Good morning, did you have a restful sleep? Do you have a micro penis?"

"I think your ass knows I don't have a micro penis, the way you were grinding all over it last night."

As the morning fog cleared, I vaguely remembered choking on my cranberry vodka when I felt him against my backside the night prior. Falling back into the bed, my face grew hot. Quincy climbed back into bed letting out a big yawn.

"What were you doing?"

"Letting the crew in and we got a gift basket delivery."

"What time is it?

"A little after nine."

Crossing my arms over my chest I wasn't sure what more to say. I knew absolutely nothing about him. It was overwhelming, I didn't know where to start.

"How old are you?"

"Thirty-five."

Nodding, I waited for him to reciprocate the question. But he just lay there in silent contemplation. "So you're not gonna ask me how old I am?" I huffed, throwing my arms in the air at his slight.

"I was going to ask but you didn't give me a chance. I'm noticing that patience … isn't your strong suit." Quincy hissed out a sigh.

Falling silent, I waited again this time for several minutes. All you could hear were my fingers drumming the mattress.

"Your brother already told me you're thirty-two."

"You could have just said that."

"Do you ask questions to learn or do you ask questions in the hope that someone will return the favor so you can in turn just talk about yourself?"

I sat up with a jerk slamming my eyes into him. "What the fuck?"

"What?"

"Where's the guy from last night?"

"He's right here. Tired and dehydrated. With a wife who's asking stupid fucking questions."

My jaw unhinged. I get not being a morning person but this was unacceptable. "OK this is a joke, right? Say sike. Say sike right now."

He lifted a blasé shoulder.

"Quincy Fucking Parrish—"

"Chester."

"What?"

"My middle name is Chester."

I sat on my knees with wide eyes studying the seriousness of his face. A row of laughter erupted from my throat as I clutched my side choking for air. "Chester?" I managed to squeak out before dissolving into laughter once again. Once

I'd regained my composure, I inched closer rubbing his full beard with my hand. "Why are you being Oscar the Grouch right now?"

Quincy stared at the ceiling. "Have you ever experienced meeting the right person at the wrong time?"

The hopeful light in my eyes dimmed. "Are you talking about me?"

"Not about you but the current situation."

Releasing my hold of his chin I said, "You said you were gonna try. You said you were invested. Was that all just bullshit?"

Quincy held his palms out lifting himself from the bed. "No ... wait, I am still invested. This isn't coming out right."

A flush of heat overtook my face and neck and confusion turned to shock. It hadn't even been twenty-four hours and this asshole was about to make me cry. "So what, you just woke up and realized you're not feeling me anymore?" I searched his face with unblinking eyes trying to understand where this was all coming from.

Had I misread everything from last night? He kissed me in that courtyard, not the other way around. One thing I knew was men, and he was just as interested as I was. But was he? He'd literally declined to have sex with me last night. I was giving off big come-hither vibes and he put the kibosh on all that. Maybe he was just being polite at the reception because of my family and friends but now that we were alone, he couldn't hide the fact that he was disappointed and I wasn't his type. Wow, I knew there'd been couples that just never clicked on this show but I never thought I'd be part of one of them.

"Oh my God, Evelyn will you just listen to me. It's not about you."

"Please don't say 'It's not me, it's you.'"

"It's not me *or* you."

"You know for a lawyer you're not very good with words." Swinging my feet to the ground, I headed for the bathroom where I could die of embarrassment alone.

What the fuck just happened? My insta-marriage was imploding before it even left the ground. Who says they're willing to try and then with little to no effort stops trying? Inching close to the mirror I examined my face. Had I grown horns in the middle of the night and now he found me so unattractive he couldn't stand to even pretend he was interested?

Quincy's voice broke through the door. "Evelyn, please open the door."

My face crumbled as salty tears tumbled down my cheeks. "Leave me alone," I sobbed.

"Are you crying?" Even from the other side of the door I registered the alarm in his voice.

"No, it's allergies. I'm allergic to assholes."

"Can you just give me five minutes ... please."

Unlocking the door, I opened it a crack to tell him to piss off, but Quincy pulled it wider, gently shoving me back inside. The camera crew close on his heels, he spun around closing the door in their faces before they could get in. Dropping his hands to his knees, he took a few deep breaths.

"Quincy?" I pulled at the toilet paper roll wiping my runny nose.

"Just let me speak." He sounded frustrated, which boggled my mind seeing how I was the one he offended. "When you walked down that aisle yesterday you took my breath away. And then you opened your mouth just confirming my inability to breathe was now a long-term chronic condition. I like you. I just wish I'd met you away from this stupid show and this spotlight." He pointed to the bathroom door. "That ... them ... it's a lot. I knew having a reality television show follow us around was gonna be weird. What I didn't count on was it making *me* weird. This morning when I answered the door, I was peppered with questions about whether we fucked last night."

"Yuck," I said, with a sniffle.

"Yeah, I just think some stuff should be between you and me. Not for the world." With the pad of his thumb, he swiped the runny snot from under my nose, wiping it on my tank top.

"Eww, why did you have to wipe it on my tank top? I mean the toilet paper is literally right here." I held up a wad of paper.

Cupping my face, his mouth met mine. His tongue was respectful but his hands were on demon time exploring my physique in the light weight T-shirt and booty shorts. As his hands traversed my body, his kisses became more aggressive, demanding all of me. His hand found my breast, squeezing tightly. Before slipping under my tank top, his fingers landed on my erect nipple, pinching it with enough force to provoke a low, breathy moan.

Listen, I was down to fuck the moment I locked eyes with him at the end of the aisle. And if our first time occurred while pressed against the counter of a hotel bathroom, I was here for it. Quincy's hand slid from my breast to the waistband of my boy shorts. Knocking on the other side of the door pulled me from my all-consuming longing for him.

"Quincy can you please open the door. You two signed contracts, you agreed to this."

His jaw slammed shut and hardened as he pulled away. Retreating several steps back, he scratched at his tapered fade. "I'm still invested, that hasn't changed."

A warmth spread through my body, the area around my mouth still prickly from his beard. "Message received."

~

QUINCY

Yes, I graduated from law school and actively practiced law, so you would think I'd be better able to articulate what I was feeling, but I bungled things with Evelyn this morning and made her cry. My circle was small and I didn't give a fuck about most people, but Evelyn made me ... made me what? This time yesterday I didn't know who Evelyn Townsend was, but she was the kind of woman that left an impression like a hot branding tool.

She stabbed the eggs on her plate, happily humming an unfamiliar tune. The tears that stained her face thirty minutes prior were a distant memory. At least she didn't hold grudges, when she said it was good she meant it.

"Hey do you want to check out the basket we got?" I asked.

"We got a basket?"

"Yeah, I told you this morning we got a gift basket."

She arched a perfectly shaped eyebrow. "The details of this morning are kind of foggy."

"Fair enough," I said, setting the fork on my plate as my cell phone pinged. "It's your brother." Evan and I exchanged numbers last night with the promise of hanging out. "Why is your brother calling me?" I whispered, eyeing her suspiciously. Had she called her six-foot-four brother telling him her jerkoff husband hurt her feelings?

Evelyn threw her hands over her head, giving her body a stretch. "Because he's clingy ... like me."

Hitting the speakerphone I answered, "Hello?"

"Good morning Big Bro. Hope you had a good night. Just wanted to check on the newlyweds."

"Hey Evan, let's try not to scare this one off. I don't think he's figured out that we're a buy one get one free type of deal." Evelyn leaned closer to the phone on the table between us.

"Oh well if you don't know now you do Q."

"Why are you so chipper? It's ten in the morning and you had way more alcohol than me." I'd watched Evan throw back several beers, one full bottle of champagne, which he and I shared, and a never-ending procession of tequila shots. All while dancing and sneaking sips from Evelyn's wine glass. The fact he was awake, speaking coherent sentences, and cheerful was proof he had a lead stomach.

"I'm not new to this I'm true to this. Last night was light work for me."

Evelyn bit into a silver dollar pancake she'd rolled over a piece of sausage, talking through chews. "What do you want, Dumbo?"

I furrowed my brow and with a look whispered, "Dumbo?"

"Because of his big ears," Evelyn mouthed, putting her hands up to her head flapping them wildly.

"I was thinking we could meet for a late lunch. I was talking to the families and most everyone's on board. Your fine ass mom said she'd come, and a few of your best men."

Did he just call my foster mom fine?

Evan continued, "The way I see it we're family now so we all need to get to know each other."

Evelyn's eyes landed on me, a soft smile on her face. If I had my way, I'd prefer to stay in bed with her all day. Ordering room service and exploring one another's bodies. But spending time with the family was fine too.

"Yeah, I think we can make that happen. When were you thinking?"

"How about three. It could be an early dinner, give people a chance to recuperate."

"Sounds cool just text us the deets."

"Cool Big Bro. See you two later."

"He's always wanted a big brother. I'm sorry ... you'll have to play catch with him on the weekends and teach him how to ride a bike."

"See, I can't tell if you're joking or not." I wrinkled my nose. As an only child, I'd wished for a brother or sister to play with when I was younger. But my childhood was not traditional and truthfully it was probably best no one else had to suffer through it. "Let's open the gift basket."

Plucking the card from the outside of the cellophane-wrapped basket, I read it aloud.

"Congratulations to the happy couple. The hard work

of getting to know one another is still ahead but all work and no play makes life very dull. So let's mix things up with a trip to …" I paused for dramatic effect even though Evelyn was already hanging onto my every word.

"Texarkana, Arkansas!" I beamed.

Evelyn's face dropped. "What? Where the fuck is that?"

"I'm guessing somewhere in Arkansas."

Snatching the card from me she reread the note. "Asshole, it says St. Lucia."

"Does it? My bad." I laughed, while trying to dodge the blows from her hand playfully hitting me.

Scooping her out of her chair, I dropped her on the couch pinning her arms overhead. Leaning in, she surrendered her mouth to mine. The sweetness from the jam and syrup clung to her lips and I kissed and sucked at her mouth until the sweetness faded before releasing my hold. The presence of the cameras was really throwing the energy off. If we were alone, my face would already be securely between her thighs on a scouting mission.

"I think we should take a nap for like an hour and then get up start packing and get ready for linner." I suggested.

"Linner?"

"Not quite lunch, not quite dinner."

Her face lit up into a glorious smile when she got the joke. I could die a happy man, I'd made the most beautiful woman I had ever come across laugh. On second thought, maybe dying was a bit premature. I still needed to make her legs shake, hear her scream my name, and watch as her lips were wrapped around me. Death could wait.

~

EVELYN

AT FISK AND CO., I found my baby brother had gone all out, reserving a private room. When Quincy and I entered the space, I spied several familiar faces from last night. Separating, we walked around the table greeting friends and family.

When I got to Walt, I gave him a big hug. "Thanks for the burgers last night. That was some elite shit."

Walt bowed his head. "It was nothing, when my bro says his bride is hungry and he needs an assist, that's what I do. I'm the fixer."

I gave his hand a soft squeeze. It was nice knowing Quincy had a trusted friend in Walt, especially since his blood relatives appeared to be in short supply. I was happy to add Walt as one of my friends. He seemed reliable and he had Quincy's back, so that was a plus.

Moving on to my brother I greeted him with open arms. "How did you pull this all off?"

"Come on Evie, you know I get shit done."

This wasn't 100 percent accurate. Evan was a procrastinator who often waited until the last possible minute before getting stuff done. At thirty-two I still had to remind him of doctor's appointments and to pay his car registration. But the one thing about Evan was he always came through for me. I could call him at four in the morning from another state in the middle of a blizzard and Evan would lace up snow shoes if he had to, to get to me.

Finally making it to my chair, I took a seat in between Quincy and Meryl.

Evan tapped his fork to his water glass focusing the

attention on him. "Before we stuff our faces, I just wanted to say thank you to Evie and Big Bro Q for getting married and making us all family. I for one am hoping for years of this. Backyard barbecues, birthday parties, and holidays. Please expect a Happy Thanksgiving and Merry Christmas text from me in the next few months because we are family now and family is everything."

I chuckled under my breath, Evan was on his Dominic Toretto kick, all he was missing was a cold bottle of Corona. This was all so surreal, like I was living in an alternate universe. It was a random Thursday and I was just hanging out with my new husband and our family. Normally I'd be at my art gallery fielding questions or working in the makeshift studio in the back. I agreed to embark on this journey, but there was so much I hadn't accounted for, like how we were going to meld our lives together. Was he an early riser? Did he go to the gym after work? Did he eat out every night? Was he a homebody or a party animal? Did he have allergies?

"Do you have any pets?" I whispered, as my brother droned on with some random story from our childhood and our twin connection.

"What?"

"Pets, do you have pets?"

"I have a dog," he said, turning his attention back to Evan.

"I just wanna say that if any of you need anything I got you. Because we are—"

"Family, we get it sweetie." I interrupted. "Sorry E but our flight leaves at nine tonight." I offered an apologetic nose wrinkle.

Evan sighed. "OK let's eat."

After a few bites of her roasted chicken Meryl asked, "So where are you two going on your honeymoon?"

"St. Lucia," I beamed.

"Oh bitch, jealous. Warm weather and fruity drinks where can I sign up?"

"You just have to marry a total stranger and you too could get a five-day, four-night stay at a mid-level hotel," Quincy said, taking a bite of his turkey club.

I couldn't read him. Was that a joke or was he pissed about something? In the morning he admitted the cameras were a distraction. When I was selected they told me to ignore the cameras and act natural, so I'm certain they offered him the same advice. But I get it, how do you act natural when everything about this is so unreal? I couldn't blame him if he was crabby.

Seated at the table were our closest friends and family but someone was noticeably missing. "Dad, where's Mom?"

"Uh, well baby she wasn't feeling too hot. So she decided to stay home. Maybe fighting a bit of a cold."

"Hmph, she seemed fine last night when she was giving her warm and fuzzy toast."

"Now Evelyn you know your mother had some concerns about this whole thing." He moved his hand in a circle through the air. "Marrying a guy you don't know. No offense Quincy." My stepdad was a Shereè apologist, even when she was wrong he always found a way to take her side.

"None taken," Quincy said.

"I don't need her to understand, but support would be nice." I tossed my napkin over the food I'd barely touched.

"You know how your mother is."

"Yeah, well I'm sick of it." My chair squeaked as I pushed it back exiting the private room to get some air.

On the empty outside patio, I shivered in the cold having left my coat at the table. Even when she was absent my mother knew just how to work her way under my skin. All she had to do was come to the dinner and smile. I wasn't asking for her approval, I was grown and didn't need it. I'd made a choice, a choice my mother was vehemently against but a choice all the same. Couldn't she just try to see things from my point of view for once? Try to get to know her new son-in-law. My mother was probably counting down the ninety days until she could throw this all in my face and tell me the dreaded words, "I told you so."

"You good?" Quincy called from behind me.

"I told you I had mommy issues." My breathing hitched as a tightness seized my chest.

"I get it. My foster mom doesn't exactly agree either."

"But she's here." A heaviness piled onto my already slumped shoulders and for the second time today, tears were rolling down my face.

Quincy took my hand in his. "Your mom's hang ups are not your burden to bear. Don't let her steal your happiness. That shit is rare." His gaze was fixated on me soft and filled with concern.

The insanely handsome man standing in front of me was right. Before we'd arrived at the restaurant I was happy and looking forward to spending time with our family and friends. I was letting my mother steal my joy and I'd been letting her do it for years.

"How did you get so smart?" I asked, wiping away the tears from my eyes.

"I'm a lawyer, remember?" He flashed a brilliant smile before throwing his jacket over my shoulders.

"I promise I'm not a cry baby." I sniffled.

Quincy pulled me close to him for shared warmth. "Don't worry about it. You haven't seen me cry yet. I'm a mess. It sounds like someone is strangling a cat the way I cry out."

A ghost of a smile crept over my face. "What's our dog's name?"

"Totes McGoats."

Rearing my head back I asked, "Are you shitting me right now?"

"Nope, you can call him Totes or McGoats, he'll even come to Totey McGoaty."

I wagged my finger at him. "See one minute I think you're super cool and then you say shit like that, which gives me pause. Long, pregnant, awkward pauses."

CHAPTER 7

QUINCY

What should have been a nonstop flight with us landing in St. Lucia in a little over five hours, turned into delays, missed connections, and layovers. Causing us to check in a day late, nearly twenty-four, full hours from when our journey began. But the hotel room helped to soothe my grumpy mood. This wasn't mid level, this was a five-star suite with a private pool and outdoor shower. When the hotel learned of our hellish trek, they upgraded our accommodations.

"This is sick, the shower has a full body shower thinga-majigger," Evelyn said, bounding out of the bathroom with an umbrellaed drink in hand.

"Not gonna lie this is nice."

"I could go for something sweet. Is it too late for room service?"

"I like the way you think Miss Townsend."

The hotel kitchen closed at eleven so it was indeed too

late for room service. Opening the mini bar, I pulled out all the sweet treats, placing them in a pile on the bed.

"Where should I start," Evelyn mumbled under her breath. While she decided, she removed the sweatshirt she'd worn on the plane. The weather in St. Lucia was a marked difference from the freezing cold of Chicago. Climbing on the bed, she picked through the full-size candy bars and bags of chips. "Do you like peanut butter?"

"Love it."

"Do you like cookie wafers?"

"Yep."

"What about coconut?"

"I'm down for chocolate covered coconut."

Evelyn wrinkled her nose.

"Was that the wrong answer?"

"There are no right or wrong answers. Just ones that are better than others." She winked.

The last few hours had been stressful, hurrying from one terminal to the next. But it was all worth it because I was sitting across from this beautiful woman who I couldn't stop staring at. Even with wary eyes and frazzled strands of hair that curled at her temples, she was still gorgeous. Running my hand over my beard, I resisted the urge to touch her. I didn't need sleep or food, I just needed to feel her warm, delicate skin under the palm of my hand.

"I'll eat whatever you don't," I said, falling back onto the bed.

Opening a Snickers bar, she split it in half handing me a piece. We sat in silence eating candy and chocolate and chasing it down with fizzy soda. Evelyn swayed back and forth humming under her breath, clearly content to no longer have to book it from one departure gate to the other. This was a moment I wanted to remember so I could duplicate it for the rest of our lives. The comfortable silence, the happy contentment I felt, like everything I wanted was right here in this room. I snuck a glance over at Evelyn with questioning eyes. How was someone I didn't know seventy-two hours ago able to make me feel this way?

Evelyn leaned back turning to face me. "Are you good? We could go in search of real food if you're still hungry?"

"I'm great. Everything is perfect." I indulged in a big yawn stretching my arms over my head to work out the kinks.

Evelyn's hands found their way to my beard, rubbing my cheek and tugging at my chin. "I like your beard."

"Thank goodness because if you hated it, we would have a problem."

"If I asked you to shave it you wouldn't?" She bit into her lower lip, diverting 25 percent of my attention to her teeth running over her plump mouth.

"No."

She gave me an understanding nod.

"But I have a strange feeling, in a few months there will be nothing that I won't do for you." I was tired, my body jet lagged, my brain was in a fog, and I was fighting an impending hard on. That was the only way to explain my oversharing.

"I'll never ask you to shave your beard."

"Good, cause what if I do and I look hideous and you hate it?" I rested my hand on her waist, my fingers finding the sliver of exposed skin peeking out from the bottom of her shirt.

"Not possible." She had moved on from my beard to my bushy eyebrows. "You're a handsome man, but you already know that."

"I don't know about that, but at least now I know you think I am."

I wasn't good at reading people but her mink eyes were screaming for me to kiss her. Leaning forward, I was prepared to test the waters but a cough from the production assistant stopped me cold. This king size bed was an island with just me and Evelyn but all around us were the crew of *Why Knot*, like sharks circling our little oasis waiting for us to make a wrong move. Without explanation, I retreated offering a meek smile before leaning back on the bed.

Evelyn removed her hand from my face turning her attention to the ceiling. Eventually her eyes drooped as she fought unsuccessfully to keep them open. I listened to the soft hum of her breathing signaling she'd boarded the sleep train. *Nothing is perfect.* This was the phrase I repeated to myself, trying to tamper down any unrealistic expectations. But by all indications the experts hit it out of the park with this match. Goose pimples raised over my flesh. *If this shit actually works I'm gonna have to send the experts a fruit basket*, I thought as I drifted off to sleep.

EVELYN

AFTER A LIGHT BREAKFAST, Quincy and I were eager to explore the resort. Oracle Resort and Spa was five-stars with pools, a lazy river, and ten restaurants to choose from. And because it was all inclusive I could eat and drink to my heart's content. That's why at 9:48 in the morning I was walking the grounds with a Lava Flow, the rum and pineapple iced drink was hitting the spot. After booking an afternoon activity with the concierge, we headed to the beach.

I'd hoped our first morning at the resort would find me walking funny from getting dicked down the night before, but jet lag put a stop to all that. This morning I awoke with the foolish belief Quincy would wake me up ready to consummate the fuck out of this marriage. But that was also a no go with him teasing me with kisses to my back and shoulders while flirting with the waistband of my shorts before hopping out of bed to take a shower. Leaving me in bed ... alone, frustrated, and dripping wet. The fact I was sleeping next to a hot-blooded male and still had to butter my own muffin to release some of the pressure while he was in the shower didn't sit right with me.

"Can you believe that a day ago we were in cold ass Chicago and now we're in paradise?" Quincy asked, taking a sip of his mojito.

"I could definitely get used to this," I said, pressing my iridescent purple toes into the gold sand.

"Don't," he said, with an insanely captivating smile.

"What? No living in the lap of luxury?"

"No, life with me is Sunday crossword puzzles and maybe occasionally ordering buffalo wings with our pizza."

I hated that I couldn't tell if he was joking. If I could hop in a time machine and zoom past the getting to know you phase I gladly would. It was embarrassing having to ask my husband first-date questions. Like, what's your favorite color? His was Sedona red which was very specific. Or how do you take your coffee? Quincy's answer was three sugars and tons of sweet cream. And then there were his questions to me, it was always what was your major in college and never do you want to come over here and sit on my face.

"Can you swim?" Quincy asked, removing his T-shirt with the characters from the Soul Glo commercial on it.

My eyes practically overheated trying to capture the Adonis-like physique before me. The light from the sun created an aura around Quincy as if God himself was confirming this man had been made with special care just for me. His skin was smooth and free from any imperfection, not a pimple not a bump, the perfect amount of hair that started at his navel and traveled downward.

His chest and abs were chiseled, almost appearing fake because they were so well defined. Then there was the tattoo on his left chest of a queen of hearts playing card. The card looked like it was stitched on to his chest like patchwork. Moving closer for a better look, I rubbed at the tattoo expecting it to be raised but my hand touched his smooth, warm skin instead.

"This tattoo is amazing." I tilted my head at every angle inspecting the work.

"Thanks."

"It looks so real, like it should be sewn on a jacket or something. Also, love that you made the queen Black."

"Of course, nothing but Black love over here," he said, letting me fondle him far longer than was necessary.

"Ok, Mr. Parrish I see you."

"You never answered my question."

"What was that?"

"Do you know how to ..."

I pulled my coverup over my head, dropping it on to the cabana bed. From Quincy's expression it was clear he was now the one distracted as he tried to take me all in. Adjusting the cups of the tangerine bikini top, I made sure to put on a show. I bent slowly, fetching the sunscreen from my beach bag, shaking the bottle with my whole body so my breast jiggled before smoothing sunscreen onto my mahogany skin.

"You just don't believe in playing fair, do you?" he asked.

"What? I don't know what you're talking about." After covering my face, neck and chest I repeated the process on Quincy, applying sunscreen to his body as well. "Will you do my back?" I asked offering him the bottle.

With a nod, Quincy massaged the sunscreen into my back paying close attention to my lower back and thighs. His hands kneading my skin caused carnal tingles to scale my body.

As he leaned in closer, his breath tickled my shoulder. "Are you ready to get wet?"

A thread of laughter ripped through me. "You have no idea, buddy."

The water was warm allowing us to jump right in. Quincy splashed me with the lukewarm water before freezing in place. "Is it cool if I get your hair wet?"

"Oh yeah, this is a wet and wavy. We're good," I said, splashing him back before flinging my arms over his shoulders.

The *Why Knot* crew remained on the beach filming us from the shore line. I suppose that helped to ease some of Quincy's nervousness since there wasn't a physical camera just inches away from us. He brushed his lips against mine pulling back before I could kiss him. He did this practice a few more times, brushing my lips with his, running his tongue over my mouth but never what I really wanted, devouring my lips with his.

A frown etched onto my unkissed mouth. "I don't like this game, let's play another."

Dropping my hands into the ocean, I found the waist-band of his swim trunks. The waist was tied too tightly for me to freely stick my hand inside. Working the string I pulled the waist loose, slipping my hand down his abdomen until I found exactly what I was looking for. The corners of my mouth lifted into a mischievous grin, he was happy to see me. With slow aquatic strokes, I stared intentionally into his face watching his eyes spark with longing, his nostrils flared and his breath slowed against my lips.

"Promise not to tease me again." I said.

"Ahh, I can't ... make that promise." He managed to speak with some difficulty.

"Hmm, what can you promise?"

"I can promise ... you ... that I intend to return the fucking favor."

"Kiss me."

His tongue slid into my mouth as he cupped my face with one hand and held onto his swim trunks with the other. Being in this man's arms was my new favorite place. The friction of my hand and the sea water, forced him to moan inside my mouth as our connected bodies floated further from shore.

"Evelyn ..." His breathing was ragged. "We should ...

probably ... stop before everyone on this beach gets an X-rated show."

I didn't want to stop I wanted to stroke him to nirvana. I wanted his tawny face to flush and his eyes to roll toward the back of his head. I wanted to watch his features contort and twist as his secret sauce emptied into my hand. Wrapping my arm around his neck I stole one more kiss, the way his tongue clung to mine wasn't the response of a man who wanted to stop. Finally, releasing him from my grip I floated away plunging my head underneath the salty water.

QUINCY

OUR MORNING on the beach was followed by swimming with dolphins. Something neither of us had done before, I thought it was cool for us to have this shared experience. Sitting poolside, we watched as the animals performed tricks; in a few minutes we would join the dolphins as props in their aquatic shows. Evelyn oohed and ahhed as the mammals' tail walked and tossed around a ball, but I was having a hard time concentrating, remembering what happened the last time I was submerged in water.

I was pretty sure this time would be rated G, highly doubting she would give me an Arnold Palmer in front of the dolphins. My mind flashed back to the satisfied look on her face. Evelyn enjoyed driving me bat shit crazy, knowing there was absolutely nothing I could do. Not going to lie I definitely ran through the calculated risk in my head deciding against fucking my new bride for the first time in the open water.

Sitting next to her now, her face lighting up with an angelic smile as the dolphins skirted across the water, I scrunched my nose, this woman was a psychopath. No less than two hours ago she had my dick firmly in her hand and now it was all rainbows and lollipops. She could fool the dolphins but she couldn't fool me. How was what transpired not the only thing that consumed her mind? It was literally all I could think about right now. Well, that and how I was going to get her alone for an encore performance.

The production team literally followed us around twenty-four seven. Well maybe not twenty-four seven, there were a few hours when I was sleeping that the camera wasn't zooming in on my face. Maybe I could book another hotel room and we could just go missing for a few hours. Our first time should be on our terms and not captured by Earl, the horny cameraman. The show *Why Knot* wasn't TV-MA, the sex was always implied, fade to black with a few moans and giggles laid over top for razzle dazzle. Even so I preferred my sex life be private. Which is why coming on a reality show was the first place I fucked up. But if I hadn't agreed I wouldn't have met Evelyn and be sitting poolside trying to come up with creative ways to fuck her on the low.

After Benny the dolphin was done swimming in circles, it was time for us to join in on the action. Benny circled around Evelyn and me before stopping and splashing us with his tail. The show ended with Benny kissing Evelyn on the cheek.

"That was fun," Evelyn said, bending at the waist to dry her legs, giving me an unfettered view of her backside. She was wearing the hell out of those little strips of fabric. The tangerine swimsuit highlighted the richness of her skin.

"It was OK. Something to tick off my bucket list, but don't even get me started on the whole ethical piece of this dolphin show."

She nodded thoughtfully. "Yeah, it's always left me a little conflicted. These animals were meant to be in the wild."

"Exactly, like my dude Benny wants to be under the sea with Ariel but he's forced to be here working. I watched a whole documentary on some of these aquatic attractions. The fishing tactics used to capture them is like the Wild West of the seas. It's pretty fucked. And when they get to one of these places they remain in a constant state of hunger and stress." Evelyn was listening intently but I didn't want to come off as a zealot so I backed off. "The worst part of all this is having some lame handler name that dolphin Benny, knowing good and well that he doesn't favor a Benny."

"Oh yeah." She chuckled. What would you have named him?"

Hunching my shoulders toward my ears I said, "I don't know, something like Fleetwood or Water Dancer."

"You are not good at naming things."

"What do you mean?" I reached for her hand as we walked back to the hotel.

"Your dog, this dolphin."

"Totes McGoats Parrish, is a fine name. Thank you very much." I said, to which Evelyn burst into hysterical laughter.

Upon returning to our room, we fell into a sleep coma, napping far longer than either of us intended. The afternoon fading into evening as we snored the time away. Now with only ten minutes until our restaurant reservation, I stood in the mirror fixing my button-down shirt. We'd decided to get dressed up for our first dinner at the resort; I'd opted for a lavender dress shirt with gray suit sans tie.

Collecting my wallet and cellphone, I yelled, "Yo, tick tock. Don't tell me you're one of those women who can never be on …"

Evelyn entered the room and I forgot how to form intelligible sentences. She was in a simple gold, silk dress that clung to her body like a second skin. Her hair was half up, half down with the longer layers cascading down her back. If she was wearing makeup it was difficult to tell, she had the most flawless skin but parts of her face, chest and arms shimmered so she must have done something. This was the first time since our wedding day that I'd seen her all dressed up. She looked amazing that night but something about the gold dress was causing heat to rise up my neck.

"I'm ready," she said, while tossing the room access card into her clutch.

"I can see that. You look nice."

Her full lips, painted a glossy peach parted into a smile. "Thank you."

Holding out a hooked arm I said, "Let's head down."

"I'm starving." She rubbed her stomach while threading her free arm through mine.

In the elevator I tried my best not to stare but she was making the task impossible. Her hair fell in soft full waves that draped over her radiant skin, if there was a power outage the illumination from her skin could light the way.

"When I said you looked nice, I lied."

Evelyn squinted, her smile fading. "You don't like it?" She ran her hand over the silk fabric.

"No, I like all of this. But saying you look nice isn't accurate." Nice was far too pedestrian of a word to describe her. "You are exquisite and honestly, I still don't think that's the right word. But it'll come to me, and when it does, I'll let you know."

Evelyn dipped her head with a toothless smile, which caused my face to pull into a goofy smile of its own. So, there we were one person smiling at their feet while the other smiled at the roof of the elevator. Both avoiding eye contact because that would make the perceptible butterflies fluttering their wings in our stomachs all the more real.

Chapter 8

EVELYN

We opted for Salsa Di Pomodoro, a quaint Italian restaurant where the wine was poured freely and the parmesan breadsticks were never ending.

"All-time favorite food?" he asked.

"Oh my God, now that's a hard question. Maybe pizza?"

"Pizza?"

"I know it's kinda basic but I love a good slice. You know the kind you have to bend to eat. Not, deep dish." I wagged my finger.

My response prompted another question from him. "Were you born in Chicago?" Grabbing his glass, he took a sip of the Prosecco Negroni.

"No." A playful smile danced across my lips.

"Where were you—"

"Guess." I leaned forward with excitement. Maybe this whole getting to know you business wasn't so boring after all.

"The world is big so I may need a hint."

Rubbing my hands together my smile was wide and gleaming. "OK first hint ... bright lights."

"That means you're from a major city. So I can rule out places like Kansas and Pocatello."

I didn't acknowledge his deductions I just moved on to the next hint. "This place has more hotels than any other location on the planet."

His eyes sparked with enthusiasm. I think he was enjoying this game as much as I was. "So it's a tourist attraction, once again ruling out Kansas and Pocatello."

"Last hint." With a raised eyebrow I rolled my teeth over my bottom lip. "Elvis."

"OK, Elvis is from Graceland. Wherever the fuck that is?"

"It's in Memphis."

"So he's from Memphis but I think most people associate him with another location that has bright neon lights and hotels as far as the eye can see."

I did my best to bite back a smile.

"Las Vegas. Final answer."

"Ding, ding, ding." I rolled my shoulders performing a dance in my chair.

"Those were easy hints." He winked. "So how long did you live there?"

"Ten years, my mom was a showgirl at the Flamingo. You know, show a little leg and ass. Tassels on the boobs."

"Damn, Momma Shereè was out there ..." He gyrated his torso.

"Yep, I'll have to show you pictures some time. She was a hottie."

"Still is," Quincy blurted out.

My eyelashes flipped open wide practically protruding from my skull. "Gross."

He raised his palms apologetically. "I'm just saying—"

"Don't just say. That's my mother, your mother-in-law." My voice was high pitched and I couldn't wipe the incredulous smirk off my face.

"And you're the spitting fucking image of her. That fat ass doesn't fall too far from the tree. That's all."

Making contact with his arm, I playfully swatted at him with my linen napkin. "Anyway, she met my stepdad one night at the casino and then six months later we moved to Chicago."

"Was it a hard transition?"

"It was weird at first but when we got to Chicago, Louis had a huge house and I got my own bedroom with one of those canopy beds like in the movies. So definite upgrade."

My mother used all of her charm and womanly wilds to land Louis. Before him, we were in a one-bedroom apartment with Evan and I sharing a pull-out sofa. Marrying Louis allowed my mother the ability to provide us with the lifestyle she'd always wanted. Fancy clothes and exotic family trips. Maybe that's why my mother was so averse to my profession, because in her eyes she'd gifted me with a head start and I chose instead to squander it on a career, that for her, ranked between vocations such as balloon-animal creator and sandwich artist.

"Are you originally from Chicago?" I asked, I wasn't going to be the only one in the hot seat.

"Born and raised."

"Were your mom and dad born in Chicago too?"

Tearing off a piece of bread, I dipped it into the seasoned olive oil.

Quincy cupped the back of his neck with his hand, taking a sip of water before answering. "Um ... my mother is from Panama and my father ... he's from Florida."

I wanted to ask him where his parents were now. He grew up in foster care and they were no-shows at the wedding so it felt safe to bet they were not a part of his life. There was a story there, but a romantic candlelit dinner was probably not the best setting for that conversation so I decided to put a pin in it.

The waiter returned with steaming-hot plates loaded with pasta and meat.

"Delicioso," Quincy said, with a thick Italian accent, his fingers raised in a chef's kiss.

"OK no." Looking up to the waiter I apologized. "I'm sorry you had to hear that." As the waiter walked away, I shot Quincy a dubious glare.

"What? I was just speaking Italian."

"You were talking like one of the Mario Brothers."

"And they're Italian." He offered a wonky smile that only lifted at one side.

I think I'd met someone whose attempts at foreign accents were worse than mine. Was this what I had to look forward to? Us traveling the world and him speaking French, Spanish, or Tagalog all poorly. I shook the thought from my head, twirling the pasta around the fork, I took a bite.

"I have another question." Quincy said between mouthfuls.

"Twenty questions with this one." I licked sauce from the corner of my mouth.

"Why'd you audition for the show?"

"Why Knot?" I laughed entirely too hard at my corny joke that left Quincy rolling his eyes. "Ba dum dum, ching."

Leaning back in his chair, he waited for my fit of laughter to settle. "Seriously."

I released a severe, tight breath. "I don't know. It's gonna sound stupid and cheesy."

"Look, we both applied to a reality show looking for love so no judgment here."

"Honestly, I have really bad taste in men. I know what I want but I get easily distracted by the shiny object in the corner. Or I'm falling for potential that may or may not ever materialize. And full transparency, when I love someone I give them all of me and oftentimes that energy isn't recip-rocated."

There was no need to hide my relationship track record. We were married and this was something he needed to know. If I were good at relationships, I wouldn't need a show to help me find my soulmate. Maybe to some that made me damaged goods but I didn't see it that way. No matter how many times I'd been hurt, I was always open to finding love again.

"So you turned to reality tv?" He said no judgment but his voice sounded hella judgy.

My shoulders flinched. "It's no crazier than going on a blind date or swiping right on Tinder."

"I'll give you that." He cut into his stuffed shells pasta with his fork.

"What about you? You don't seem like the type of guy who would do this kinda shit."

"Too smart?" he quipped.

"Too calculated."

Quincy's jaw moved from side to side. "I did it as a joke."

My smile faded, did he just call this a joke? Who would inconvenience their entire lives for a joke? Marrying a stranger wasn't for the faint of heart. The process involved inviting someone into your life in hopes that love followed. This wasn't some viral social media dance or a night at the comedy club. Those things were jokes, this ... our marriage was very real.

Quincy continued completely oblivious that his words were feeding my silent fear that I was already too invested. "My friend, AJ wanted to audition for the show. You met him at the wedding. He convinced me to come with him and I completed the application and interview process for laughs. I didn't think I'd ever get selected. So when they told me I had a match ..." He placed his hands next to his temples and flared his fingers out. "Mind blown."

"So you weren't even looking to settle down." I tried as best I could to keep my tone even but there was a tightness in my chest and Quincy's words were the vise around my heart twisting slowly.

"I hadn't really given it much thought. But when someone claims they've found your perfect match it's kinda hard to walk away from that."

"Right." I took a long drag from my wine glass hoping to settle my nerves.

Quincy examined my face, my temples dotted with sweat, the cut of my glare doing nothing to hide my mistrust. "Not the answer you expected?"

"No, I guess it doesn't matter how we got here or for

what reason." I was doing my best to tamp down the insecurities that were bubbling up.

I didn't know what reason I was expecting but "I did it as a joke," wasn't it. How does someone who wasn't even thinking about marriage three months ago end up on a honeymoon? If he saw this experience as just a bit of fun how could I take any of his intentions seriously? The last thing I wanted was to fall alone. Been there, done that. Falling in love while the other party's feet are firmly planted is a long descent to the ground, with rocks and bramble along the way.

"Well, if it helps, I'm happy I listened to my gut and said yes." He reached for my hand entwining his fingers with mine.

And just like that my head took off spinning willing to ignore all the bright red flags that littered this conversation. Why was he so fucking handsome with a smile that muddled my senses? Quincy's finger gently massaged my hand, I was 85 percent certain there would be a wet spot on the seat of my dress when I stood. All this from holding hands, imagine what would happen if I could just feel the weight of his body pressed against mine. Our reasons for being here were very different but he claimed he wanted to try, and I had no reason not to believe him.

"Here's to listening to our guts." I clinked my glass into his. Hopeful by the end of the night he would be rearranging mine.

Quincy excused himself to the bathroom while our plates were being cleared from the table. My pasta and shrimp dish was delicious. I wanted to eat the entire serving and lick the plate clean but the thought of dessert stopped me. When Quincy returned minutes later he offered a meek smile, his face slick with sweat.

"You OK?" I asked, taking stock of his damp face, something was definitely different about his countenance.

"Geesh, I don't know I'm feeling a little queasy." Quincy wiped at his forehead, coughing.

"You look a little off."

"I do?" He grabbed his glass of water taking shaky sips.

"Do you think it's something you ate? Because I may have eaten the same thing."

"I don't know but I feel cold and nauseous." He pressed his hand to his mouth as if to suppress the urge to hurl.

"Maybe we should call a doctor?" I surveyed the room calling over our handler, Jared.

"NO! No doctor," he said with vigor before descending into a weak frown.

"What's up guys?" Jared asked.

"Quincy's not feeling well. And he looks even worse."

Quincy shot an unamused glare in my direction.

"What seems to be the problem, Quincy?" Jared asked, bending to get a better look.

"I feel like crap right now. I think I ..." He gagged before swallowing hard.

Pushing my chair back, I went into full on caretaker mode. "OK we need to get him back to the room. You're not well, you need to rest."

"I don't wanna ruin our dinner. We just ordered dessert."

"Barfing all over my very nice dress would be one way to ruin the night. Let's get you upstairs." I did my best to reassure him with my eyes that he was not ruining our dinner. It didn't matter to me if we were at a fancy restaurant or on the bathroom floor, I just wanted to be with him.

Quincy allowed Jared and I to help him to his feet. "Can we just call it guys. You're not gonna get anything useful from me for the rest of the night. Unless me clutching the toilet bowl is the B footage you're looking for."

Jared made a call, following closely behind, while I helped Quincy out of the restaurant and to the elevator banks. "OK we'll wrap filming for tonight. If you're not feeling better in the morning, you're going to the resort doctor," Jared instructed.

Quincy leaned on me for support while the intern helped to remove the mic packs attached to our bodies.

"Understood, I'm sure I just need to puke it out, drink some ginger ale, and get some sleep. Thanks guys." Quincy gave a faint wave as we entered the elevator alone.

As the elevator doors closed I propped him against the wall. "Listen it's gonna be OK. If you vomit, I'll hold your hair back," I joked. Touching my hand to his forehead I realized I didn't know what I was doing. "You don't feel warm, but I'm not really sure."

He deliberately uncurled his vertebrae, his face relaxed. "I'm suddenly feeling much better."

"What?" My head flinched back slightly.

"I'm fine. I was just pretending." He smoothed down his dress shirt releasing a long sigh of relief.

"Why would you do that?" I was looking forward to my cannoli crepes.

"Because ... now we're alone." His eyes snaked along my body. "All alone."

"Oh." Swallowing hard the weight of his words sunk in.

"Yeah, now you have to back up all that shit you've been talking."

"You don't think I can?" My pulse quickened. This man had gone full Denzel Washington downstairs just so he could be alone with me. Impressed wasn't the word. We had all night, I could finally start making a dent in my list of ways to drive Quincy wild. I'd only started the list three days ago but it was already as long as my arm. Heat whooshed up my body at the thought of this man's hands on my most delicate and sensitive parts.

"Nope."

My laughter sprinkled the air. "I sure hope you're hydrated."

The cocky smile fell from his face, his lips quivering he said, "Wait what?"

QUINCY

BACK IN THE HOTEL ROOM, Evelyn squealed. "What's all this?"

"I knew my little stunt would end our dinner early so I ordered a dessert sampler from room service while I was in the men's room."

"Impressive." She snagged a bite-sized brownie popping it in her mouth. "So how long were you plotting the scene in the restaurant?"

"Since you kissed me in the ocean this morning." I fidgeted with my wedding band. I wasn't used to wearing jewelry and the past few days I'd taken up the habit of twisting the matte-black band around my finger.

I hoped my little stunt wasn't too over the top. But I just couldn't figure out another way to get Evelyn alone. If I'd let the crew come back to the suite I would have to wait it out while they pointed their stupid cameras in my face waiting for me to do or say something interesting. By the time the crew left Evelyn would probably have trouble keeping her eyes open. The last thing I wanted was to go another night without our bodies entangled all naked and sweaty.

Evelyn unlatched her high, strappy heels tossing them to the side. I was starting to realize my blushing bride was lackadaisical when it came to her things. She'd undress and leave clothes lying on the floor. I was always able to find her because her discarded items led me to her like bread crumbs. Picking up her forgotten shoes, I tucked them next to the couch. The last thing I wanted was to stumble over one of her heels in the middle of the night and be impaled by the stiletto. Losing an eye would definitely dampen the rest of our trip.

She stared at me expectantly waiting for me to make the first move. Normally I'd know exactly what to do, but this was different. I was married to this woman; she wasn't some one-night stand I would never see again. Evelyn was my wife and I didn't know her favorite sexual position or if she liked foreplay or preferred to just jump right in.

What if my moves, which I'd honed during years in the swampy waters of the dating pool, didn't curl her toes? Worse yet, what if she was forced to fake it in hopes that my cumbersome act at seduction would end. And if she faked it,

I wouldn't even be able to tell because I didn't know her body and how it naturally responded.

I shifted from one foot to the other looking for an opening. "Do you remember when we were in the elevator before dinner and I said I felt stumped trying to find words that best described you?" I asked, slowly moving closer.

"Yes."

"I think I have the word now." I whispered softly.

Her eyes narrowed to mere slits as she braced herself for my next sentence.

"I think the word is divine."

"Wow, that's a pretty hefty word."

"It fits ... because you're heavenly and goddess like." My eyes, soft like satin, focused on her.

"And you're full of shit."

"I was actually being serious." Throwing my hands in the air I released the thought. "You know what never mind."

Evelyn seized my arm giving it a reassuring squeeze. "No, don't do that."

"What?" My shoulders sagged. Her response left me feeling a bit deflated.

"Don't just brush it aside. I'm sorry. You were speaking and I'm all ears."

Pursing my lips, I took note of the sincerity in her voice deciding it was safe to continue. "I settled on divine because there is something mystic and ethereal about you. Maybe because I don't really know you yet and everything you do kind of leaves me in awe. Seriously God was in his bag when he created you, because you are beyond perfect." My fingers were skipping up her arm. "It was stupid but there it is."

Evelyn shook her head, stretching slightly to reach for

my mouth, she kissed my lips like she was testing the temperature of the water, eager yet reluctant at the same time. My body responded to her instantly, my groin ached as my dick expanded and throbbed inside my pants. I reached under the skirt of her dress, the warmth of her skin making me hot and feverish.

That one kiss sent us into a frenzied hunger, hands flying, articles of clothing dropping to the floor in quick succession. We slowly stumbled to the bedroom, my shoulder and Evelyn's head knocking into walls and door jams along the way. I unhooked her purple embroidered, strapless bra, exposing her round, raised, brown nipples. Evelyn pitched in, tugging off her thong panties, tossing them aside with her feet.

Bumping up against the bed, she tumbled to the mattress. Her naked body displayed before me caused rapid fire heartbeats in my chest. My eyes meandered over her features, her supple breast, the curve of her waist, and her long legs slightly agape ready to receive me. An unruly twitching overtook my fingers, which ached with a need to touch her.

Leaning in, I whispered, "You are the most beautiful woman I have ever married." We laughed against one another's mouths. "How are you still single?" I tucked a tuft of hair that covered her eye behind her ear, grazing her forehead in the process. Even the simplest touch made my pulse quicken its throb.

Tugging at my chin she replied, "I'm not. I'm married to you, remember?"

"I guess the appropriate question is, how did I get so lucky?"

She slid her tongue in my mouth grabbing my face so she could have full control. The soft moans that escaped from her lips were driving me insane. Evelyn made those same sounds when she took a bite of delicious food. The thought that I could satisfy her was very rewarding. Pulling back to catch my breath, I surveyed her form trying to decide where to start first. I settled on her breasts, they were perfect; a little more than a handful, they spilled over the sides of my hands when I tried to cup them.

With the pad of my thumb, I smoothed the peaks of her breasts before circling her nipples with my tongue. The night ahead would be a long one because I'd just made it my mission to kiss, lick, and suck every part of her body. After the right breast I moved on to the left, showing it the same focused attention. Evelyn's hand patted my head letting me know I was a good boy.

Traveling down her body, I laid kisses on her stomach, which made her whimper, and the side of her torso which caused her to giggle. I took a mental note of each varying reaction to my touch. When I got to her thighs her body tensed in anticipation. Grabbing a leg, I rubbed her feet before wrapping my mouth around her big toe. This move caused her to sit up and take notice.

With her toe still stuffed in my mouth, I mumbled, "I'm sorry is toe stuff off limits?"

"No, I'm down for toe stuff." She was working hard to regulate her breathing.

What a relief, I didn't want to come off as some foot-fetish guy. That wasn't what this was about. I was just totally enamored with this woman and wanted to please her in every way.

With a grateful smile, I tickled the sole of her foot with my tongue causing her to squirm.

Dropping to my knees, I began my ascent upward. Once I kissed the soft skin of her inner thigh, Evelyn's hips began to move in a small circle longing for that initial lick of her clit. Sliding my hands under her ass, I settled in between her legs. The first lick caused her back to levitate from the bed. The next few twirls of my tongue sent her falling backward fisting the bedsheets. She was warm and gushy like those chewy exploding candies I kept in my office at work.

This was the best view in the house, watching as Evelyn twisted into a pretzel, her inner lips against my mouth as I slurped, sucked, and drove my tongue inside her. Her breathing took on a panting quality when I settled onto her bud. Parting my mouth, I tongue kissed her nerve center, causing Evelyn to drive her nails into my arms. Halfway through, I froze mid lick inching my head back hovering between her legs, which required Evelyn to move her hips against my stiff, outstretched tongue. This woman didn't disappoint, bracing her feet and using my ears as handlebars, she pulled closer swiveling and thrusting her center against my mouth. When her legs grew weak, shaky from ecstasy I finished her off, flicking and sucking her moist core until she exploded.

"Fuck ..." Her breath ragged, she squirmed trying to escape my tongue that was still softly teasing her. "You're gonna make my head explode," she said, pushing me away with her legs.

Sliding off the end of the bed, she landed in front of me, still crouched on the floor. She wrapped her arms around my neck kissing and licking herself from my lips and beard. If we weren't already married I would pop the question right now. This woman was perfection.

EVELYN

"FOR MY NEXT trick ladies and gentlemen." Licking his lips, he stood surveying the room.

Quincy sifted through a bowl of condoms sitting on the bedside table. You would think we were filming a porno with all the condoms scattered throughout the suite ... in the main living area, on both bedroom night stands and in the bathroom. The crew of *Why Knot* had us covered for wherever the mood struck. Grabbing a condom, he flipped it over in his hands. *Was he reading the label?* I really needed him to hurry the fuck up.

"Take your time. There's just a hot and horny naked woman in your bed."

"Calm down eager beaver."

Nudging him with my gaze, we exchanged a shared chuckle. "Eager beaver," I repeated feeling like I was on a natural high.

Quincy's tongue acrobatics were next level. I don't think we as a society celebrate the power of good cunnilingus. It's all about teasing and tension. Teasing me to the point I was ravenous and begging for release before pulling back and resetting, allowing me to catch my breath before he brought me to the edge once more.

Back at the foot of the bed, Quincy handed me the condom before tugging his boxer briefs off. He stood there naked making ridiculous Greek god poses, which I allowed because the man was indeed a work of art, with his chiseled stomach and smooth, copper-hued skin. And then there was the third limb that casually occupied the room making it hard ... all the puns intended ... to focus on anything else. Opening the condom wrapper, I pinched the tip of the latex before rolling it over the length of his plumb penis.

Quincy worked two fingers into my mouth before sliding those same two wet fingers inside of me. Kissing his stomach, I stretched my limbs wide giving him full access. As his thumb floated over my clit my insides wriggled, forcing me to bite down on his flesh for fear I'd scream out his name. Positioning himself directly in front of me, he removed his fingers and inch by inch replaced it with his erect member. An unchecked hitch interrupted my breathing, my body taut as I took him all in, only managing to release short puffs of air as he filled the void inside of me.

After the first few strokes I called out, "Motherfucker." Biting down on my lips I refocused my eyes on the light fixture hanging from the ceiling.

"We good down there, Evelyn?" His mouth curling into a wicked smile.

Through clenched teeth I replied, "It's impressive. Not gonna lie. You're only a few strokes in and I'm impressed."

I should've saved my compliment because it went to his head and his next few hip thrust were slow and angled, causing me to crumble into the bed. My body shifted into system overload, with my pulse crying in my ear and my deepest parts igniting with shades of pinks, reds, and vivid burgundies. Quincy increased his pace grabbing one of my legs so he could dive deeper.

When he dared to pull out stopping the momentum, I flashed him a disapproving warning, no one told him he could stop. Quincy got the hint and with a lurid smile he drove into me once again causing my vision to falter. Lifting from the bed, I grabbed for him, needing to feel his body on top of mine. The warmth of his skin hit the spot, Quincy hooked his arm above my head burying his face in my neck licking or sucking with each thrust.

"Kiss me," I begged.

Without missing a beat, he kissed me with such raw emotion, the pad of his thumb caressing my cheek. The taste of him silenced all my fears. You couldn't tell me this wasn't my forever. Wrapping my legs around his waist, I angled my body closer; returning his thrust with one of my own.

"Dammit Evelyn." He groaned into my ear.

Hearing his voice stripped down and primal sent shivers sailing up my spine. Quincy was millimeters away from my face, his pupils dilated as he trained his intense brown eyes on my reaction to his every thrust. His all-knowing gaze made my chest grow tight, it was too intimate and personal and when I looked in his eyes, I felt something akin to love. Which was ridiculous because I'd only known this dude for what ... five days? I pinched my eyes shut, silently reminding myself it was too early for the head over heels antics I often found myself giving in to.

Resting his forehead against mine, Quincy commanded, "Open your fucking eyes, Evelyn."

Without hesitation I obeyed and was immediately rewarded with his adoring gaze as his wide eyes registered my face. The downward movement of my hips was met by his thrust making it difficult to deny this man was specifically made to please me. My body tensed, the only sounds I could produce were moans and groans so primordial, I had a hard time believing they were coming from my mouth. As he retreated and entered me I shuddered, scraping my finger-nails down his back.

Our lips once again connected as his powerful strokes intensified. I could barely return his kiss, distracted by the sweet release ripping through me. Lifting from my embrace, Quincy claimed hold of my waist, ensuring I squeaked out every drop of pleasure. My hands balled into fist and my toes curled as I screamed out obscenities.

Quincy grabbed my legs, continuing to thrust, pump, and swivel. Maintaining my focus was a daunting task as the heat radiating from my center sent shockwaves to the rest of my body. But I mustered up enough energy to cry out, "Come for me, baby." My words produced the intended response, Quincy's body seized and his face contorted, as he shouted out loud grunts and expletives. Collapsing next to me, we laid in silence for several minutes as he gently rubbed his hand over my breast.

By the time he switched positions so he was hovering above me, his breathing had returned to normal. "I just had sex ... *WITH MY WIFE.*" The last three words he said in a Russian accent like Borat.

I dissolved into laughter. "Please don't make me laugh. I'm sore all over."

He flooded my face with kisses before arranging the bed sheet and blanket to cover us. Settling onto his chest, Quincy wrapped his arm around me playing with the strands of my hair. I knew I couldn't stay like this forever; eventually I'd have to get up, wash my face and slap a scarf over my head.

But that could wait because I didn't want to think beyond this moment, about what we were going to do when we got home, or how we were going to make this thing work. I just wanted to indulge in this perfect moment with my husband on our honeymoon.

Chapter 9

QUINCY

In the mirror the next morning, I examined the scratches on my arms and back. Hard-fought battle scars in the fight to snatch Evelyn's soul. Wetting my toothbrush, I couldn't help but smile when I remembered last night, and three o'clock this morning.

"Good morning," Evelyn said, entering the bathroom.

"Morning." My line of sight drifting from her face. "I'm not gonna lie, I'm having a hard time looking at you after all the filthy shit we did."

Evelyn rummaged through her toiletry bag pulling out a bottle of face wash. "The feeling is mutual, buddy."

Gnawing on the bottom of my lips, I ventured to ask, "So when can we do that shit again?"

Her hooded eyes popped open, an expectant expression taking over her face. "Right now."

"Yes, absolutely the fuck yes." I muttered, trying not to spit minty fresh toothpaste in her eye.

"OK, let me at least brush my teeth." She laughed.

My electric toothbrush was all that could be heard as we snuck glances at one another. The crew would be at our room to start filming any minute if we were going to do this it would have to be a quickie. I didn't know if I could be quick with her. When we connected, I found something new to fixate on and right now it was the three, tiny moles on the back of her arm forming a mini constellation. *How had I missed that last night?*

After rinsing my mouth, I leaned in, kissing that exact spot. Standing behind her, I toyed with the waistband of her cotton sleep shorts before slipping my hand underneath. Gently kicking her legs open with my feet before plunging two fingers inside, she was still dewy, coating my fingers as I slid in and out.

Evelyn's head lolled back, landing on my shoulder. I watched our reflection in the mirror, her body pressed against mine, mouth agape, struggling to breathe. Pulling away, I stumbled to the bowl of condoms on the bathroom counter searching for my size. A knock on the hotel door made my hands search faster.

"We don't have to answer that." I pointed in the direction of the rapping knocks.

"We kinda do." Evelyn was straightening her clothes like this morning's rendezvous was over.

"OK, so answer the door and tell them I died and we can do a *Weekend at Bernie's* for the rest of the honeymoon."

Her brow mashed together. "Weekend at Bernie's?"

"Yeah, guy dies and his friends pretend he's still alive so they can party in his fancy house."

"That was a movie?"

"Yeah, it's really funny. You'd love it. Trust me." I finally find my size pulling the condom from the bowl. The knocking on the door sounded more like banging now.

"I have to get that."

"I thought you liked to break rules." Did I just wanna stay in the room the rest of the day and fuck and suck Evelyn … yes. If I had my way, today's itinerary would consist of morning sex in the bathroom, followed by a finger bang in the patio pool. We'd break for hydration and sustenance and then jump into some doggy-style action. Nap. Second meal of the day which would feature Evelyn as the main course … My thoughts were interrupted by Evelyn who was speaking with flailing arms. "What?"

"I said if we don't answer, they'll just barge in.

"We can barricade the door."

"No," she chuckled.

Frown lines creased the corners of my mouth like a three-year-old child who was denied a sugary cereal.

"Rain check." She grabbed hold of my chin turning me to mush.

"Promise."

Evelyn hovered over my lips before giving me a kiss. "I promise."

EVELYN

AFTER GETTING DRESSED, we decided to leave the resort and explore the island. As we drove around, the Pitons, two mountain peaks that ran along the coast of the island, were an ever-present sight. I'd won the game of rock, paper, scissors which granted me the privilege of driving; I enjoyed zooming through town, the breeze whipping through my hair. Quincy wasn't enjoying it quite as much. He clutched the hand hold in our golf cart staring straight ahead with wide eyes.

"Eyes on the road," he ordered. "Car ... there's a car."

"Are you having fun?" I yelled over the sound of traffic.

"You might wanna slow down just a touch." He shouted back.

I weaved in and out of traffic like our rented golf cart was a high-performance vehicle.

"Brake .. apply the brakes." His shoulders were hovering around his ears.

"You're doing a lot right now."

"I'm just trying to stay out of a St. Lucia jail for vehicular homicide."

Pulling into a parking spot, I placed the cart in park. "We're here, so you can unclench your cheeks." I thought it was funny how uptight he got. He always appeared laid back and chill but relinquishing control was not one of his strong points. I would have to help him with that.

"My life literally flashed before my eyes." He exited the vehicle, mopping his brow. "Do you even have a license?"

"No, I do not."

His eyebrows climbed up his forehead. "Evelyn—"

"But I'm a good driver."

"No, you are not." He sliced his head left to right.

In the souvenir shop we perused the aisles looking for items to bring back to our friends and family. I was all for enjoying the sites of St. Lucia but I would rather be enjoying Quincy. Last night had me eager for more, I wanted to shove my tongue down his throat and pull on his hair. But for some reason, people tend to frown at public displays of affection, especially when it involves tongue kissing and finger blasting.

"Do you think Walt would like this shirt?" He held up a powder-blue polo shirt with the map of the island on the front.

"No."

He returned it to the rack. "I hate souvenir shopping. I never know what to get."

"That's because souvenirs kinda suck. Have you ever gotten a souvenir you actually used when you returned home?" I said.

"No."

"It's a weird social contract that when your friends or family go on a vacation they are obligated to bring you back some lame hat or keychain. And when you open it you're required to smile bright and thank them for thinking of you."

"You have really strong views about five-dollar magnets," he said, rotating a glass tumbler in his hand.

"Let's just get a bunch of shot glasses and call it a day."

"That's fine with me. But I have to get Naomi something special because I promised I would." He picked up a large seashell pulling it up to his ear.

I appraised his face considering his words. "How long did you live with Naomi?"

"A little over two years."

Two years wasn't that long of a time but clearly a bond had formed. "You guys pretty tight?"

"Yeah, she's the closest thing to family I got." He showed me a stuffed bear wearing pants.

A swift no shook my head. "What did she think when you told her you were getting married?"

"Honestly, I don't think she believed me. Even when I was getting fitted for my tux, I really think she thought I was joking. Like the longest episode of Punk'd." Turning the corner, we headed down the next aisle. "But you made an impression. She's been texting me asking when her daughter-in-law is coming over for dinner."

"I can't wait. I'd love to get to know her better and all the people you love."

"Well, you met Naomi and you met Walt so you're pretty much caught up."

"So you keep your circle small?" I threw a dog toy in the basket for Totes McGoates.

"Minuscule."

"Why's that?"

Scratching at his forearm, he considered my question. "Because at the end of the day the only person you can rely on is yourself. Everyone has their own shit going on and nine times out of ten people are looking to extrapolate things from you. Money, attention, energy. So I just tend to keep to myself."

His response left me dumbfounded. Quincy wasn't an introvert, the way he schmoozed my family, with the exception of my mother, saying all the right things. Maybe that was the rub, he said the right things so no one would look deeper to examine what was below the surface.

"I'm not a hermit crab I have friends." He was clearly trying to mollify some of the uneasiness that bulged from my eyes. "There are plenty of people I hang out with, but I choose to share my true self sparingly."

Was he hiding his true self from me? A facade of perfection to shield who he really was.

"We should get these glasses and go," I said.

"OK."

While I loaded shot glasses with St. Lucia etched on the front into our basket, Quincy moved his hips from side to side.

"You do realize you just randomly dance at the weirdest moments." He danced unprovoked two hours earlier while we were standing in line for the golf cart.

"When the beat moves me I can't control my feet."

"The beat?" I looked around the half empty store.

"You don't hear that?" He pointed to some imaginary sound in the air.

"There's no music playing."

"You don't *hear* that?" Taking the basket from me he set it in the corner. Quincy placed his hand on my waist pulling me close against him. Pressing his mouth to my ear, he whispered, "Can you hear it now?"

"I think I can kinda make out the sweet harmonics of a piano," I said, playing along.

"After the piano comes the mellow groove of the saxophone."

I followed his lead as he moved us two steps forward before swaying in a slow circle.

"I hear it. It kinda floats in on a wave." My hand cradled the back of his neck.

"Up next are the trumpets filling in the gaps left

behind." He made a sound very similar to that of a trumping horn.

"Are those drums?"

"Yeah, you can feel it in your chest, right?"

I nodded looking up at him in awe. This man had created a full symphony in my mind, making the nonexistent music come to life. Swaying back and forth, we danced to the music that only we could hear. It didn't matter that we were blocking the magnet rack that an eager tourist had to walk the long way around to access. All that mattered was that I was in his arms.

~

QUINCY

"Did anyone else feel like they were going to faint while waiting at the altar?" Sarah asked the group.

The production of *Why Knot* set up a dinner date with the other two couples who were also a part of the social experiment. Evelyn and I weren't the only ones who'd married a stranger in the last few days, there was also Jace and Michelle and Elliot and Sarah. Meeting the other couples was a bit surreal because these were people who could relate to this very unique experience. Evelyn was being a social butterfly, so excited for the couple's date night. I did not share her enthusiasm; I wasn't looking to make friends and I had no intentions of trading war stories. The chef was far more entertaining and I was content to watch our cook light an onion tower on fire or catch his spatula behind his back.

"So, Quincy what do you do for work?" Elliot, a pale man with a dad bod asked.

"I'm a lawyer."

"Really, what type of law?"

Evelyn's eyes turned to me, she was probably just as interested in the answer as everyone else at the table. Since we were on vacation work talk hadn't really come up.

"Uhh, contracts."

"Contracts, hmm that's cool. What about you Evelyn?"
"Elliot asked.

"I'm an artist."

"So you don't work." Elliot laughed at his own words. "Luckily, you married a lawyer. Congratulations on hitting the jackpot, sweetheart."

My eyes darkened; a twinge of anger laced my voice. "I'ma need you to watch the way you talk to my wife." The table fell silent, even the hibachi chef stopped flipping his utensils.

Elliot held up his palms. "Chill man. It's just a joke."

"Yeah well, jokes are often used to hide true feelings." There was a hint of a smile on my face but if Elliott was smart he would take my words seriously.

Evelyn placed her hand on my knee under the table. "It's fine."

Crinkling my nose I disagreed. "Nah, it's really not." I wasn't trying to be a wet blanket but in my experience when you give someone an inch they just keep advancing forward until one day they've walked a mile on your ass.

"No disrespect intended." Elliot inched his bushy eyebrows to his hairline.

I was ready to call it, this guy was an asshole. The food

hadn't been served and we were already bumping heads, my expectations were low for the rest of the night.

"Girl, I love art." Michelle chimed in. "What mediums do you work in?"

"Mostly paint, I also do some photography."

"Do you have an exhibit? I would love to see some of your pieces."

"I have a gallery, The Townsend, downtown. Some of my pieces are on display."

Michelle squealed. "Hold up. I know that place. It's an art gallery but you also have paint and sip nights in the back.

"Paint and sip?" Sarah asked.

"You've never been?" Michelle replied. "You can get your Picasso and Prosecco on at the same damn time. I love that place, it's such a vibe. I had my bachelorette party there."

"Awe, I'm glad you had a good time." Evelyn placed her hand over her heart a smile brightening her face.

"A good time? It was so much more than a good time ... it was an experience. The painting project was Black love themed and the music was old school R&B. When Tevin Campbell's, 'Can We Talk,' came on it was an entire sing-a-long."

All I could do was listen. I didn't know any of this. My wife was a business owner with a popular gallery space in downtown Chicago. *Did she have employees and a payroll?* The thought of Evelyn balancing budgets and writing employees up for being late tickled me. I made a mental note to review her legal paperwork, lease, and other business documents to make sure she was straight. There had to be at least one perk to marrying an attorney.

"Do you have a tax guy?" I whispered,

"Turbo Tax."

I nodded, adding connecting her with my tax lady, Jill, to the list of my Evelyn to dos.

"I'm just gonna ask the question because I'm dying to know." Sarah, a mousy brunette with a blunt bob said. "Has anyone consummated their marriage?"

Under the table I gave Evelyn's thigh a quick squeeze. I hoped she was receiving the message, which was don't share our personal business with these people we just met. What we had or hadn't done sexually wasn't open fodder while eating at the Hibachi Kitchen.

There was a long pause as everyone at the table looked from one face to the other.

"Fuck it, we'll go first." Michelle said. "Yes, we've had sex. I mean have you seen my husband?" She gave Jace an inappropriately long, open-mouthed kiss.

Elliot chimed in next. "We decided to wait. We have all the time in the world." Elliot's strained expression let me know that decision was 100 percent his wife, Sarah's doing. I didn't blame her for giving that pompous prick the stiff arm.

"What about you two?" Michelle posed the question to Evelyn and me. "Because you two look like a match made in heaven."

"We're playing it by ear. No timetables." I said.

Evelyn nodded her head in agreement. Team Parrish in full effect.

The other couples eyed us skeptically. I didn't care if they believed us or not, the topic was a non-starter for me. When I agreed to be on this show I knew it meant giving up an expectation of privacy. The crew of *Why Knot* and eventually millions of viewers would watch this relationship play out in real time. Allowing people into my private life would give them license to critique, criticize, and comment on me, Evelyn, and the viability of our union. Our lives were on display but that didn't mean I couldn't play a role in controlling the narrative and how people perceived us.

EVELYN

The tropical vacation was coming to a close. For our last night in St. Lucia, Quincy surprised me with a romantic, candlelit dinner on the beach, just the two of us and the cameras. After five days of filming, I'd managed to ignore the crew, often forgetting they were there. Maybe because I was so focused on Quincy and getting to know him and I wasn't going to let the inconvenience of being on a reality show negatively impact my chances at love. Quincy tended to be far more distracted, often opening his mouth to speak only to stop short like he remembered the cameras were present.

After dinner, Quincy had one last surprise for me. Changing into our swimsuits, he led me to a private underground cave with a pool and dim lighting.

"How did you find out about this place? I don't remember seeing this in the hotel guide."

"I just asked the concierge if he could recommend a romantic place for our last night on the island, and voilà." His smile was ten times its normal size, clearly very pleased with himself.

"Well thank you, this is really nice." My eyes pinged

around the room in an attempt to take it all in. "There's a bed in the corner."

"There is?"

Biting down on my lip, I was already plotting how I was going to repay him. "Let's get in."

Quincy removed his T-shirt and as always, I couldn't help but stare. After our week together you'd think I'd get used to the sight of his toned arms and muscular chest but no, every time he took his clothes off I felt a push of blood flow through my veins. Dropping my cover up, I piled my hair atop my head before walking into the surprisingly warm water. The medium-sized pool had jets like a hot tub circulating the water around us. Quincy poured two glasses of Champagne placing them within arm's reach on the side of the pool before joining me.

"Can you believe our honeymoon is already over?" I asked, taking a sip from my glass.

"At first, I thought it would be a long five days having to spend all that time with someone I didn't know. But it really flew by." He scooped up a handful of water before allowing it to slip through his fingers.

"Are you excited to get back to your normal life?" I asked, wading over to him.

"Yes and no. I'm gonna have a shit ton of work when I get back and then we have a lot to figure out."

"Yeah, we do. First up, where to live."

Upon our return to Chicago the real work would begin; we would have to meld our lives together and create new routines and traditions. Marrying a stranger was crazy enough but marrying a stranger right before the holiday season was a whole other level of insanity. We would be celebrating Halloween in just two weeks followed by Thanksgiving, my birthday, Christmas, and New Year's. When I stopped to think about it, it made my head spin like one of those cartoon characters with little birds floating above them.

Quincy poured a palmful of water onto the bare skin of my shoulders. "So on a scale of one to ten of all-time best honeymoons, how would you rate this one?"

My pulse skittered as I tugged on the heart-shaped pendant on the necklace I hadn't removed since Quincy gifted it to me on our wedding day. "Definitely a ten … higher. Best honeymoon ever." Pressing my body against his, I waited expectantly.

Quincy's eyes shifted to the two cameras in the room, his body tightening with trepidation.

If Quincy acted like this every time the cameras were nearby it was going to be a long three months. I wanted him to feel comfortable enough to relax and be himself around me. If the crew of *Why Knot* caught me face down ass up so be it. I wasn't going to repress my desire to touch this man whenever and wherever I wanted. They wanted a show and I had no qualms giving it to them because when I was into a guy all I did was show up and show out.

Grabbing his chin, I instructed, "Eyes on me."

Quincy's gaze softened focusing on my face, his hands, which were balled into tight fists against my waist, relaxed. His eyes fluttered closed as my hands glided up his stomach and over his chest before coming to rest on his neck. With his hand securely around my waist, he pulled me closer, mind you we were already insanely close.

Maybe it was because our honeymoon was drawing to a

close and I was both skittish and eager for what the next few weeks held for us, but this embrace felt weighted with all our hopes and dreams for the future. Quincy slowly leaned in to kiss me, but I pulled my mouth out of reach so his kiss didn't connect. He flashed me a vexed look, causing me to release a sputtering laugh. I was starting to read this man's moods, and the look he just gave clearly said, "Stop fucking with me."

Running my hand over his face, I scratched at his beard before brushing my finger across his mouth. I replaced my finger with my lips smiling against his mouth daring him to kiss me in front of God and the entire *Why Knot* crew. Quincy parted my lips and the taste of him silenced all my fears. It was just us two, no producer whispering indistinct instructions into a headset. No heavy footsteps from a cameraman trying to capture the perfect angle. No Jared preening in my face asking me if I wanted another drink to ease my inhibitions.

All I could feel was Quincy, his body pressed snugly against my chest and the urgent kisses like I was his only source of oxygen. Pulling at the strings of my bikini top, Quincy pulled it from my body, the floral top floating away in the water. It caught me by surprise, he was a bit timid when it came to public displays of affection. As opposed to me who was ready to hold my breath, submerge underneath the water and suck him dry if he let me. I wrapped my legs around his waist never letting the connection of our lips falter.

There was rustling around us followed by foot falls ascending the stairs.

Jared called out, "We're going to leave you two alone. Have a good night."

When the footsteps abated Quincy cupped my face, his hold on my lips intensifying, any lingering hesitation gone with the exit of the crew. Using my feet I tried to remove his swim trunks but couldn't get a proper grip. Quincy helped, pulling his shorts down with his free hand.

Moving away from my lips, he scattered kisses along my neck and chest. "We need to get out," his voice was thick and raspy.

I held on tight as his strong legs took assured steps carrying us out of the pool before dropping me on the cabana bed in the corner of the cave. Reaching for his towel, he unfurled it and condom packets scattered to the ground. He picked up one of the packets, drying his hands before ripping it open. I worked on undoing the strings of my bikini bottoms so I could be ready to meet him. Pulling me to my feet, he walked forward causing me to retreat until my back hit the rough cave wall. In one swift movement, Quincy picked my leg up securing it at his waist before sliding inside as I held my breath until he was snugly in place.

Quincy slipped his hands under my butt, wrapping my other leg around his waist, I circled my arms around his back. Taking my cues from his movement, I rocked my pelvis back and forth. His firm, warm body in contrast with the cold, hard wall against my back heightened the pleasure. How had I been matched with a man who knew how to please me without even trying? Loud moans pinged off the walls of the cave and reverberated in my ears. With an arch to my back, I grabbed his neck pulling his face toward my breasts, watching with great delight as his tongue kissed and sucked my sensitive nipples.

Quincy inched away from the wall until only my shoulders touched, I swayed my hips in either direction in tandem with his thrust. The slight change in position increased the pressure. As Quincy's thrust intensified, my body shuttered, my center pulsated and my face grew hot. A delicious tingly warm wave crested inside of me as I moaned over his mouth. My body falling limp, Quincy held on to me with his strong grip that would leave indentations in my side. I found it hard to maintain my hold on his waist, my legs had gone hollow from the first orgasm. Adjusting for my sudden bout of weakness, he used his quads and glutes to support my weight giving me a quick hoist.

The elevated position forced me to cry out ... a low protracted moan that was laced with profanity.

"I love it when you moan," he said breathless.

And I loved it when he provided positive affirmations. His deep and prolonged gaze made me feel heady. "What else do you like? I wanna make it a reality." This was me giving away the store, good dick had that effect on me. And Quincy's dick was very good.

"Call my name," he ordered.

"Make me." My response was more of a plea than a demand.

Spoiler alert ... he did. He claimed hold of my ass and worked it over his shaft again and again until all I could see were blurry, twinkling lights. He teased my pert nipples with his tongue until he was drooling. He slapped my ass cheeks with just the right amount of force, skirting the line of pleasure and pain until I had no choice but to give him what he wanted as I crashed into my second orgasm of the night.

"Quincy Chester Parrish." I screamed. Yes, his full government name ... because he deserved it.

Using the wall to brace us, his final thrust made his legs twitch as he bit down on my shoulder with a loud growl. His limbs clearly spent, he took wobbly steps dropping me onto the cabana mattress before collapsing next to me.

"Evelyn?"

"Yes." My voice was a smile.

"Let's try really hard to make this work," he said still short of breath.

With a clipped nod against his chest, I agreed. Of course, I wanted desperately for this to work and I planned to do everything to ensure that at the end of our ninety days together he couldn't imagine his life without me.

CHAPTER 10

QUINCY

Once we exited O'Hare airport, I knew the honeymoon was over. It was cold and rainy, a drastic change from the sunshiny days in St. Lucia. Landing at eight in the morning, we decided to head to Evelyn's place first before ending the day at my house. As part of the show the couples had to tour each other's living spaces and then determine where they wanted to live. Not gonna lie, I was hopeful this process would be fairly painless and we would end up living at my house for the next ninety days.

When the RideX car pulled up to Evelyn's apartment, I was surprised to find she lived roughly ten minutes from my place. *How had we not crossed paths before?* I found it hard to believe that we didn't frequent the same restaurants or stroll the same aisles at the Trader Joe's, perusing the specialty items just steps away from one another.

"This you?" I pointed at a multi-level apartment building.

"Yep," she said, wrapping her scarf around her neck.

"We're neighbors, I'm about a ten-minute walk away. I'm probably in this area a few times a week. There's a great bakery just down the street with the best lemon custard donuts."

"Heavenly Dough, yeah I love that place." Evelyn twinned my broad smile.

Inside we rode the elevator to the seventh floor. Opening the door to a corner unit, she moved aside so I could enter with luggage in tow. Her apartment was open concept with a wall of windows which probably provided great sunlight on less gloomy days. Style wise the aesthetic wasn't what I was expecting. The place was dark and non-descript ... chocolate leather sofa, deep walnut hardwood floors, I'd imagined her place would be brighter with pops of color. There were a few accent pieces, an area rug, throw pillows, and plants that cheered the place up a bit.

"OK, this place is nice. Look at you." My face pulled into an impressed expression. "This is a great neighborhood."

"Yep, I like it." She tossed her back pack and coat on the floor heading to the kitchen to make some tea.

"One bedroom or two?"

"One," she said, pulling large mugs from one of the cabinets.

While she made the tea I walked around checking out the bedroom, which was a contrast from the living space. This bedroom screamed Evelyn, it was warm and colorful and even though the room was fairly large it still felt cozy. I could see myself in the queen-sized bed with her body curled around mine. In the bathroom, I opened the medicine cabinet taking a peek. It was pretty benign: toothpaste, lotions and creams. In one of the drawers, I found a supply of birth control pills and condoms.

"Are you done snooping?"

I jumped at the unexpected sound of her voice right outside the bathroom door. "I wasn't snooping. I was just evaluating the space."

"Is that what you were doing?" She closed the drawer with her hip wrapping her arms around me. "You should take off your coat and stay awhile. I turned up the heat and made us tea."

I planted a soft kiss on her lips, but with all things Evelyn, one kiss, one glance, one smile was never enough; I always craved more. Leaning in, I snuck another quick peck.

"A place in this neighborhood gotta set you back a few thousand a month."

Evelyn dropped her arms, stepping away. "Uh-huh."

Her gallery must be pulling in a pretty penny for her to be able to afford to live in Logan Square. Back in the living room, Evelyn poured us both generous cups of tea. "Do you like your tea like you like your coffee?"

"Yeah, sugar and creamer if you've got it," I said, shrugging off my coat.

I stopped at a shelf with a picture of some random guy in snow gear, maybe on a ski vacation. It wasn't Evan. *Why did she have a picture of this guy on display in her apartment?* Maybe she'd just forgotten to remove this old picture before the wedding. Evelyn wouldn't find any photos or memorabilia from any of my exes at my place. I'd scrubbed it clean. The old photos I kept in a shoebox. The forgotten panties from the one-night stand I had before I was selected for the show, random earrings, clothes, or hair ties all trashed. The stuff I wasn't ready to get rid of I'd given to Walt for safe keeping.

"Let's sit down and write out our monthly expenses. It'll help us decide which place best suits our needs," I said. Picking a place to live was a big decision and laying out our finances would help to make the choice clear.

After setting the mugs on the two-person dining table, Evelyn went off in search of paper and pens. I hoped this exercise would help dissuade her if she felt strongly about keeping this place. She had to be paying three thousand a month in rent. My monthly mortgage was half that and I had a backyard.

Evelyn returned, taking a seat at the table, pens and paper in hand.

"We'll each make our list of monthly expenses and then we'll exchange them."

"Got it." She shifted back in her seat, concern marred her features.

We worked in silence writing out our list. As a lawyer, I assumed I made more than her and I was fine with being the breadwinner as long as she was willing to contribute her fair share. When we exchanged papers, I noted that my list was way more detailed than hers. Her list was also far less accurate with a few items listed with question marks next to them.

"You forgot to list your rent." I flipped the sheet of paper over.

"You said to list our living expenses." Evelyn lifted her mug to her lips taking a long loud sip.

"Yeah, and rent is a pretty big living expense."

"I don't pay rent." She chewed on her bottom lip.

Blinking owlishly, I asked, "What do you mean?"

"Just that, I don't pay rent." Her throat wobbled as she swallowed.

"What, did you win this apartment from HGTV or something?" I teased with a half-cocked smile.

Evelyn cleared her throat. "No, this place belongs to a friend. That friend lets me stay here rent free."

Leaning back in my chair, I studied her face. "Your friend just had an apartment to spare?"

"Yeah, he travels a lot for work. So I'm essentially house sitting."

I pulled my face into a frown. "OK, so this world traveling friend of yours ... is a dude."

"Why does that even matter?"

I wrinkled my nose. I'm a dude. I know dudes. And not many of them were willingly giving up their homes without the expectation or at the very least the hope that this thoughtful gesture would result into a pass to smash.

"I'm just saying it's unusual that old boy let you stay at his place out of the *kindness* of his heart."

"He was helping a friend. He had an empty place and I needed somewhere to stay."

"OK." I gave my shoulders an indifferent bounce.

I looked around the space with new eyes. This explained a lot, like how she could afford to live in the area. And why this place seemed off when I first walked in, because she didn't contribute to the decor of this space. It felt false and uninviting. I pinned my arms over my chest.

"So that's it?" She eyed me suspiciously.

"It's clear we don't see this the same way and that's fine."

I was grappling with strong fight or flight vibes and thought it best to end this conversation before it started.

Inhaling deeply, her nostrils flared. "You don't seem fine."

"I don't know what you're expecting me to say. You just told me that your *friend* lets you stay in *his* place rent free." Pushing back from the table, I jerked to standing. " I hope you're an organized and efficient packer."

"What's that supposed to mean, you're just counting my place out?" Her head jerked upward flashing me a incredulous stare.

"It's not even *your* place so it's not a viable option. I own a house and you're living situation is untenable. The answer is clear." I clasped my hand to emphasize the finality of the subject.

"You're being a bit unreasonable." There was a stubborn bend to her jaw.

I pulled on my coat working the scarf around my neck before looping the buttons. "I think I've seen enough. I'm gonna head downstairs and call us a RideX while you lock up." Slinging my duffle bag over my shoulder, I pushed past the cameraman heading for the elevator.

Standing outside of the apartment, my stomach congealed with doubt. To avoid conflict, I'd often shutdown. Pretend to be OK when I wasn't. Tolerate shit I shouldn't. I wasn't interested in arguing over something that wasn't up for debate. My place was better suited to meet our needs. But more importantly we couldn't establish a life together in someone else's space. She had to see that.

The car was six minutes away and she still hadn't come down. I hated personal conflict, because nine times out of ten, I was bound to insert my foot in my mouth. The only way to avoid this was to keep my mouth shut and my feet planted on the ground while I slowly retreated. Mopping my hand over my forehead, I gulped down some steadying breaths. *What if she stays upstairs?* Pinching the brim of my nose, I closed my eyes offering up a silent prayer. *Maybe I should go back. I wasn't ready for this to be over.*

Turning, I made a bee line to the apartment entrance, I mashed the elevator button waiting for it to descend. When the doors opened Evelyn was on the other side; a ribbon of relief unfurled inside of me. I squared my shoulders trying my best to erase the concerns from my face. Evelyn exited the elevator, luggage in hand, not meeting my eyes. Her features normally bright and full of life were subdued, her jaw rigid like it was carved in ice. I reached for her luggage wheeling it through the lobby. Holding the door open, I gave her a wide berth, my nonverbal way of extending an olive branch.

"Our driver will be here in four minutes," I said. I wanted to reach for her but instead plunged my ice-cold hands into my coat pockets as we waited on the curb.

"Great."

~

EVELYN

THANKFULLY THE DRIVE to Quincy's house was short because the tension between us was suffocating. I'd predicted a few days prior Quincy was an asshole and that divination was correct. Yes, my living situation was unconventional but Simon was just a friend. Any romantic relationship we once shared ended years ago before I ever moved into his place.

This was an arrangement of convenience. Simon traveled for work and pleasure and his Chicago apartment was often vacant. He was rarely in the city as his primary residence was in London. When he did come to Chicago and needed a place to crash, he stayed on his couch. Or sometimes I would bunk with Meryl or Evan until he was gone. There was no hanky panky.

Quincy was quiet for the duration of the ride. I couldn't tell if he was upset or indifferent. He spent much of the ride with his face focused on his phone checking what looked like work emails. I don't really know which was worse the silent treatment or an all-out verbal slug match.

Kicking the can down the road was never my MO; I preferred to tackle things head on. I was getting the distinct impression that Quincy was more like my dad, walking away before things turned left. But unlike my dad who walked away to cool off, Quincy exited stage left hoping that when he returned the audience would forget he flubbed his lines. The car turned onto a tree-lined street slowing to a stop. Exiting the vehicle, I looked up and down the nicely manicured block.

"You're back." An older gentleman called out to Quincy.

"Hey Otis, how's it going?"

"You know, same shit different day." Otis pointed to our *Why Knot* entourage. "What's all this?"

Quincy tossed an irritated eye at the crew. "Nothing, just some side project."

His words were meant to dismiss the crew but I'd be

lying if I pretended like I wasn't also hit by a stray, verbal bullet.

"And her?" The old man pointed his chin in my direction.

"Oh, this is ... she's my ... we actually—"

"I'm Evelyn." I interrupted extending my hand which Otis pressed to his lips for a kiss.

"Happy to meet you, Evelyn. It's nice to see Quincy with a friend. I was starting to worry he was one of those loners who'd end up on the five o'clock news one night. Thought I'd have to say he was a nice young man who mostly stuck to himself or some shit like that." Otis coughed out a laugh.

"Mr. O is my next-door neighbor and he also thinks he's a comedian."

"I made your pretty young thang laugh. She probably hasn't had much to laugh at if she's hanging with you."

"I like this man." I gave Otis a playful wink.

"Well, I'm right here don't be a stranger."

"I'll probably head to the grocery store tomorrow, so have your list ready," Quincy called after him.

It would appear Quincy wasn't such a hard ass when it came to people as he claimed. His trust issues hadn't stopped him from finding a place in his heart for that old man. Luggage in tow, he headed to his front door.

Inside I walked around deliberately looking for something I could call him out on. It smelled the scent of clean, reminding me of my favorite detergent. The large living room with kitchen and dining that looked out to the backyard were spotless. On our honeymoon he unpacked all his belongings utilizing the drawers and closet space. When he removed an article of clothing, he would fold it before returning it to his duffle bag. *Was my husband a neat freak?* I'd also noticed the clothes I discarded on the floor of our suite would often end up neatly folded and stacked in a nearby chair.

The space was nice with a large, gray sofa and a huge, flat screen television. Taking stock of the space, the television was the only thing on the walls. No art, no photographs, no mirrors or accent pieces.

"It's nice." I lifted a blasé shoulder. It took everything within me to spit out a compliment, I didn't want to give him the satisfaction of that admission.

"Yeah, it has a kitchen, utilities, and no strings attached." Sliding his hands into his pockets he lounged against the kitchen island.

"Are we going to talk about this? I wasn't sleeping with Simon if that's what you're thinking."

"I don't care. It's fine." He pursed his lips before continuing. "It's minutes away from the L. Walking distance to restaurants and shops. It's quiet at night, a safe neighborhood with couples our age." He droned on like a realtor in a monotone voice.

Clearly everything was not fine. He was pressed about my current living situation. Throwing my hands in the air I asked, "I'm just gonna call a duck a duck. You seem bothered."

Quincy pulled his face upward. "I'm not."

"He was being a friend, helping me out."

"There ain't that much friendship in the world." He scratched at his beard.

"You know not everybody has a nefarious ulterior

motive. Some people are just genuinely kind. Helping and expecting nothing in return."

Quincy scrunched up his face. I could tell he wanted to say something but he was biting back his words. His facial features relaxed and in a calm affectless tone he responded. "Everybody wants something. You really can't be this naive."

I narrowed my eyes to slits. "So what's Mr. Otis's ulterior motive?"

"I don't know. I buy his groceries, so he can eat, so he doesn't die. So, I guess survival."

"No, *you* really can't be *this* jaded."

A shrug rolled over his shoulders.

"You are unfuckingbelievable."

Performing a visual sweep of the room, I looked for an escape. I needed to get far away from this man before I said things that would be difficult to walk back. Spotting a door in the corner of the kitchen I took hurried steps in that direction. I blindly swung the door open and walked in, closing it behind me.

"That's the pantry." Quincy called from the other side.

"I am perfectly aware this is a pantry." Looking around I took note of the canned goods and boxes of cereal.

It's hard to argue with someone who refuses to argue back. And truthfully, I didn't want to argue. I just wanted to work through the issue. When you leave things unsaid, they don't magically disappear they tend to linger, popping back up at the most inopportune moments.

"Can I come in?"

"No." I fumbled with the doorknob trying to lock myself in.

"The door doesn't lock ... because it's a pantry." His voice called again.

Turning my back on the door, I spied his well-organized shelves, fisting packages of chocolate chip granola bars I dumped them in the bucket reserved for oatmeal. Next, I rotated all the cans so the labels all faced in the wrong directions.

Quincy's voice interrupted my organizational mayhem. "If money's an issue I can continue to make the payments on this place. I don't expect for you to contribute to a mortgage when your money stacks differently than mine."

The swinging pantry door clipped his shoulder when I opened it unexpectedly. "I can afford to contribute." I snarled. "It's just that my money isn't consistent. I could make five grand one day and nothing for weeks. But I'm not looking for a handout."

"You are literally living in a handout."

My eyebrows stitched together as the muscle under my eye twitched.

Quincy clicked his tongue, taking a step back. "I think we need a minute." The next sentence he intended for his ears only. "Shit maybe more than that." Heading for the door he announced. "I'm gonna go get my dog."

My jaw fell slack from surprise. "You're leaving?"

"Yep," he said, patting down his pockets looking for his keys.

Not even two hours ago I was on cloud nine and now I was bracing for a bumpy landing. How did we go from kissy face to needing space in a matter of hours?

"I wanna finish this conversation." I stood in his path to the door, my eyes practically pleading.

"And we will, when I get back." He gave my shoulder a pathetic pat before brushing past, leaving me alone in his place.

∼

QUINCY

Totes McGoats leapt panting excitedly at my return. Crossing the threshold of Walt's house, the *Why Knot* crew was left to wait outside. Walt declined to sign the friend and family waiver which would have allowed the show to film in his home. If Walt was at my place or at a public event, he was fair game but his home was off limits. After reading the contracts it was the choice I advised all my friends to pick. It allowed me to have a place of reprise when I wanted to get away.

"There's my boy." I provided generous belly rubs as Totes ate it up. "Thanks for watching him while I was gone."

"Sure thing. He was no trouble at all." Walt said. "He actually told me he prefers it here but I told him he has to go home ... you need him."

"Hmph." I rolled my eyes. Totes couldn't talk but if he could he would never pick Walt over me.

"So how was the honeymoon?" Walt rubbed his hands together in anticipation of some salacious details.

Removing my coat, I reached under my shirt turning off the mic pack. This was an A and B conversation and the *Why Knot* crew could C their way out of it. "The honeymoon was great. The last few hours not so much."

"Why what's up?" The smile fell from Walt's face.

I filled Walt in on Evelyn's unique living situation. "And so I left because I didn't want to fight."

"What's this about? Is this about Evelyn living in some random guy's place. Or is this about you and Evelyn moving in together?"

My shoulders wilted. "It's a big commitment."

"Yeah, sure it is."

"She's gonna be there every morning and at night. And she's messy. She's so messy. She doesn't close drawers. She leaves wet towels on the floor. She'll fill a glass with water and only drink a couple of sips and just abandon the glass."

My temperature rose and my chest grew tight. While Evelyn slept on the plane, her head resting on my shoulder, I ran through all the possible outcomes like I was Dr. Strange. All I could think about were all the ways this wouldn't work. All the ways she could hurt me. And even worse, how I could end up hurting her.

"So what are you going to do?" Walt led me to the kitchen, handing me a cold one from the fridge.

"Well we have to move in together so I think we should stay at my place."

"Has Evelyn agreed to that?"

"No, I'm making an executive decision." I took a swig of my beer.

"I hate to break it to you but you're married now. It's a partnership."

Sure, Walt was right, but I had no intentions of leaving my place and squatting in Evelyn's *cozy* apartment. This was one of the many reasons I was single, I'd compromised for much of my childhood. Being placed with a random foster family with no voice in the matter, oftentimes exposed to shit I didn't ask for and forced into situations I didn't deserve. So when I turned eighteen I decided no one would tell me what I could and couldn't do and that my wants came first. Fucked up way to be I know, but I'd settled my entire life ... settled for hand-me-downs, for affection, for a semblance of family.

"My place is the right option and why she needs to go back and forth on it is beyond me. I don't care that she's living at a *friend's* place. She could be shacked up with the seven dwarfs but at the end of the day my house, with multiple bedrooms and an outdoor living space is more desirable than a place with pictures of *Simon* on the slopes or next to the Leaning Tower of Pisa."

"You're coming at this totally wrong."

"Excuse me?"

"You negotiate for a living." Walt reminded me.

"So what do you suggest I do?"

"Apologize, listen to her side, make your case, then come to a mutual decision. Honestly, it's not really that difficult."

I scrubbed at my face with my hands. "Whose side are you on exactly?"

"Yours and Evelyn's because you guys are a team now."

Walt was married once before. After his marriage ended, he had a lot of regret regarding how it all went down. I didn't want to end up like Walt alone, running a bunch of shoulda, woulda, coulda scenarios in my head.

Walt was right and I hated it. Because he would no doubt throw this rare occasion when he was right in my face for years to come. "Thank you for listening. I didn't mean to dump this all on you."

"It's a speed bump not a roadblock. You two will be

fine." Walt clinked his beer bottle into mine. "So back to the honeymoon, did you two Shamma Lamma Ding Dong?"

"What are you twelve?"

"I'm trying to be respectful. So did you?"

A smile spread across my face despite my best efforts. "Yes ... yeah."

"Was it good?"

"Yep."

If Evelyn were some random hookup I would probably provide Walt with a play by play. But she was my wife, so Walt would just have to get the message from my goofy smile and bulging eyes. If I didn't fix things with her soon this stupid smirk may end up being all I had left of her.

When I opened the door to my place Totes trotted inside, stopping in his tracks when he saw Evelyn asleep on the couch. She was curled up in a ball with her coat over her body as a blanket. Seeing her so peaceful made me feel even guiltier about the way I'd acted all day. Totes hopped up onto the couch climbing on top of the mystery woman giving her face curious licks. Her eyes fluttered open to find him staring at her.

"You must be Totes McGoats." Her voice raspy with sleep. Sitting up she allowed the French bulldog to invade her lap while rubbing his head and body.

I sat on the antique trunk I used as a coffee table, reaching for Evelyn's knee. "So, I think it's safe to say the honeymoon is over," I half joked.

She rubbed the sleep from her eyes.

"If you were wondering why I had to go on a reality show to find someone, now you know." I chuckled nervously hoping I hadn't already ruined this. "I don't like conflict. It immediately puts me on guard. I handled this poorly and I own that. This was all me. I just keep pinching myself because you're kinda too good to be true. So when I heard about your living situation it just fed into fears that were already there. And I'm a bit of a fatalist."

"You were dismissive and rude."

"Yep, those are my go-tos. When in doubt, dismiss, deflect, defend. It's kind of baked into the cake. I'm like that with everybody. But I don't want to be that way with you."

Arguments were never easy but having the crew watch as we disagreed and the knowledge that millions would watch this moment and choose sides was stressing me out. Scrambling to my feet, I grabbed Evelyn's hand pulling her toward the master bedroom, locking the door behind us.

"I don't wanna fight." I breathed out.

"I don't want that either." Her shoulders curved.

Totes scratched and whined at the door probably upset I'd locked him out like this wasn't his place too.

I scrubbed my face releasing a long sigh. All the nirvana I'd brought back with me from St. Lucia was slowly dwindling. "I'm sorry. Tell me what I need to do to make this right. If you want, we could put both addresses in a hat, or play rock, paper, scissors. I just really want us to start out on the right foot … together."

"I don't care where we live." She brushed this issue aside like it was settled law. "I just don't want you to push me away when we have an argument."

I nodded in agreement. "Yep, that's fair." My therapist, who I did not tell I was getting married, was going to get an earful next Tuesday. "Are … you …OK?"

"Uh-uhm."

"Are ... *we* OK? Because honestly all I care about is this moment, right now and those lips." I cast my gaze toward her full, luscious mouth.

Evelyn allowed a smile to peek through.

Slipping my hand under her sweatshirt, I removed the microphone pack from her body and then did the same to mine. I turned them off before tossing them into the master bathroom, closing the door. Without batting an eye, Evelyn pulled my shirt over my head, her hands gliding over my muscles which twitched at her touch.

"Take your clothes off," I whispered.

Standing back, I watched with eager eyes as she complied, stripping off her yoga pants and sweatshirt. Why the fuck had I spent all day fighting with her when we could have been doing this? Rookie mistake, I wouldn't let it happen again. The air in my lungs seized as she removed her bra and panties. My hands found her warm body, in the dying light of the afternoon sun, caressing the underside of her breast. Softly kissing her lips, I maneuvered my fingers inside of her studying her face, every twitch, lip bite, or gasp for air. I wanted to please her, I wanted her body to yearn for my touch because I always hit the right spot.

Removing my fingers, I licked them clean before whispering against her lips. "I'm sorry I ruined our first day back home."

"You'll just have to make it up to me." She breathed out.

"Let's christen the fuck outta this place," I said, undoing my belt buckle.

CHAPTER 11

QUINCY

"**D**amn Evelyn, what do you got in here?" Walt asked.

Evelyn flashed him a coy smile. "You're big and strong you can handle it."

"I *have* been working out." Walt smiled, flexing his bicep.

"Can you two please stop whatever the fuck this is." I interrupted. "We have a few more things and we're done." I brushed past them carrying a large box into the house.

Today was move-in day. Aside from clothes and shoes, Evelyn didn't really have much to move. Since she was house sitting most of her stuff was already in storage. This was a plus because we wouldn't have to fight over which toaster to keep. That would also make things much easier if this didn't work out, I wouldn't be down a wife and a toaster.

Back outside I found Otis and Evelyn chopping it up.

"Evelyn just told me she's moving in," Otis said. "I guess

when God gives you a good thing you don't waste too much time trying to figure it out."

"Mr. Otis was telling me about his wife."

"Clara. We went on one date and got married a week later. She ain't hardly talk the entire date. Maybe that's what I liked most about her, she let me talk and was content to just listen and hold my hand." He smiled at the memory. "We went on like that for fifty-three years, just talking, and listening, with her hands in mine."

"That sounds heavenly." Evelyn smiled, her eyelids fluttering.

"Yep, she really was that. Sweetest woman I'd ever met."

"To have all those years and memories with one person is pretty special." Evelyn playfully nudged her shoulder into me.

"I suppose if you try hard enough you can get there too. Word on the block is you two got hitched or whatever."

"Yeah, we did." I leaned on my car which was loaded with Evelyn's stuff.

"It's also been said that you two barely know each other."

I rubbed the back of my neck. It was surprising to hear I was a topic of gossip on the block. Mostly, I minded my business only exchanging neighborly pleasantries. But I guess a camera crew following me around would get tongues wagging. I could only imagine the stories my neighbors were spinning.

"Do you think we're crazy?" Evelyn asked.

"I've done crazier shit for less prettier women." Otis tagged me on the shoulder.

Otis and I talked almost every day but I'd never mentioned the show. Probably because there was a fifty-year age gap and I assumed he would judge me harshly for looking for love on a reality show. I wanted to spare myself the back-in-my-day speech. You know the kind, "Back in my day a man would just walk up to a woman and start a conversation. Young fellas nowadays are soft too afraid of rejection." But his response today was more curious than anything else. "To each his own, young man." Otis would often say. I'm sure at some point he would corner me and ask me to explain how all this worked.

"When we're all settled in you should come over for dinner one night." Grabbing a box, Evelyn headed inside.

"Piece of advice." Otis said.

I nodded my head.

"Communication and when that fails, flowers." Otis chucked up the peace sign as he headed back to his place.

With the last of Evelyn's things neatly stacked in the house, I called for pizza, which was the only way I could convince Walt to come and help.

"How does it feel? It's official now." Walt teased.

"I guess we're just an old married couple." I threw my arm around Evelyn resting my hand on her shoulder.

"I sure hope not." She narrowed her beautiful, brown eyes at me.

"No?" I leaned in, wanting to kiss her.

"Nah-uh." Evelyn elevated onto her toes, planting a kiss near the corner of my mouth.

Walt cleared his throat. "Could you stop," he asked. "You two are doing that thing again. We talked about this. Can we save the mushy gushy stuff for when I'm gone?"

Evelyn tossed Walt an evil eye as I dropped my arm from around her. "Cockblocker," she whispered.

Walt returned her glare with a playful middle finger.

It was crazy how Evelyn fit right in with Walt and I. We'd went from the dynamic duo to the three musketeers in no time flat, it never felt awkward or forced. She laughed at our lame jokes and listened to our heated debates about superhero movies or binding precedent, chiming in with her informed opinion, mostly on the movie stuff not the legal stuff.

Grabbing beers from the fridge, she changed the subject. "I was thinking, Halloween is less than two weeks away ... so, what are we doing?" She traded glances with Walt and me.

Both of us offered blank expressions.

"Please don't tell me you guys don't dress up for Halloween, or worse wear a stupid T-shirt that says 'This is My Halloween Costume.'"

"No, I dress up." My eyebrows mashed into a frown.

Evelyn tilted her head to the side. "When was the last time you dressed up?"

"I don't know." I shrugged, having been guilty of wearing minimalist costumes to Halloween parties in the past.

Walt flipped his beer cap on the kitchen counter. "It was three years ago. We went as the kids from that sci-fi show with the monsters. It was Quincy, me, AJ, and V."

I cleared my throat loudly.

"Who's V?" Evelyn leaned her hip onto the kitchen island.

"Q's ex-girlfriend." Walt took a sip of his beer oblivious to the laser beams shooting from my eyes.

I'd dated Victoria for close to four years. The relationship ended badly and the last thing I wanted to do was exhume the ghost of girlfriends' past. I hadn't thought about Victoria in years. That was a lie. I thought about her after awkward first dates, when *The Office* was on television or late at night when I was alone in bed fearing I'd never find whatever it was I was looking for. But these past two weeks with Evelyn, Victoria never crossed my mind.

"That's cool." A smile sprang across her face as she looked up at me. "Do we wanna do something like that? A group costume, or maybe a theme."

"I'm down for whatever." I scratched at my forearm.

Evelyn's face lit up. "How about a Batman theme?"

"I'm Batman." Both Walt and I said in unison.

"Really?" I asked. "I hate to say it but you don't really have the physique for Batman."

"And you do with your bird chest. How much do you lift?"

"I can lift way more than you." Turning to Evelyn I asked, "How much do you weigh?"

Evelyn screwed up her nose. "Did you just call me fat?"

"No, baby ... fat where?" I placed my hand on her curved waist. "The only thing fat about you is dat ass. Ain't that right Walt?" I was hoping he could help dig me out of this hole I'd fallen into.

Beads of sweat formed on Walt's forehead as I needled him with my eyes waiting for him to back me up. "Umm ... I mean this with the utmost respect. The ass pokes out."

I followed that up with a compliment of my own. "The ass is sitting, you hear me."

"That ass is fatter than a mug." Walt tossed out.

"Like is it an ass or a side table because I was about to put a coaster, drink and a hardbound copy of War and Peace on dat thang."

"When it comes to asses—"

"OK ... no ... thank you but that's enough. I get it." Evelyn raised her palm to stop our rambling.

"It's a perfect derriere." I added, kissing her on the cheek.

"Can we focus, I have a vision for Halloween. Walt is gonna be Batman."

"Yes." Walt pumped his fist. "I am vengeance," he said, with a raspy deep voice.

"What? Come on." I grumbled. "What happened to team Parrish?"

Evelyn turned to me. "You my darling are gonna be Two-Face. I'll do your makeup and we'll get you a slick suit. He was handsome and tortured, two qualities I find very hot."

I let the Batman slight slide. She just told me she thought Two-Face was hot so I'd dress up as Two-Face or Papa Smurf if it turned her on. "Who are you gonna be? I asked.

"Duh, with all this ass there's only one choice, Catwoman." She purred pretending to scratch at me. "So we have the outfits now we just need a party to go to."

The room fell silent as we searched one another's eyes.

Evelyn rolled her shoulders. "OK, not a problem we'll just throw our own."

"Where?" I asked.

"Here. What's the point of having a house if you don't invite people over, have them get shit-faced drunk and throw up in your backyard?"

"All of that sounds terrible." Aside from my house-warming party a few years back, I didn't invite people over. My home was my refuge, not *Prysm Nightclub*.

"Don't worry about it, sweetheart you just leave it all to me." She latched on to my chin, which she had to know by now was my Achilles heel. "Send me a list of who you want me to invite. The more the merrier."

"Ten people." I weakly protested.

"The more the merrier. I expect a list from both of you."

EVELYN

AFTER WALT LEFT I took to unpacking. I'd read somewhere about what you should do when a partner moves in with you. Top on the list was making room for them so they didn't feel like an inconvenience or an intruder. Quincy had done just that, moving some of his clothes to the second bedroom closet and emptying out half the dresser drawers so I had a place for my stuff. That was a good sign; it showed effort and intent. For the next ninety days this was *our* home.

After a luxurious shower in his bathroom that sported a full body shower feature, I ambled to the living room where Quincy was scrolling through his phone in the dark except for the light of the fireplace. The *Why Knot* crew left hours ago when they realized all they were getting was boring footage of me smelling random clothes before deciding whether to chuck them in the hamper or hang them up.

"You all squared away?" he asked, as I plopped down next to him.

"Yes. I love your bathroom by the way."

"Yeah?"

"Great lighting and the shower is perfection." I offered up a chef's kiss.

"I aim to please." He tossed his phone on the table focusing all his attention on me.

Damn, he was one good looking man. He was happiness to my eyes causing giddy excitement to flutter inside of me. I tried my best to swipe modest glances at his face but I wanted to stare shamelessly ogling him with my eyes until I got my fill. His intense, brown eyes never shied away, he didn't seem to mind my curious gaze.

Tucking my hair behind my ears, I wished I'd taken more time pulling myself together. My hair was damp from the shower and I was wearing a red and black flannel robe. Did I have plenty of sexy lingerie I could have slipped into? Yes. So why did I pick this robe that gave off the kitchen is closed type vibes?

Quincy wasn't deterred by my grandma-style garb, his hand grazed my leg before it slowly inched under my robe. His touch made my chest heave like I was in one of those Harlequin romance novels my mother loved reading.

My eyes traveled to his kissable lips. "I don't wanna be that couple that just has sex all the time." I blurted out.

"Were we just about to—"

"Oh yeah, big time." His hand was still resting on my thigh.

"We shouldn't fight the feeling." He leaned in for a kiss but I stopped him, placing a finger over his eager lips.

"We're supposed to be getting to know one another."

"We are. Sex is the most intimate thing a couple can do.

If we didn't have sex, I wouldn't know how your eyes light up right before I slid inside of you."

My flesh grew hot and my lady parts throbbed so intensely I could feel the pulse in my ear. With much difficulty I ignored all that and said, "You know what I noticed?"

"Are you wearing anything under this robe?"

"No." He didn't have to ask, his wandering hands that cupped my naked ass cheek were providing the answer. Quincy made a second attempt at a kiss. "I noticed you don't have any art on the walls."

Quincy sunk back into the sofa accepting we were going to talk. "What?"

"Your walls are bare all throughout the house." I pointed. "No art, no photographs, not even a mirror."

He shrugged, reaching for his glass of wine he took a sip before handing me the glass.

"How long have you lived here?" I took a gulp of the red wine, tucking my cold feet under his thigh.

"Almost two years." He looked around the room.

"Two years? And your walls are butt booty naked."

"I don't know. I guess I've just never found a piece of art that spoke to me."

"Have you even looked?" I drained the glass, giving it a shake. "More."

Pouring us another glass, he handed it back to me. "Not really."

"I know tons of artists. If you stop by the gallery you might find something you like."

"So are my naked ass walls a deal breaker?"

"It's embarrassing. You're married to an artist." I chided. "Your place is hella nice, it just needs some warming up."

"Really, like what?" He brought the almost empty wine bottle to his lips.

"Art on the walls. More than one pillow on the couch. Maybe a few plants. *IKEA* has some great stuff."

Quincy rumpled his face. "I don't shop at *IKEA*."

I pulled my face in an "excuse me" expression. "Oh, my bad. I didn't realize you were bougie."

"I'm not. I just believe in paying for quality."

"I have an *IKEA* night stand that has lasted me for years."

"If we must, we can go to *Crate and Barrel* or *Restoration Hardware*."

I audibly gagged. *Restoration Hardware*? I didn't know people actually shopped there. Even my fakey faker mother got her furniture at *Ashley's Home*. When we wrote out our budget a few days ago, Quincy placed his salary at well over six figures, so I knew he had money to blow, but spending six thousand dollars on a dining table, sans chairs was insane.

"Stop, have you ever even been?"

"In *Restoration Hardware*? No, because every time I walk past that store it calls me a broke bitch."

"The store said that?"

"Loudly, for everyone in the mall to hear. 'Broke ass bitch approaching.'" I imitated an uppity British accent for the last part.

"That is the worst British accent I have ever heard."

"I'm still workshopping that one. Now, my Australian accent is flawless."

"Let me hear it."

Taking a sip of wine, I handed him the glass. "Crikey, blimey."

Quincy shook his head. "No, somehow that was worse than the first accent." He laughed uncontrollably, hysteria rolling through him so intense he almost spilled the wine. "Oh God Evelyn, I love yo ... Yuletide logs." He shouted out shooting a nervous glance in my direction.

I tried my best to hide a smile. The slip of the tongue was not missed by me. "Oh yeah, the dessert or the actual burning log?

"The dessert." He gave me an appreciative smile, probably relieved I didn't call him out on his near miss confession.

"What do you like most about it?"

"It's chocolaty, decadent, and then there's the cream filling." His eyes were hooded and dreamy. I wasn't sure if it was from wine or wanton.

"Eww, I'm sorry I asked." Reaching for his phone I handed it to him. "Unlock your phone."

Passing the phone back to me he said, "My phone isn't locked."

"What, you don't lock your phone?"

"No why would I do that?"

"To hide things."

"Like what?

"Naked pictures, porn, slutty text messages, or screenshots of Trevante Rhodes whom you've never met but if you did you would let him destroy your life."

"That is wildly specific."

"He's a very good actor," I said earnestly.

Opening up the search engine, I pulled up the Two-Face costume I'd found for him, turning the screen so he could see. "I found this at a costume shop. I rented it and the Catwoman outfit."

"So you were serious about all that?"

"Yes. Like the bubonic plague."

"Do you go all out for every holiday?" He rubbed his hand over his forehead and eyes.

"Holidays are huge in my family. Most events are awkward and cringe but at least we're all together." I pasted on a fake smile.

"Family discord. It's the reason for the season. So we have Halloween figured out, what about Thanksgiving."

"Big family gathering. Aunts and uncles from out of town. A cousin I may have made out with."

"Excuse me?" His eyebrows jogged up his forehead.

"I didn't know we were related at the time. We met at a bar the night before Thanksgiving. He was fine as hell. I was horny as hell. Not my finest moment. Anywoo, Thanksgiving usually ends with happy birthday and cake cutting."

"Happy birthday?"

"Yeah, Evan and I were born on November twenty-fourth. Well, I was born on the twenty-fourth and he was born eleven minutes later on the twenty-fifth, so my family always celebrates on Thanksgiving."

A deep-set frown lined his face.

"What?"

"There's just so much I don't know about you. It's weird cause I feel like I've known you forever and then you say some shit like that and I realize I have so much to learn."

"I'm sorry I wasn't trying to overwhelm you." My face fell as I fidgeted with the sash of my robe.

"No, you didn't. That's not what I meant." Quincy

stood, grabbing the wine bottle, he placed it into the recycling bin.

When I was a kid my teachers noted on my report cards, "Evelyn is a good student but she talks entirely too much." This was my MO. I moved too fast, falling too soon. Playing it cool wasn't in my vocabulary. Hard to get. What was that? I was honest, and shared things I shouldn't, like the fact I almost fucked my cousin. Probably should've kept that piece of Evelyn trivia to myself.

"I talk too much. I'm sorry. I know. My mother always said you don't have to speak every thought; women should be a mystery. A lesson lost on me because I never liked mysteries."

Quincy retook his seat next to me on the sofa. "Evelyn, I like listening to you talk. I enjoy talking to you. Are you the weirdest woman I've ever met? Yes. But I am surprisingly into your special brand of weird."

My fears slowly abated as his words sunk in. Straddling his lap, my warm smile returned. "When's your birthday?"

"September third." He undid the sash of my robe.

He was a Virgo, that made sense. Virgos were known to be one of the most intelligent signs but they were also big-time overthinkers. Tapping my forehead, I said, "Locking it in. The weather will still be nice. Maybe we could do a beach party or rent a yacht." My face lit up. "Ooh, let's rent a yacht."

"Maybe."

September was a long way away, we may not even still be together. I had to learn to pace myself. If it were up to me I'd get tangled up in him like Christmas lights making it damn near impossible for anything to pull us apart, but I needed to stop planning for the future and live in the moment.

"Or not. We can figure it out later."

"What do you want for your birthday?" His hands were playing with my breast. My eyes crossed when he pinched down on my left nipple.

"I don't know." My hips were already floating over his lap in preparation of what was to come.

"You gotta want something." Quincy leaned in kissing the space between my chest.

"Hmm ... you."

"Me?" His breathing had grown shallow.

I continued to circle my hips feeling his penis come to life in his pajama bottoms. "Uh-huh, just you over and over again."

"You already have that." Quincy cupped the back of my neck, his thumb stroking my throat.

"I want more. I'm greedy in that way." I shrugged off my robe letting it drop to the floor.

"OK, I mean I'm still gonna buy you a gift so you don't yell at me."

Sliding off his lap, I knelt in front of him, tugging at the waistband of his pajamas.

"What are you doing?" Quincy asked with wide eyes.

"Unwrapping my birthday present early."

CHAPTER 12

QUINCY

After my first day back at work, I hopped on the L riding a few stops. I was headed to Evelyn's gallery to check out some potential art for my walls. This was week three of being married to a stranger but to my surprise it was going pretty well. Don't get me wrong, it was an adjustment sharing my space with someone else after living alone for so long. Evelyn was messy and loud. When she cooked she used every pot and spoon in the house. She was always losing her keys. In the middle of the night, she would kick the covers from her body screaming, "I'm hot. Are you not hot?" She peed with the door open. She'd beg me to watch a movie with her and then promptly fall asleep.

And then there was Totes McGoats who acted like Evelyn was the bringer of light. He followed her around the house, weaseled his way in between us when we were sitting on the couch, and he would whine incessantly at the front door when she went away. My dog was a traitor, falling for a pretty woman who smelled savory and full with hints of amber, wood, and vanilla that lingered on our bedding long after she'd gone.

Townsend Gallery had large windows that showcased the space with concrete floors and white walls so all the attention remained on the art. The space took after its owner, alluring, immediately drawing me in. The sound of *Rachel Chinouriri* floated through the air, playing softly.

"Can I help you?" a woman with tattoos up and down her arms asked.

"Ahh, yeah. I'm looking for Evelyn."

"Is she expecting you?"

"Yes, I'm her ... I'm Quincy."

The woman's face brightened as she gave me a thorough once-over. "Be right back." She threw another quick glance over her shoulder as she walked away.

The word husband was still foreign on my tongue. I'd rolled it around in my head several times but it still got stuck in my throat each time I attempted to verbalize the word.

"You came." Evelyn's face was a song as she walked toward me in a color-block outfit of pinks and reds.

I was used to seeing her in swimsuits, jeans, or nothing at all, but professional Evelyn was quite the turn-on. Her wide-legged, fuchsia slacks hugging the curve of her backside and a chunky, red sweater pulled off one shoulder offering a peek-a-boo of skin.

"Hi." My face pulled into a goofy smile. It had only been ten hours since I'd last seen her but the way my heart was kicking feral beats in my chest you'd think it had been longer.

"Hi." She returned a goofy smile of her own.

"Hi." The tattooed lady waved from behind Evelyn.

Evelyn stepped aside. "This is Dotty, my assistant who keeps the lights on for me. I'd be lost without her. And Dotty this is my ... Quincy."

"Nice to meet you. I've heard so much about you." She extended her hand giving mine a firm enthusiastic shake.

"Not that much." Evelyn shook her head brushing the hair from her neck.

Dotty waved her off. "A lot. You said he was fine but you didn't say he was *fione*."

"Is there a distinction?" I asked.

"It's in the way you enunciate. Any dude can be fine. But not every dude is *fione*." She pinched her finger and rolled her neck.

"I get it. Thanks." I winked.

"Well, I'ma leave you two lovebirds alone. See you tomorrow, Evie." Collecting her things, Dotty left the gallery, locking the front door behind her.

"Sorry about that."

"No, she seems nice."

Evelyn fidgeted with her wedding band. She seemed nervous but I couldn't figure out why.

"Are you OK."

"Yeah, it's just kinda weird having you here." Her tongue poked at the inside of her mouth.

"Do you want me to leave?"

"No, I just mean the last two weeks everything's kinda been compartmentalized and now things are bleeding over into our lives."

I tipped my head forward in agreement. "Shit just got real."

"I'm sure shit got real for you the minute I moved in and invaded your home."

"Yeah, it did because you're messy and you snore."

"No, that's your dog." She pouted.

"Nah, it's definitely you ... high pitched nasally."

She tried to walk away from me but didn't get far because her hand was locked in mine.

"Did you have a good first day back at work?" Evelyn ignored my tongue in cheek insult, fingering the button on my coat.

"Yep. I would have preferred to just be laid up in the bed with you ... but maybe later."

Evelyn's hand floated to the necklace I'd gifted her on our wedding day, a smile tugging at the corners of her mouth.

"This is a great space. Your personal studio is here too, right?"

"Yeah, I work back there." She pulled on my arm, leading me to a small space separated by a partial wall.

The smile melted from my face. "Not much of a space."

"Tell me about it."

"This place is far from the house. What if you're inspired to create in the middle of the night?"

"I hop on the L." She jerked her shoulders in a shrug.

"No bueno."

"I know. I'm looking for a new spot but this is all I can afford right now. A dedicated studio is a luxury."

"No, I totally understand." I made a mental note to check with some of my real estate friends, maybe they could find a place closer to the house that would meet her needs.

"OK, so walk around check out the pieces if you find something you like just give me a holler."

After a kiss that was far too quick, she busied herself on her laptop while I cased the joint. The gallery housed sculptures and wall art in different mediums. There was also a wall filled with a series of portraits of Black and Brown faces both young and old. I stopped at a black and white piece of a couple, the woman kissing the man on his neck. It made the bottom of my stomach flutter because it reminded me of the kisses Evelyn would plant just underneath my ear.

"What can you tell me about this piece?" I called out.

Raising from her stool, she walked over standing next to me. "It's a watercolor done in black and white. The piece is called *The Embrace*. Do you like it?"

Holding my hand to my chin, I moved closer inspecting the canvas. "Yeah, I'm feeling this."

"Yeah?"

"Yeah it's dope. Is it an original or a print?"

"It's the original. No prints."

"Ah, so it's one of a kind."

"What do you like about it?" Her hands were clasped behind her back.

"I love the simplicity, the clean lines. But most of all I love the feminine and masculine energy. The couple seems love locked in that all-consuming ... if I could live inside you it wouldn't be close enough type a way."

"Have you felt that before?" Her eyes were velvety.

God, I loved the way she looked at me. Her gaze was curious with a hint of mischief, and a dash of seduction.

"Um." Scratching at my forearm, I deflected. "I ... I don't know. I don't remember." That was a lie.

"Do you wanna look around some more? I have a few pieces in storage in the back."

"Nah, I want this one. How much are we talking?"

Evelyn winked at me. "I know the artist I can get you a deal."

I rubbed my palms together. "Cool. So, when do I get to see one of your pieces?"

"You just did." She pointed to the painting I'd just agreed to purchase, before walking away.

EVELYN

"Would you stop squirming?" I ordered.

"I'm itchy." Quincy complained, twitching his nose.

"Where?"

"My nose, just right inside."

I slipped my finger in the tip of his left nostril giving it a quick scratch.

"Better?"

"Yes, thank you."

Tonight was the Halloween party and I was finishing up his face makeup. It was very possible I'd bitten off more than I could chew, but luckily Meryl arrived early to help with the finishing touches in the living room. In less than twenty minutes, close to fifty people would show up in their festive fits. Quincy and Walt both texted me a list of friends's numbers and with that and the contacts in my phone I'd sent a mass text message inviting everyone to the Halloween Party at Quincy's ... our place.

Quincy's hands kept exploring my latex costume that

made my tits and ass look phenomenal if I did say so myself. We would have been finished sooner but we lost fifteen minutes because he couldn't stop kissing me. Quincy looked amazing, one side of his face was discolored and raised as if he'd suffered severe burns. His suit was a contrast to his split personality, one side professional, the other side loud and obnoxious. Spinning him around I waited with bated breath as he checked out my handy work.

"I look diabolical." Pulling the large two-sided coin from his pocket he tossed it into the air. "Should I kiss this latex queen or should I chuck her the deuces." The coin landed in the sink spinning before revealing heads. Leaning in, he tapped his makeup-free cheek, I complied giving it a kiss.

In the living room, I checked on the board of assorted meats and cheeses laid out on the length of the dining table. The home was dimly lit with flameless candles spread throughout. I'd spent all last night carving and drawing on pumpkins which were now arranged in front of the fireplace. The huge spider attached to the ceiling, which I made out of streamers and balloons, added a creepy effect in the low light. I spared no detail, even placing eyeballs in the hand soap mason jar in the guest bath.

"Everything looks great. Thanks so much for helping me." I pulled napkins and plates from a paper bag placing them on the dining table.

"Glad I could be of assistance."

"Did you ride the L like that?" I pointed to Meryl's sexy Chucky costume.

"I had a coat on."

"I didn't know a homicidal, possessed doll could be sexy, but here we are."

"So," Meryl looked back toward the bedroom where Quincy was still getting ready. "How's it going?"

A smile eased wide across my face. "It's been pretty good. I don't know if he's just on his best behavior but he's nice."

"You like him." Meryl squealed.

I shushed her not wanting Quincy to overhear. Which was silly because if he didn't know I was into him, he wasn't paying attention. "I think it's safe to say I like my husband."

Meryl inched closer. She'd been out of town for work so this was our first chance to catch up since returning from my honeymoon. "How's the sex?" she whispered.

I knew the cameras were probably zooming in on my face waiting to capture my response. I also knew Quincy would kill me if I was caught on tape gushing about our sex life. Focusing on Meryl until our gaze locked, I bulged my eyes wide, a smile dancing across my face. We'd been best friends since childhood so we knew how to communicate without saying a word.

Meryl pulled a whole dill pickle out of an open jar giving it a shake.

I clipped my head in a quick no.

Next Meryl picked up a thick uncut salami still in the wrapper.

My eyes flickered in approval.

"I know you're fucking lying, bitch." Meryl jumped up and down laughing.

"What are you two plotting in here?" Quincy asked, strutting into the room.

"Oh so that's why he walks like that?" Meryl whispered, with a nod of her head.

"Nothing." My face was flushed and I felt a little guilty. But Meryl was my best friend and I told her everything. If the cameras weren't around, I would have given her every dirty little detail, girth, feel, and taste.

I started the Halloween playlist and the Backstreet Boys, "Everybody" started to play. Meryl and I spun and twirled in sync to the beat with hand moves we perfected over years of friendship.

~

QUINCY

A LITTLE AFTER eleven and the party was in full swing. My house was filled with ghouls, goblins, and five sexy nuns. Evan was in the middle of the living room dressed as the Joker doing the running man to the Geto Boys. Apparently, Evelyn also coordinated her brother's outfit for the night. Taking a swig from my beer, my eyes were drawn to the front door. A woman dressed as a sexy Raggedy Ann entered the party and my heart functions stalled.

Is that Victoria? Closing my eyes, I counted to five because I was clearly seeing things that weren't there. When I reopened my eyes, there she was hugging my friends and laughing.

Walt approached out of breath. "Dude?"

"What the fuck is she doing here?"

"Maybe she heard you were having a party and decided to crash."

"Well that's hella bold." Grabbing Walt's cape, I pulled him into the chilly backyard.

"Who just shows up at their ex's house ... uninvited?" Walt asked.

"Victoria, because she chooses chaos every fucking time. Oh, Quincy's gotten married and is moving on with his life. Let me show up to his house and piss on his fucking rug," I shouted.

"Or maybe she just came to congratulate you."

"No, she came to check out Evelyn and compare and critique."

"Probably more likely."

"Well she's in for a rude fucking awakening. When Victoria sees Evelyn. When ... she ... sees ... Evelyn." I punched a fist into my palm after every word. "She's gonna see I upgraded."

"Like Beyoncé."

"That I leveled the fuck up."

"Like a boss." Walt cosigned me.

"Like a fucking boss," I yelled.

If Victoria thought she could just stroll in here, kick sand in my face and steal my ice cream she had another thing coming. I couldn't wait to see the look on her face when she saw Evelyn. Evelyn was smart, funny, and a good person, yadda yadda, yadda. But her face was a showstopper rendering me speechless every single time. Her big brown eyes, her huge luminous smile that was so bright it could warm a small room. Her perfectly rounded lips that begged to be kissed and then there was her buxom frame soft in places, like the curve of her long neck while firm and unforgiving in others, like her thighs which held me captive as our bodies moved in syncopated time.

"What's up?" Evelyn shouted, entering the backyard.

"I'm drunk." She teetered, reaching for my hand to steady her.

A flush crept over my neck and face. "Nothing, just chillin."

"Nothing?" Walt's eyes widened. "Victoria's here dude."

Walt was the worst wingman ever.

"Who?" Evelyn drained the rest of her Frankenpunch, lime sorbet mixed with tequila.

Blowing out my cheeks, I released a breath. "For some reason my ex, Victoria, is here. I think I may have included her number when I was giving you the guest list."

"Oops." Evelyn laughed hysterically.

"This isn't funny." I pursed my lips folding my arms across my chest.

Evelyn straightened, clearing her throat. "No, it's not funny, Walter." She shot a look in Walt's direction hitting him on the arm. "This is serious. So what can we do?" She paced back and forth before snapping her finger. "I know ... we could kill her and bury her in the backyard. And of course, we could never talk about it again and then in the summer we'd get a note that said I know what you did last summer. Wait, it would say I know what you did last Halloween and then this killer with a hook would pick us off one by one. And plot twist ... it was your ex all along because we never really killed her."

I tilted my head narrowing my eyes. "What the fuck is wrong with you?"

"I'm drunk, so ..."

"Listen, I can ask her to leave," Walt suggested.

Evelyn nodded trying her best to focus. "If it makes you uncomfortable ..."

"I'm not uncomfortable." I tsked, fidgeting with my suit. "I don't even care. I just don't want things to be weird for you. But I'm straight. Not pressed."

"I like weird. Plus, it's Halloween." The creaking sound at the beginning of Michael Jackson's "Thriller" caught her attention and Evelyn danced away joining her brother on the makeshift dance floor in the middle of the living room.

"Wow." I rubbed my forehead, Evelyn was wasted.

"I know, how is she still able to twerk in that tight ass latex suit?" Walt asked.

Even though it was thirty-six degrees, I was still in the backyard rocking side to side. I wasn't interested in talking to Victoria and so I thought it best to just keep my distance even if I could no longer feel my toes.

"Hey you." A familiar voice called from behind.

Victoria never played fair. She knew me well enough to know I was avoiding her. She wasn't going to let the fact that she was at her ex-boyfriend and his new wife's Halloween party, which she wasn't invited to, spoil a good time.

"Quincy, it's good to see you again." Victoria leaned in for a hug, she smelled like a field of flowers and I immediately felt my allergies starting to act up.

"Sexy Raggedy Ann. I see you more as the grim reaper or Medusa. But this works too."

"There was a grim reaper outfit but it didn't show off my legs." She ran her fingers across her striped, thigh-high, red and white stockings.

"Yeah, I guess you're right." I laughed out a puff of air.

"So you got married?"

"Yes, that is something that happened." I looked into the

living room and found Evelyn on top of the coffee table trunk doing the snake with her brother and a fake skeleton.

"For reality TV?" She pointed at the camera.

"For love." I surprised myself with how hard I laughed, having a difficult time believing my own words. Victoria didn't share in my humor. When we were dating, she rarely laughed at my jokes. She'd call me childish and said Walt and I needed to grow up. Victoria was a wet blanket. I still don't know how I was able to wrap myself around her all those years.

"Are you hard up for money?" Her face feigning concern.

I was not going to be goaded into a fight with my ex-girlfriend. "How have you been?"

"Great, close to making partner at the firm."

"Wow, well you deserve that you always made work your first priority."

"Because work was actually fulfilling."

You fucking bitch. "Nice to see some things haven't changed."

Evelyn came dancing into the backyard performing some complicated footwork to the Ghostbusters theme. "Why aren't you inside grinding on me and sticking your tongue down my throat?" She wrapped her arms around my neck.

Victoria coughed. "Hello, you must be Quin's new wife."

I paid close attention as Victoria's eyes scanned Evelyn. She was clearly looking for flaws but she wouldn't find one because Evelyn was a masterpiece. She was the *Mona Lisa* and Victoria was one of those exaggerated caricatures you got for ten bucks at the local state fair. It was satisfying seeing the woman who told me I could never find anyone better than her slowly realizing I could and I did.

"Yes. I'm Evelyn Parrish. Wife to Quincy ... wait I know this. You told me your middle name. It was hideous."

"Chester." Victoria said.

"Yes." Evelyn snapped her fingers. "Wife to Quincy Chester Parrish. You must be his ex. I've heard nothing about you but nice to meet you all the same. Thanks for coming to our little soirée."

I didn't think it was possible, but Evelyn was drunker now than the last time she came to check on me.

"Ahh, yeah, congratulations by the way. I have to admit I was surprised when I heard Quin got married."

"Stranger things have happened," I said.

"Yeah, but I thought you were opposed to the whole institution."

I wasn't opposed to marriage; I was opposed to being locked in the institution with Victoria.

Evelyn's eyes moved from Victoria and landed on my face.

"Nope, just waiting for the right person," I countered.

"And a stranger you met on a reality television show was the right person? No offense." Victoria extended her hand toward Evelyn.

"Absolutely none taken. But to answer your question when you know you know and sometimes even *then* you don't know until you *know*."

I blinked rapidly. "She's drunk. But what she said."

Victoria rolled her eyes, if Evelyn noticed she didn't react. "Was that queso dip I spotted on the table in there?"

"Yes, personal recipe. It's delicious." Evelyn leaned in, whispering loudly in Victoria's ear, "The secret is hot sauce."

Victoria cringe smiled in that annoying way she always did. "I think I'll make myself a plate. It was good seeing you again Quin."

Evelyn watched as she walked away before looking up at me. I braced myself expecting her to rip me a new one. "You've been out here almost all night. Are you not having fun?"

"No, I'm having a great time. Everyone is because of you." I played with a lock of her hair which was voluminous and wild like a feral cat.

"You seem distracted."

"Nope." I took a drag of my stale beer.

Evelyn threw a glance into the living room. "Flip your coin. Heads or tails. Whichever way it lands is how you get to fuck me tonight."

I choked on the pale ale nearly spitting it back up. "Heads or tails?"

"Uh-huh." She swept her tongue over her lips.

Reaching into my pocket I retrieved the oversized fake coin, tossing it in the air I caught it closed fist before slapping it on the backside of my hand. Slowly I pulled my hand away and every drop of blood in my body diverted to my dick when I saw the results.

"Tails," I said. Not even sure what that meant. Was it doggy style or something else?

Lifting to her tip toes she whispered over my lips, "Come dance with me."

Clasping her hand in mine, we re-entered the party space.

"Big Bro," Evan yelled across the room where he was standing way too close to a woman who was not his girlfriend.

Pulling Evelyn to the designated dance area in the middle of the living room, I swayed from side to side as her body undulated against mine. I'd spent too much time letting Victoria's presence ruin my vibe. It was Halloween, my wife was wearing a costume that highlighted her best assets, and she was eager for some skin-on-skin contact.

Cupping the back of her neck, I pulled her close, my lips enclosed onto hers holding nothing back. My hand gripped her ass while the other bore down on her neck. I didn't give a fuck about the cameras, Victoria, or the fact that Evan's six-foot-four ass was standing on my couch in his outside shoes. All that mattered was the way this woman ran her fingers through my hair before discreetly dropping her hand, rubbing it across my member.

"Aren't you glad you danced with me?" She teased. Strike that ... it wasn't teasing because everything this woman claimed she backed the fuck up.

WITH THE LAST of the guests gone, Evelyn and I moved across the space picking up trash and clearing food.

"This was so much fun." She gave her body a mini stretch.

"Thanks for putting this all together. It was a fun night. Sorry about the shit with Victoria." I wanted to gauge her temperature now that she was coming down from her giddy drunken high, just to ensure we were good.

"So that was your ex?"

"Yep."

"She's really pretty." Evelyn balanced several empty beer bottles in her arms.

"I just hope her being here didn't make things awkward."

"Nope. We both have a history. It's cool. I actually thought it was kinda funny watching you squirm."

"I noticed that." Pulling the plastic bag from the recycling bin I held the bag open while she tossed the bottles in.

"So was she the one that got away?" Evelyn asked, sifting through the almost empty Halloween candy bowl.

"She was the one that I couldn't get away from fast enough."

"There's no lingering feelings?"

"God no. Victoria was a lot of work. I get that relationships take work and need to be nurtured ... blah, blah, blah, but everything with her was a fight. She wanted me to be this corporate sell out guy and that wasn't appealing to me. I'm all for growth and change but at our base level we are who we are. And if I can't be who I really am with the person I'm supposed to love then what's the point."

"When was the last time you saw her?"

"Maybe a year ago? At a legal conference." I decided to omit the fact we had sex in my hotel room at that conference. Like Evelyn said we both had a past.

"Admit it. It felt kinda good to show her you are thriving and flourishing."

I lifted a blasé shoulder, I'd had my fill of talking about my ex and was looking to shift the topic. "What I'm interested in is that coin flip."

Evelyn's gaze grew intense as she moved closer, erasing the distance between us. She kissed me on my neck just like the couple from her art piece that hung on the wall in the dining area. Grabbing her waist, I lifted her to the kitchen island, closing my eyes as her lips touched mine, her mouth tasted sweet from the Halloween candy she'd consumed the entire night. The thick zipper on the front of her costume slid down with ease and her ample breast popped out like a Jack-in-the-box. My knees grew weak as my heart accelerated in my rib cage. Burying my face in between her chest, I teased her skin with my tongue. A sigh parted her lips as my tongue grazed her nipple.

"I've been wanting this all night." I nipped at her lips.

"What do you want?"

"I want you to sit on my fa—"

"Whoa, you two better not be having sex." Evan called, shuffling into the living room.

"Shit." Evelyn hopped off the counter zipping her suit. "Evan."

"Why are you still here?" I asked.

Evan wobbled back and forth. "Because I'm drunk, duh."

"We have talked about this. Boundaries." Evelyn reminded him.

"I was minding my Black ass business. It was you two who decided to be some big ole freaks ... on the kitchen counter no less."

"So what, you're just staying here tonight?" I tossed him a side eye.

"Yeah. Ooo, maybe we could get breakfast in the morning at that one spot, The Giddy Griddle."

"I'm sorry," Evelyn said softly her lips curled out dejectedly.

With a roll of my eyes, I turned my attention back to Evan. "Tomorrow, I'm getting bottomless mimosas and your ass is paying for everything."

"I got you covered Big Bro."

CHAPTER 13

EVELYN

It was almost nine in the morning on a Sunday and instead of being in our warm bed with my naked body pressed against my husband, I was at church. Once a month Quincy accompanied his foster mother to church and this Sunday, he invited me to attend. After service Naomi and I sat in the lobby while Quincy was busy chatting up someone he recognized from work.

"I'm happy you decided to come out. I know you young folks like your sleep," Naomi said.

Ms. Naomi was fifty years old but she looked like she and I could be contemporaries, so hearing her talk about herself like an aging senior citizen tickled me.

"No, I appreciate the invite. I want to be a part of all of Quincy's traditions. And spending time with family is important."

"Things are going well with you two?" Ms. Naomi pulled on her gloves.

"I think so. I mean there's still a lot to figure out but I'm game."

"When Quincy told me he agreed to appear on this show I was shocked. He's always been so private." Naomi rolled her shoulders. "I guess it's a bit of a coping mechanism."

I nodded my head thoughtfully.

"When you've suffered as much loss as he has it can be difficult."

My brows compressed over my eyes. "Yeah, of course … right."

Naomi studied my face. "You have no idea what I'm talking about, do you?"

I offered a sheepish grin. "No, Quincy's kind of been secretive about his childhood."

"Quincy can be a hard nut to crack because he's constantly looking for flaws. He doesn't trust easily because almost everyone he trusted as a kid hurt him. He's funny, I'm sure you've noticed that. He's always used humor to cover up the pain. So much so, that if you bring up a topic he doesn't want to discuss he'll make a self-deprecating joke to distract from the fact that he isn't sharing."

"He does joke a lot." My mind raced at the realization. Every benign conversation I was running through my head with fresh eyes.

"Don't let him get away with that stuff. He will push you away and have you thinking you're the one who decided to leave."

"I'm a good listener, but he has to wanna talk." There was nothing I wanted more than for Quincy to mentally unload on me. Whatever he was carrying we could sort through it together. I wanted to be his soft place where he could escape from the world and just find comfort in the warm embrace of my love. But to do that he had to open up.

"The thing is he desperately wants to share himself with someone the good, the bad, and the ugly. He just gets in his own way."

"What about his ex, Victoria? Did he share stuff with her?" According to Quincy he and Victoria dated for years so surely he'd opened up to her.

"No." Naomi let out a dry laugh. "I think he told that girl one thing and she flipped out because it was messing up the upper middle class dream she had inserted him into. She can't be rubbing elbows with the mayor if her father-in-law is a convicted felon."

My eyes flickered with confusion trying to process Naomi's words. Were we talking about Quincy's father? I know it sounds morbid but I just assumed his father was dead. This news, while unexpected, didn't change anything for me.

I knew plenty of people whose fathers went to jail or were still currently behind bars. We are not responsible for our parents' choices. And it was clear Quincy worked hard to sever any connection his apple had to that tree. I had follow-up questions but this revelation was Quincy's to share. When he was ready for me to know, he would tell me, I decided not to press the issue any further.

"Don't get me wrong, when he loves someone he loves them with all he has. He just fights like hell not to get attached."

"Why agree to do a show in which the whole purpose is to fall in love?"

"The one thing Quincy is scared about right now is you. Because you, he didn't expect."

Scared of me? She couldn't be serious. I was on his side, Team Parrish and all that jazz. Quincy appeared to have it all figured out incorporating me into his life with little to no interruption. Plus, this show and the entire process was ultimately a joke to him so if this failed ... if we failed, he'd be no worse for wear. Me on the other hand, I was swimming in feelings if not love then love adjacent. If anyone should be shaking in their boots about the prospects of our future, it should be me.

After leaving church, we headed up the stairs to the L train. Quincy picked up the pace clutching my hand, he whispered, "Run."

Without hesitation I followed his lead, running for the approaching train. The crew of *Why Knot* had a difficult time keeping up. Letting go of my hand we ran past a group of slow walkers before he claimed my hand again pulling me onto the waiting train, the doors closing behind us. Jared made it to the platform and slapped the door staring daggers into Quincy's face through the window of the train door.

"Get off at the next stop." He screamed through the doors.

"What, I can't hear. What are we supposed to do?" Quincy smirked as the train pulled away from the station.

Dropping to a section of empty seats, I breathed out a heavy stream of air. "What did we just do?"

"I don't know. I thought they would catch up." His words implied innocence but his face told a different story.

"When we get home they're going to kill us." I tugged at my scarf, beads of sweat forming on my forehead.

Ditching the crew was a no no. Before we started filming ... before I ever met Quincy, I sat through a whole conversation with one of the producers about never trying to evade or ditch the crew. Something about legally binding agreements, breach of contract, and civil litigation. I wasn't sure what all of it meant but I did know they could sue us.

Quincy's face lit up. "Then I guess we should take our time."

"What?"

"If we're going to be in trouble anyway, we might as well make it worth it. Stand up." Pulling off our coats, he removed our mic packs taking the batteries out of each unit so we couldn't be tracked. Stuffing the dead packs in my oversized purse, he asked, "What should we do first?"

QUINCY

MY LEGS WOBBLED as we circled the ice rink at Millennium Park. It had been years since I'd ice skated but as we made slow rotations around the rink, it was coming back to me. I felt brave enough to let go of Evelyn's hand and propel myself forward on my own.

"When we were younger my stepdad would take us to ice skate every year around this time. Evan would speed through the rink, practically knocking people over. And Erica would hold on to my parents crying the entire time. She was a really annoying baby." Evelyn shook her head skating backward. "What about you, any favorite childhood family memories?"

My eyes narrowed. "Since I grew up in foster care I don't

have a ton of warm and fuzzies associated with family." I always hated these types of conversations. Why people were so excited to relive their childhood was beyond me. My childhood was something I preferred to forget.

"Oh my bad, I'm sorry." Evelyn's face fell. "That was insensitive. I know our childhood experiences were likely very different."

"No, it's all good."

"How old were you when you entered foster care?"

"Eight."

Evelyn's eyes grew wide and she gave me that look. The look that shadowed everyone's face when I mentioned growing up in foster care. It was a mixture of sympathy, pity, and relief that it wasn't them. I sped up hoping to outrun this particular topic of conversation, gliding past couples and families all laughing and enjoying their Sunday morning. Eventually I'd share my past with her but I wasn't interested in unpacking my childhood trauma in the middle of Millennium Park.

"I'm getting better at this," I said, after catching up with her again.

"You are. You didn't fall once. Impressive."

"Do you know any tricks?"

"I know all kinds of tricks." She gave me a rascally smile.

"I was talking about skating." Wrapping my arm around her, I pulled her close for warmth.

"Yeah, I know a few. When I was a kid ..." Evelyn stopped abruptly, a pained contortion to her face.

"Hey, don't do that." Grabbing her hand, I pulled her to the rink railings. "Just because my childhood sucked doesn't mean I don't wanna hear about yours."

"Not gonna lie here. I feel a little guilty."

"For what? Having a normal upbringing."

"Because it sounds like you didn't."

"And none of that is your fault. Look, life is like a box of chocolates and I just happened to get the gross white chocolate with cherry filling."

"That's disgusting."

"It really is the worst chocolate out there. Calling it *chocolate* is just wrong."

Grabbing my coat, she pulled me toward her lips. The cloud from our breaths commingled as it escaped our lungs. As I parted my lips her soft, warm tongue drew me in. Her kisses ignited a fire deep inside, time slowed and quickened in the same breath. How she made the world around us disappear with a kiss was beyond me. Somehow, I was free falling but I didn't remember jumping.

EVELYN

It was my turn to pick the next stop on our impromptu ditch day; I decided on the Art Institute of Chicago, mostly because we were frozen after the ice rink and I thought this would be a great way to thaw out. With hot chocolate in hand, we walked the exhibits.

"When did you know you wanted to be an artist?"

"I've loved drawing for as long as I could remember. I just didn't know it was something I could make money from. When I went to college I kinda fell in with the artsy crowd and it was a wrap. There's just something about creating an image in your head and then using your hands to birth it, giving it life for others to appreciate." My eyes gleamed with a far-off look, which often happened when I discussed my work. "Finding someone who loves what you created because of the way it makes them feel, or 'cause it unearths a long forgotten memory … there aren't words for that."

Quincy stopped at a painting called *Reclining Woman* of a figure that was choppy and crudely drawn. "OK, what does this painting say to you? Because honestly, I don't get it."

I examined the canvas before responding. "I've studied this artist. He had an interest in geometric shapes. It was his goal to showcase art in a more accessible way by painting the mundane. Personally, I see it as empowerment to just rest with a book. We're taught our value is connected to what we offer. How hard we work. How much money we make. And this piece says the reclining woman is enough. Rest is a form of rebellion.

"But you don't have to see what I see. That's the beauty of art. Two people can look at the same piece and pull completely different points of interest or dislike. Art is always gonna make you feel something. Doesn't always mean those feelings will be positive. There are some pieces I strongly hate and I love them for that because it connects with something deep inside me that sometimes can't be expressed in words. Maybe it's a frown, or tears, or a smile that makes your cheeks hurt."

Quincy's eyes pinged across my face as if he was looking at me for the first time. "I'ma bone up. Learn more about this stuff so we can have deep philosophical discussions about art and life."

The thought of him taking an interest in the thing I was most passionate about made my heart warm. Well, maybe art and Quincy were tied for eliciting intense fiery emotion.

"I for one would love to have deep conversations with you." My hands twitched as my fingers brushed against his.

Quincy's gaze dipped to mine, his face serious as he licked his lips. "How deep are you trying to go?"

My lady parts throbbed as familiar heat warmed my cheeks. "Like, buried treasure at the bottom of the sea deep." I shoved my free hand in the pocket of my coat, knowing if I touched him I wouldn't want to stop.

"Evie, you know I will fuck the shit out of you in front of this *Reclining Woman*, right? We will go viral and possibly to jail."

My face softened with the subtle raise of an eyebrow. "You called me Evie."

"Yeah." He bumped a shrug.

"You never call me that."

"Is that weird?" He crinkled his nose.

"No, I like it." I considered his face for a long time. A month ago, I didn't know this man and now I couldn't picture my life without him. "Can I show you something?"

"Sure, lead the way."

I led him to a section of the museum that housed a collection of art from local Black and Brown artists. Stopping in front of a large colorful canvas, I trained my eyes on him.

"Wait is this yours?" Pointing to the painting of four Black girls he moved closer.

"Yeah."

His tentative smile grew bigger as my words sunk in. "Oh my God. Evelyn."

"I know." I wrung my hands. Other than the piece in the gallery, this was the first time I was sharing my work with him. I wanted him to like it, if he didn't like it then he didn't like me because my work was essentially my soul laid out on a canvas.

"Baby, this is huge. Your work is in the Art Institute."

"It's just one piece. It's a collection of local Black artists and I was one they selected."

"Wow, this is major. When did this happen?"

"A couple of weeks ago. I haven't really told anyone. I didn't wanna sound like I was bragging."

"This is a huge flex. You should brag. Your shit is amazing ain't no need to be humble about that." Stepping back, he continued, "You know how this piece makes me feel?"

"No how?"

"The girls remind me of the neighborhoods I grew up in. They look like the girls I went to school with. The hair, the facial expressions. The curious look in that one's eyes." He pointed to a girl in overalls. "Your work feels familiar, it feels like home to me."

A mother and her daughter approached, examining the piece.

"That piece, was created by this beautiful talented woman right here," Quincy said.

My face grew hot.

The mother smiled and the daughter looked at me with

awe. "It's nice that my daughter can see art that looks like her."

"Representation makes all the difference." I agreed.

"If you like this you should check out the Townsend downtown. A gallery filled with nothing but Black and Brown artists, including my wife."

"Quincy." His endorsement was causing me to blush.

"I love your piece," The woman said before moving to the next canvas on the wall.

"Have you told your family at least? Your mom?"

"No." My eyes grew cloudy. "She wouldn't understand."

Cupping my face, Quincy said, "I'm so impressed by you and proud, immensely proud."

Tears welled from deep inside and coursed down my face. "Thank you." I managed to stammer out.

Quincy touched his forehead to mine. "From now on consider me your biggest fan." He brushed away one of my tears with his thumb.

My eyes danced over his face, with a short intake of breath I whispered. "I love ... yuletide logs."

"Welcome to the club," he said, against my lips.

QUINCY

I DIDN'T REALIZE how hungry I was until I was halfway through my burger. Reaching for more truffle fries, I grabbed three and greedily shoved them in my mouth. "This is so good," I mumbled.

Evelyn smiled at me with an agreeing nod, wiping burger juice from her lips.

We'd decided to end our night at The Gwen Hotel downtown for drinks and much-needed sustenance. My phone vibrated in my pocket. The production for *Why Knot* had been blowing up our phones every hour on the hour since we'd been on the lam. I sent every call straight to voicemail. We would have to deal with the fallout of our ditch day but that could wait.

After several more bites my stomach caught up with my eyes and I tossed my napkin on my plate.

"Was being a lawyer your dream job?" Evelyn asked.

"No, making money was the only goal. I don't like the sight of blood so I decided to become a lawyer instead."

"Contracts law. Exciting?"

"It sounds boring but it actually can be pretty intense, negotiations, breach of contract. We're talking about billion-dollar corporations so there tends to be a lot at stake."

"And what's the long game with that gig?"

"I don't know. It pays the bills and allows me to do what I really enjoy."

"Which is?"

"Helping others." I laughed, that sounded corny as hell. "I grew up poor and I didn't have a lot of options. I saw so many kids get caught up in the system with no advocate or guidance. So I offer pro bono services to people in the community who couldn't otherwise afford it."

"Like at risk teens?"

"Teens, families, single moms, women looking to get out of unstable situations."

"That's really admirable of you. Most people get out the

hood and never look back. Only talking about their struggle as some kind of bragging point."

"It's selfish really. I wish there was someone who could have helped me and my mom when I was younger. Maybe things would have turned out differently."

Evelyn's mouth hung open, I could tell she wanted to ask about my mother. This was actually the first time I'd mentioned her. I was sure Evelyn had questions. Her gaze was heavy as she weighed the pros and cons. Dropping her eyes, it was clear she'd decided against probing further.

"What do you think's gonna happen when we get back home? She finally asked.

"I'm sure they'll be waiting for us and we will get a thorough talking to which will include them pulling out the contracts we signed to remind us what we agreed to."

"Ugh, I sure hope not. This has been a perfect day. I could do without the scolding."

"Well, we could always kick the can down the road."

"And how exactly would we do that?"

"We could escape to Canada or Mexico."

"Outlaws?" Her eyes flashed.

"Yep, we would have to change our names. I'd probably have to shave my beard."

"I'd rather get caught than lose that marvelous beard." She leaned forward rubbing my bearded face, I naturally tilted my head into her hand in dutiful submission. Grabbing her arm, I pulled her toward me so she was as close as possible without being on top of my lap in our small circular booth.

"I'm gonna change my name to Percy." I said softly, slipping my hand under her dress rubbing her knee.

She rolled my new name on her tongue. "Percy, Percy. I could get used to that. I'll be Mary."

"Mary?" I frowned.

"It's plain and unassuming no one on the run would willingly change their name to something so mundane." She licked a little residual ketchup from the corner of my mouth.

My hands were on the move gliding up her long limbs, I grabbed at her hip.

"We'll open up a small paperie shop where you can sell hand crafted cards. Mini pieces of art." The table cloth and dim lighting provided some cover as Evelyn opened her legs wide for me. My fingers brushed against her soft, wetness over her panties. "I could provide notary services in the back. We'll settle in a small town. The type of place where everyone knows everyone."

I pushed her thong aside, running my thumb over her slick flesh. Evelyn buried her face into my shoulder angling her pelvis so I had better access. "Maybe we can make jam or banana bread. I've always wanted to learn to make bread. We could sell our wares at the local farmers market every Saturday." Evelyn hooked her leg over mine as I inserted one finger then another slowly moving in and out, plunging deeper each time. She clutched my sweater whimpering in my ear. Using my thumb to stimulate her, my stomach trilling when she kissed the space right under my ear. "Does that sound good?"

"Yes," she moaned.

"It'll be hard at first." I pulled her hand from my chest sliding it down to the stiff member in my lap. "But I'm sure we can come to some sort of arrangement that works for both of us." Her hand worked over my pants.

"All done?" The waitress stood in front of our table.

In one smooth motion I removed my soaked fingers and turned to smile at the waitress. "Yes, thank you. Every ... thing was great." My voice hitched as Evelyn's hand ran up and down my member. Her face, still tucked away in my neck.

"Might I suggest getting a room," The waitress said, clearing our plates. "After all this is a hotel."

It took five minutes for us to secure a room and make our way up to the fifteenth floor. Inside the dark space, I pulled back the curtains to let in some light from the city below. Evelyn unzipped her boots kicking them off before shrugging her coat to the floor. She didn't wait for instructions, pulling her dress over her head she crossed the needless distance between us, falling to her knees.

She unbuckled my belt and pulled down my zipper, stripping me out of my pants and boxer briefs in one motion. She grabbed hold and eagerly took me into her mouth. My back hit the glass window panel of the sliding door. I leaned into it thankful for the support. Removing me from her mouth, she worked her tongue from the bottom to the tip licking me like I was a lollipop and she was craving something sweet. When she plunged me back into her wet mouth my hand fell to her head gently helping her maneuver the length of me.

Evelyn's eyes looked up into mine, spiking my heart rate and causing my knees to feel woozy. This woman was like a dream. And not just because she had her plump mouth wrapped around almost all of me. I was hoping for my perfect match but I could have never imagined her. She was smart, and talented, and knew how to circle my dick with her tongue, driving me completely bonkers.

"Goddamnit Evelyn." I pulled her to her feet kissing her as we wobbled toward the bed. Pushing her to the mattress, I watched as she removed her bra and panties. Ignoring the condom in my wallet, I wanted to forgo it, desperately needing to feel her without anything between us.

"Is this OK? I pointed to my naked dick that was subtly bobbing midair.

"Yes." Evelyn reached for me kissing my stomach and licking the crease at my waist.

She kissed the sensitive skin all around my penis which jumped in anticipation of her. Pulling me into her mouth once more, she sucked my dick like a learned professional. Nothing compares to the feeling of someone wanting you. And right now, Evelyn wanted every inch of me, her hands massaging my balls while her mouth worked me over.

"Turn around," I instructed. Without hesitation she complied, which turned my insides into molten lava.

She spread wide, arching her back. Grabbing hold of her waist, I slid inside, the sound of her breath hitched as I delivered the first thrust. I ran my hands over the curve in her back as our bodies worked in tandem. Resting my hands on her shoulders, I watched as her firm backside slammed against me again and again.

The view was enthralling, Evelyn's ass working overtime. When I paused the action she took the lead rotating her hips over my length before touching down her ass cheeks, twerking like she was dancing on the dick. Widening my stance, I rested my left foot on the bed with an appreciative ass slap, I grabbed her waist slowing the tempo. I wanted her to feel that shit in her diaphragm. Evelyn was incoherent, but I was able to make out her pleas for more between whimpers.

Craving eye contact, I switched positions, sitting on the king bed I pulled her on top of me. I angled myself so she could slip me in, and as I disappeared inside, her eyes fluttered closed. She stayed in the down position for a minute allowing my presence to sink in. With her hands draped over my shoulders she began to rock over my lap. Tipping her face upward, I locked in watching her facial expression change with every increasing stroke. Her mouth agape and even though no words were uttered I knew exactly how she felt because I was feeling the same thing.

"Quincy, please." She finally managed to breathe out.

"Beg for me baby," I whispered, kissing her neck.

Evelyn proceeded to tell me how much she needed me and how good I made her feel. Which is all I wanted, I wanted to please her and hearing the confirmation set my chest ablaze.

Tucking her feet underneath my thighs, she moved slowly back and forth. My entire body shivered as tremors vibrated through every part of me. She was done letting me passively fuck her preferring to now take the lead. Tilting back, she rode me like she was breaking in a bull, all that was missing was a cowboy hat. I bit into her shoulder a little too hard leaving an impression of my teeth. Evelyn performed supernatural gymnastics across my lap making it impossible to regulate my breathing

"Evelyn." Her gaze landed on me and I stared back my eyes hooded and clouded. "You are so beautiful."

I rested my head in between her chest. I needed to calm

down before I said something stupid. A weak chuckle tickled my throat, the fact I thought I was ever in control amused me. Evelyn pressed against my shoulder, sliding up my shaft all the way to the tip before floating back down.

"Oh fuck, oh my God. Evelyn." I squirmed underneath her, my toes curling, I blew out puffs of air. Wrapping my arms around her, I dug my fingers into her thigh pressing hard on her flesh. God, I hope I wasn't hurting her. My thoughts were in cursive and my filter was gone. I tried to choke back the words creeping up my throat uninvited, sweat beading my forehead. As she slowly inched upward again I cupped her face, crying out. "I fucking love you, Evelyn." My bottom lip trembled.

Her eyes grew wide as she slid down shuddered against me. She moaned loudly her body convulsing before turning to mush. That was all the motivation I needed to release, pushing her hips into my pelvis, my entire being spasmed as I growled over her lips. I wrapped my arm around her, not ready to let go. Evelyn rubbed my back while I twitched uncontrollably every few seconds. Her hips still softly floating over my lap didn't help matters much.

I gave her ass one last slap causing her to coo seductively. Loosening my grasp, I allowed her to drop next to me, before also collapsing to the bed. My eyes stared at the coffered ceiling of the hotel room. *Fuck, did I just admit I loved her?*

CHAPTER 14

QUINCY

"Look who finally showed up to work." Walt followed me into my office.

"Hey." I tossed my satchel on the desk.

"You do realize you're not fooling anyone with the old 'I'm working from home this morning, be in later' right."

"Yeah well, I needed to get home, shower, and deal with the *Why Knot* crew bitching us out."

"Why what happened?"

"Evelyn and I kinda ditched them yesterday." I sunk into my office chair.

"Yikes, I'm sure they were pissed."

"Super pissed. Talking about our contractual obligations."

"That's rich."

I buried my face in my hands letting out a long sigh. "Could you close the door."

Walt complied before taking a seat in front of my desk. "What's up?"

"I think I may have fucked up last night." The *Why Knot* crew didn't film me at work so I was allowed to talk freely.

"What do you mean?"

"Evelyn and I … we." I shook my head, deciding to just say it. "I told her I loved her last night while we were having sex."

Walt raised his coffee cup. "Congratulations, a month to fall in love that's a record for you."

"You said, 'Fuck my life,' wrong."

Walt wasn't understating the facts. I didn't say the L word until I was all out of options. Even when I was head over heels for a woman. That short little sentence, I love you, always changed everything. It made people behave differently because now they thought they had me on lock and they could essentially start treating me any which way and taking me for granted. Which in a way was true, it took a lot for me to fall in love, but once I was there I often ended up stuck well after the love had passed its expiration date.

Victoria and I dated exclusively for eight months before I told her I loved her and the minute I did, she took that confession as her cue to go all DIY on a brother trying to renovate who I was. Loving someone romantically had never made things better for me. How the fuck the experts of *Why Knot*, after intense interviews and reviewing my completed five-hundred-question survey, thought I was ready for a committed relationship was beyond me.

"Did she tell you she loved you back?"

"See that's the thing. She didn't." The fact that she didn't throw in a courtesy "Me too," was my second problem.

"What did she say?"

"Not a gotdamn thing." I pursed my lips, shaking my head in disbelief.

"Maybe she didn't hear you."

"I was looking in her eyes and purposefully articulated every word."

"Then why wouldn't she say the same?"

"Oh I don't know Walt. Maybe because she doesn't feel the same way."

"To hear you tell it, you don't genuinely feel that way either."

I flashed Walt the evil eye. "That's not the point," I said taking a sip of my lukewarm coffee.

"No? Let me ask you this. Do you love her?"

"No. I barely know her. It was an excited utterance. She was doing very exciting things. Evelyn has a way of scrambling my senses. Before I could even stop myself the words were tumbling out of my mouth." My hands were flailing around as I tried to explain.

"OK, let me restate the question. Are you falling in love with her?"

"Objection, asked and answered."

"I asked, but you damn sure didn't answer. You deflected."

"Look, I'm not gonna lie I enjoy having her around. She's great. But no one's perfect and the last thing I'm looking to do is fall in love."

"Says the guy who went on a reality tv show to find love."

I bounced my shoulders.

"So what are you going to do?"

Reclining in my chair I said, "What I do best."

"Avoidance and gaslighting?"

"Whoa, that was a dark characterization of me."

"Listen, I like Evelyn and more importantly I like what she brings out in you. Don't let fear turn into regret."

"I'm not scared." I eyed my friend to see if he was buying my lies. Walt's bushy, raised eyebrow told me he was not. "Who meets the love of their life on a reality tv show? What if she's just playing a role for the cameras and once they're gone she goes all Jekyll and Hyde on me? What if I'm getting too attached and she doesn't want this?" I looked down at the palms of my hands. I didn't realize I had all these thoughts floating in my head until I spoke them out loud.

"What if the inverse is true and Evelyn loves you ..."

I wrinkled my face.

Walt rephrased. "What if she likes you just as much as you like her?"

My phone pinged and I looked at the screen with an eye roll, that was my third problem. "And then there's Victoria."

"What now?"

"Ever since the Halloween party she's been texting me. Wants to get together for drinks."

"And you said no, right because that would be a cosmically bad idea."

"Of course. I've told her work has me slammed but she is being persistent. She's like one of those whammy's from that game show. When everything is going well she pops up out of nowhere ruining your life." She'd even sent me a picture of her from the party in her sexy outfit, why I hadn't deleted the photo I couldn't explain.

"I bet seeing you with Evelyn made her feel some type of way."

"Well, she's acting all chummy like we are best buds. I should just block her number."

"You should."

"Yep, I should."

"You're not going to, are you?"

"Nope."

After work I got drinks with Walt, ignoring Evelyn's calls as the night weaned on. I just needed some space to think and I couldn't do that with Evelyn's doe eyes staring up at me all night. This little marry-a-stranger experiment was moving way faster than I anticipated. I'd read somewhere once when you place individuals in extreme situations they will often act in ways they wouldn't normally if not under those pressures. Maybe that's what was happening with me and Evelyn. Forced to live with someone I was attracted to, I was starting to feel things I would not otherwise if I'd met her in the normal setting at a bar or a coffee shop.

After Walt left, I lingered at the bar not in any hurry to get home. It was past eleven and Evelyn had called me at least three times. Each call I sent to voicemail before turning my phone off all together. Ordering one last drink, I chatted up a leggy blonde, when she placed her hand on my knee I knew it was time to close out the tab and head home.

"Where have you been?" I hadn't even moved completely over the threshold before Evelyn accosted me.

"I went out for drinks with Walt." The *Why Knot* crew was still there, no doubt to catch the fireworks from what I assumed was about to be a fight.

"You could have called and told me."

"My bad." I dropped my bag in the cubby bench near the front door.

"My bad? I made us dinner." She pointed to a plate on the kitchen counter covered in foil.

I hoisted an unapologetic shoulder.

"I called you a bunch of times it just kept going to voicemail. I thought maybe something happened to you."

"My phone was off, I'm fine."

Evelyn's probing questions grew more pointed. "OK, what are you doing? What's going on?"

Unlike me, Evelyn liked to confront issues attacking them head on. I preferred to let things fester, getting gross and oozy until it required antibiotics or worse, an amputation.

"Nothing, I'm tired." Hanging up my coat, I brushed past her walking to the bedroom.

"Quincy?" her voice shouted behind me. The sound of her bare feet hitting the hardwood let me know she was in hot pursuit. "If I did something like this you'd be fuming."

I spun on my heels and said, "You know I've been thinking."

This was the point where I should head to the bathroom take a long hot shower and let the tension gripping my shoulders slip away. That is what I should do. But when it came to matters of the heart I rarely ever made the easy choice.

"OK, what does that mean?" Her eyes darted over my face looking for clues regarding where this was headed.

"I don't have to check in or explain myself to you because at the end of the day I don't know you. And I don't owe you a damn thing."

I was ruining this, I was purposely saying things I would regret in the morning. Statements once uttered I couldn't later claim I didn't mean. After years of cultivation, I'd created a safe little bubble in which I chose to live. If you asked me to do something that would disrupt the delicate ecosystem of my comfort zone, I would politely decline. Evelyn infiltrated my bubble, like ivy, innocent to the untrained eye but when left unattended it multiplied rapidly claiming everything in its path until the environment was unrecognizable.

Her shoulder slumped under the weight of my words. "You're being an asshole."

"This is moving really fast. Too fast." I knew my arrows were hitting its mark when the cameraman pulled closer.

"I ..." Evelyn's chin trembled as she critically scanned my face before looking to the others in the room.

"I just don't wanna give you false hope that this could be more than ..."

Her eyes welled over and before I could finish my sentence the first tear fell. The look in her eye made my heart sink. *Why am I doing this?* I'd come home to the smartest, funniest, most interesting woman I had ever met. And instead of cuddling up with her on the couch while we shared laughs and stole kisses, I was doing this.

Evelyn exited the room, heading for the front door she slid into her purple tie-dye Crocs.

"What are you doing?" I swallowed hard.

"Leaving." She coughed out.

The vein in my forehead pulsed underneath my skin. A pronounced aching in the back of my throat left my mouth dry as beads of sweat formed on my upper lip. "Evelyn, no please don't—"

"Why? So you can hurt my feelings more." She swiped at her wet face but it was no use as the salty tears she wiped away were replaced by fresh ones. "You don't think I see what this is. I see what it is. I'm scared too. But you don't get to do this. You don't get to say that you don't care, when I know you care. And you don't get to tell me that what I'm feeling isn't real. Or that it's all in my head. Fuck you, Quincy. I see the way you look at me. I'm not making that shit up."

I wanted so badly to pull her into my arms and tell her I was stupid and she was right. But years of pushing others away left me blank faced and still. I needed to protect my heart and if that meant breaking Evelyn's so be it. "Maybe I just don't want what you want." I spat out.

"You want it, you're just too chickenshit to admit it. I jumped Quincy because I thought you were jumping too." She wiped at her runny nose with the sleeve of her sweatshirt. Grabbing her bag, she left, leaving me alone in my thoroughly wrecked bubble.

EVELYN

"ARE YOU SURE THIS IS OK?" I asked as I climbed into Meryl's bed.

"Girl, don't be silly. If I had a sex life maybe the answer would be different. But truthfully this is the most action the left side of the bed has seen all month."

After my fight with Quincy, I didn't want to be alone and Meryl being the supportive friend she always is, suggested I crash at her place for the night.

"He was being such a dick."

"You know why that is. You guys have been playing house for what a month now and he's starting to realize he can't live without you."

"Honestly, I feel stupid. I'm a grown ass woman believing in love at first sight and prince fucking charming."

"Couples fight it's no big deal."

"It didn't seem like he was starting a fight, it felt more like he was initiating a breakup."

"Evie, that man is into you. I've seen it with my own two eyes. Can you think of anything that would suddenly make his feet chilly?"

"Well, he did say he loved me on Sunday night."

"Bitch, you are holding back intel." Meryl smacked me on my arm. "How am I supposed to properly assess the situation if I don't have all the facts?"

"Sorry, do you think that's an important fact?"

"That depends. When did he say it?"

"During sex."

"I know that's right." Meryl stuck out her tongue and did a little dance. "You hit him with the jerk and slurp, didn't you?"

"Not exactly, more like the rock and rolla."

"What did he say and how did he say it?"

I imitated Quincy's deep voice. "I fucking love you, Evelyn."

"Sounds like he was balls deep in that good good and his

brain betrayed his heart. Wait, did you tell him you loved him back?"

"No." This was not my first time at the rodeo. My hip swirl had this same effect on many men.

Meryl pointed in my face, nearly poking me in the eye. "And there you have it my friend."

"What do I have exactly?"

"You *had* the upper fucking hand. And he decided to even the scales by giving your confidence in this relationship a kick in the ribs."

I slid deeper under the bed covers until only my head was poking out. This made sense, it definitely felt like he was picking a fight and throwing words at the wall to see which ones would stick. Why were people such cowards when it came to expressing their feelings? Everyone wants to claim they're adults and grown, but when it comes to communication they show their true emotional age every time.

I wasn't an expert on the topic but I knew some very basic truths. Words had power. They could block blessings or open doors to opportunity. Words also elicited actions. So what response had Quincy hoped for when he'd said those things? Was he intentionally trying to push me away?

My phone rang, it was Quincy, I declined the call, sending it to voicemail. I wanted him to know I'd seen his incoming call and purposely sent him to voice message purgatory.

"You don't think he's gonna come over here looking for you?"

"No, he doesn't know where you live. Because at the end of the day we don't even know each other. I can't believe he said that. He doesn't know me but since we've been having sex he's come inside of me raw three times."

"Raw?" Meryl's eyebrows arched.

"We were both tested for the show. I'm on birth control. We're married."

"OK, I wasn't judging." Meryl showed her palms in submission. "So what are you gonna do?"

"First, I'm gonna eat this entire carton of ice cream even though my ass is lactose intolerant. Second, I'm gonna feel sorry for myself a little bit longer. And then finally he and I are gonna hash this all out and let the chips fall where they may."

"Ohh let's watch a sappy movie and cry."

"I like the way you think."

Meryl turned on *If Beale Street Could Talk* and fifteen minutes in I was bawling.

The next morning, I gathered my things and headed home waiting well until after eight, when Quincy typically left for work. All that crying from the night before left my muscles achy, and my eyes puffy and ashen. Dropping my keys in the wooden bowl Quincy purchased so I would stop misplacing my keys, I stopped in my tracks when I heard the refrigerator door shut.

"I thought you would've already left for work?"

"I called in sick." He set a carton of orange juice on the counter.

"Are you not feeling good?"

"I'm not good with how we left things."

Dropping my bag, I tugged my hoodie down over my face, hoping to shield my eyes. "Do you want me to leave? If you want me to leave, say it. Say it now."

"I don't want that." He was still in his pajamas; his eyes were red and his face was haggard. It looked like his sleep was as restless as mine had been.

Staring into the gloomy backyard, I burrowed my hands into the pockets of my oversized Grambling State University hoodie. My eyes filled with fresh tears. "Fix it." I just wanted to rewind back to our perfect date and the promise I felt for our future. My throat felt tight and my breathing was labored as tears rolled down my cheeks. "I need you to fix this."

Quincy nodded stammering out a crude sentence. "Evelyn, I had a lot to drink last night ... I got into my own head ... said things I shouldn't have."

"Things you meant."

"Things I shouldn't have said because I haven't worked it all out in my head yet."

His tone was rehearsed like he'd lost sleep practicing those very words and now in the light of day he was regurgitating these tired lines. Saying all the right things even though they felt hollow to me. Admittedly, it was an alcohol-fueled rant, was an easier pill to swallow than the idea he couldn't see himself with me when this was all over.

"You called me a stranger," I said through sniffles.

His eyes canvassed the room. I guess the scripted portion of the apology was over and now he was struggling to find the right words. "Evelyn, it's been a month and there is still so much we don't know about each other. It's not a bad thing it's just a fact." His tone was pleading.

"It's been a month and you just want to focus on all the things we don't know but what about the things we do know. I know you make the best avocado toast I've ever tasted."

Quincy stood silent for a moment overanalyzing like he always did. Loving me was never gonna make sense. It was always going to be scary and exhilarating at the same damn time and the sooner he accepted that the better. He needed to think bigger but he was still over there biting his tongue.

His tense posture eased. "Fair enough," he finally said. "I know you can't carry a tune but I would listen to you sing off key in the car any day of the week."

I wiped away a rogue tear. "I know you talk in your sleep."

"I do?" A wrinkle cut across the expanse of his forehead.

"You do."

Quincy's eyes widened and he moved from behind the kitchen island toward me. "I know when you're frustrated you get a little crease at the side of your mouth. I know from your text messages you don't know how to spell the word probably to save your life. I know that when you walk into a room I stop breathing. It's just for a split second but I literally stop breathing."

Tingles licked up and down my skin. Blood scrambled through my veins in a tizzy. My heart quaked pushing against my ribs. I didn't like the tension filled space we'd worked ourselves into and I wanted to get out.

"I'm sorry." He swiped a quick glance at the crew, lowering his volume before continuing. "You're right I am scared. This … the possibility of it all terrifies me. I don't let a lot of people in. And in the past when I have, they've been the wrong people and I've gotten hurt. So now I'm at a place where I want to let you in but if I do, then I could get broken. And I've spent the last few years working really hard to put myself back together.

"Evelyn, you're the type of person who falls off the horse and gets right back on. I'm the type of person who falls off a horse and swears off all forms of elevated riding and then goes home to construct a passionate think piece on why horse riding is dangerous and should be avoided at all cost." Quincy reached for my hand. "I didn't expect to like you this much. I'm not as brave as you."

"I'm not brave. I'm just as scared as you are. I didn't know what to expect but I didn't expect to feel this way a month in."

"When you left last night, it allowed for a lot of time to think and it all kinda clicked. For me, the thought of being without you is far scarier than being with you."

He grabbed my wrecked face and kissed me. Leading me to the master bathroom, he only stopped kissing me to help me shed clothes with every step. He was oblivious to the camera and crew who were following close behind with bated breath, until we were safely in the bathroom and the crew was forced to wait outside. Turning on the shower, we shrugged off the rest of our clothes before entering. I hoped the steamy hot water would help to wash away all the doubt and uncertainty between us.

I craved the feel of his body against mine. Quincy's hands ran through my hair which had coiled into tight, soft curls from the water. Our breathing was heavy, when I breathed out, he would inhale me in. My heartbeat thumped in my ears as the erratic beats thudded then stuttered in time with his own unpredictable pounding.

As the water bathed over us, Quincy lifted his face from

my neck to confess, "I really am sorry, I hurt you and I wish I could take it back. I just got into my head."

Cupping his face, I said through tears. "I understand, but you just can't not show up. You have to show up for me every time. You have to wake up every day and choose me ... choose us."

"What if ... what if I can't?" He sniffled, his eyes turning foggy.

"Then you'll lose me."

Quincy's jaw tightened as if it was carved out of steel. His eyes turned stormy, my words sinking in. He planted his feet and scooped me up, sliding inside without hesitation. When he used his strong arms to hoist me over his length I could feel his regret and desire all rolled up in his intense thrusts. When I agreed to do the show I knew the odds were against me, that the likelihood of being hurt were far greater than finding true love. But this man made me want to fight. I would wake up and choose him one hundred times over no matter what the cost.

CHAPTER 15

QUINCY

"Hey, what about pumpkin pie?" I held up a box.

"Excuse me?"

"Pumpkin pie." I smiled, waving the box as I performed a quick two-step.

It had been almost two weeks since our fight and I was relieved we'd returned to our well-worn groove. Evelyn was cautious initially, but after a few days the overly affectionate wife I'd grown to lo ... fondly appreciate returned. Kissing me for no reason, cuddling with me on the couch and sneaking into the shower in the morning to conserve water ... of course. My feelings hadn't changed, I was still pessimistic but Evelyn's glass-half-full mentality was starting to rub off on me.

"You mean sweet potato pie." Evelyn ambled over to the table with a variety of sweet treats.

"I don't know how to break this to you and quite frankly I'm shocked the experts didn't think about this before matching us but I love pumpkin pie."

"Wow, this is quite troubling. I marry a guy, he's smart and funny, but he's a pumpkin pie zealot. I don't know if I can get past this."

"So my pie choices are a deal breaker?"

"A small penis and pumpkin pie. Those are my deal breakers. Lucky for you Quincy Jr. is adequate."

"Adequate?" I moved close, dropping my voice to a whisper. "This adequate dick had you calling me daddy just an hour ago."

"I never said that. I never did." She tugged at my coat lowering her voice so the customers in Mariano's grocery store didn't overhear.

"Oh my God, Evie." I leaned in, resting my forehead against hers.

"I said dandy."

"Fuck outta here." I retreated at the blatant lie.

"You misheard."

"No, no. You called me daddy and you told me it was mine." I said that entirely too loud feeling my face flush.

"I said you were doing a dandy job and that I didn't mind." Evelyn was having a difficult time keeping a straight face.

I threw my hands in the air and trumpeted a laugh that floated through several aisles.

"If you want we can get the pumpkin pie. My family will probably disown me but it's fine and *dandy* with me." Evelyn placed pumpkin and apple pies in our cart before heading for the ice cream section.

"Thank you. So kind."

Our first Thanksgiving together had been low key. Since Naomi was out of town visiting her sister in California,

Evelyn and I had slept in, spending most of the day in and out of bed. Lazy days like that were my favorite. Sometimes Evelyn would read to me while I rested my head in her lap. Sometimes we'd have sex, at times fast and frantic all hands and limbs like the world was gonna end. Other times soft and slow with her sweet, warm breath fluttering my eyelashes. I really couldn't get enough of this woman and if I could, I would crawl inside her skin and make it home. Yes, I do realize how crazy and psycho killer that sounded, I'm just trying to say I like her a lot.

"So is there anything I should know before we get there?" We were headed to Evelyn's parents' house for Thanksgiving dinner.

"Yes, my two uncles Bert and Barry were married to the same woman not at the same time. She was married to Uncle Barry then they divorced and a year later she married my Uncle Bert. They lasted for ten years before they split and just last year she remarried my Uncle Barry."

"That's messy as fuck."

"It doesn't help that Uncle Bert and Barry are identical twins."

"Yeah that's worse."

In the forty-five-minute car ride Evelyn brought me up to speed about the hot mess that was her family. "So basically, we'll start out with some pleasantries, followed by mean-spirited ribbing. Thanks to you no one will be able to ask me when I'm gonna settle down and find a nice fella. While we're passing the candied yams and cornbread, we will begin to air our grievances. I can guarantee someone will say something like 'You know what your problem is' or 'I just find it funny how.' There will be yelling. There will be tears.

There will be loud obnoxious singing, that last part will be me."

As we pulled up to the massive brick house with a red door, I placed the car in park. The Townsend residence reminded me of the house in the movie *Home Alone* which was also located in Chicago.

Evelyn leaned in smiling. "Have I scared you off?"

"No, I'm a messy bitch and I live for drama." I smiled, giving her a quick peck on the lips before exiting the car.

Inside, the house was already at capacity. Evelyn took my coat and headed to a guest bedroom to drop our things in.

"Q, over here," Evan yelled, waving his arm excitedly. I made my way to the living room where Evan was standing with a group of people. "I wanted to introduce you to the cousins. The middle ones at least, the young ones are running around the house like bad asses."

While Evan rattled off names I scanned the room. The house was impressive. Who knew a car dealer pulled in this type of dough? The massive living room was already decorated with a Christmas tree that almost touched the twelve-foot ceiling. Stockings were hung, there were presents already wrapped under the tree and anytime the front door opened, a jolly voice would shout out "Ho, Ho Ho." There were two types of people in the world. People who waited until the last minute to decorate and then people like this.

Shereè Townsend had this house fully decked out for the holiday season with two Black five-foot nutcracker soldiers flanking the front door, fresh garland and mistletoe displayed throughout the sprawling home, and Nat King Cole singing about toasty chestnuts pumping through the surround sound speakers. I'd seen shit like this on television but never with my own eyes. Maybe at the office Christmas party. But Hoyt, Benson, and Hilderbrand was a law firm and this was a personal residence. The Townsend's took this holiday stuff seriously.

After the introductions, Evan pulled me to the side. "What did you get my sister for her birthday?"

I chuckled. "I haven't given her her gift yet and I'm not telling you because you don't know how to keep a secret."

When we'd left the house I let Evelyn know her birthday gift would be revealed when we returned home. She probably thought I was going to wrap a bow around my penis and call it a night, but I had something far more exciting planned for her. Wait ... not that my dick isn't exciting, shit you know what I mean.

"Did Evie say I can't keep a secret?"

"Evie, Louis, I think your mom may have mentioned something."

Dinner at the Townsend residence felt like a state dinner at the Elmsworth White House. I would love to hear other family members' opinions on all this unnecessary showboating. Place settings featured a small pumpkin with the guests' name written in calligraphy. Dinnerware was gold and heavy in my hand so I knew they weren't cheap. Each wine glass was engraved with the letter "T." The long dining table which took up the whole dining room was a buzz with guests settling in with plates from the kitchen buffet.

Evelyn came in with two plates. "I got you a little bit of everything." She smiled, setting my plate in front of me loaded with ham, greens, yams, mac and cheese, cranberry sauce, a few slices of turkey, some mashed potatoes, green beans, and a jell-o like substance I'd never seen before.

The table was a whisper as the family dug into the first round of food. All I'd eaten today was a bag of Doritos and Evelyn's ass so I was famished and shoved a generous serving into my mouth, my fork a mix of savory and sweet.

"So is anybody going Black Friday shopping?" Erica, Evelyn's baby sister asked.

Shereè frowned. "The types of gifts I purchase you can't get at a Black Friday sale."

Evelyn leaned in whispering in my ear. "She's right. She gives the best gifts."

"I'm fittin to be out there. Daddy needs a new flat screen tv." Evan high fived his cousin who was seated next to him.

"The food is delicious, Mrs. Townsend." I offered.

"Who are you?" an older gentleman with a Bluetooth earpiece in his ear asked.

"That's Quincy, Evelyn's husband, Uncle Barry," Erica said.

"When did Evelyn get married? I don't remember being invited to no wedding."

"It was intimate and kinda last minute." Evelyn added.

"Well, congratulations. Shereè ain't said nothing about it."

"I guess I was just waiting to make sure it actually stuck," Shereè said.

Evelyn stabbed a cube of candied yams with her fork.

"Mom could you not," Erica said.

"What? What did I say? Evelyn ran off and did what she always does. I'm not going to enable this kind of behavior."

"You really can set your clock to it." Evelyn blurted out.

"To what?" her mother asked.

"To your passive aggressive bullshit."

"Evelyn Rae," her stepdad shouted.

You could hear a pin drop all eyes were on Evelyn and her mother. Except Evan who was shoving forkfuls of garlic mashed potatoes into his mouth.

"Who made the mac and cheese? This is cheesy." I tried to redirect the conversation.

"So what Momma just gets to say whatever she wants and we all just have to take it?"

Louis gave Evelyn the stern father look, narrowing his eyes. "We taught you kids better, you will respect your elders."

"Yeah, and that respect should be reciprocated."

"Well, if you gave me something to be proud of maybe I could," Sheree said, reaching for her glass of red wine.

There was an audible gasp from the end of the table and I could practically see the steam emanating from Evelyn's ears.

Evelyn covered her face in her hand releasing an incredulous laugh. "I just find it funny how—"

"Evelyn." I placed my hand on her knee giving it a little squeeze. My eyes bore into hers which were lit with anger. Her mother threw out the bait and Evelyn fell for it every time. I didn't release my hold of her gaze until some of the fury retreated from her eyes. Today was her birthday and this day should be nothing but good vibes only.

"Looks like Q is the Evelyn whisperer," Evan said, a little too loudly.

Evelyn placed her hand over mine and her shoulders, which were hunched close to his ears, relaxed.

Even though this evening was rowdy and I was peppered with questions I was happy to be here. Happy to be a part of a family that believed in traditions even if a little drama ensued. Happy to witness the kids at the children's table who were poking and prodding one another. The hum of activity and the sense of community and playful ribbing. If Uncle Bert and Barry could move past their differences nothing was impossible.

I cleared my throat addressing the table. "Once I had Thanksgiving dinner at a shelter with canned vegetables and a ham loaf. So, I just think we should all be happy to be with family even if we don't always agree. And since Thanksgiving is all about giving thanks, I wanna say that I am thankful for my wife who is a dreamer in the best possible way. You make me hope for things I never thought were possible. And I'm thankful for my mother-in-law who on this day gave birth to the dynamic duo."

Shereè's face softened. "I was in labor for twenty-seven hours with those two."

I lifted my beer bottle. "Happy birthday to Evelyn and Evan and happy Thanksgiving everyone."

While Evelyn was learning the newest viral dance from her teenage cousins, I decided to tour the residence. My interest was drawn to a library with books neatly shelved from floor to ceiling and a fireplace in the middle of the room that was warming the space. I ran my fingers along the spines of the hardbacks that adorned the shelf, pulling out a first edition red leather-bound book and examined the first few pages.

"I got that for Louis's birthday a few years back," Evelyn's mother said her British accent in full effect.

"I'm sorry I didn't know anyone was in here." I replaced the book, moving backward toward the door.

"Stay, have a drink with me."

Eyeing the exit, I had no choice but to comply. "OK sure." Taking a seat on the brown leather couch opposite her. She poured me a glass of wine and handed it to me before she reclaimed her seat.

"Are you having a good time?"

"Uh ... yes. This is one hell of a family dinner."

"How do you normally celebrate the holidays?"

I shrugged. "With my foster mother, sometimes alone if she's out of town."

"So you're not really big on family traditions."

"No, I'm big on family traditions just kinda short on family."

This was probably the first time in a long time I was excited for Christmas because I wouldn't be spending it alone. Sure I could tag along with Walt but that was his family and I always felt like a third wheel. I hadn't told Evelyn but I was ready to lean in hard to the Christmas spirit. I'm talking decorating, peppermint bark hot chocolate, a gingerbread house, and matching pajamas.

"Well, for as long as this little marriage experiment lasts you are always welcome here."

"The whole marrying a stranger thing still not sitting right with you?"

"It's foolhardy. Love requires time to grow."

"From what I heard you and Louis had a whirlwind romance."

"That was different." She tilted her perfectly coiffed head narrowing her eyes.

"Maybe Evelyn and I are different."

"What do you see in my daughter, Quincy?"

"I don't know. I guess all the things you don't."

"Do you love her?"

I swallowed hard, I was not saying those words again. "I don't know exactly where we are on the timeline but I can definitely see a future with her."

"See that's what I mean ... different." She took a long sip from her glass. "I guess I should thank the Lord for small favors, with you being a lawyer at least I know my daughter will be taken care of."

"Quite honestly Mrs. Townsend, your daughter will probably end up taking care of me one day. She's an amazing artist. She has a piece on display at the Art Institute downtown."

"Really? Why hasn't she mentioned it?"

I wanted to say "She hasn't mentioned it because she knows you would find some way to belittle her accomplishment and make her feel small," but I opted for, "Yeah, she was selected out of hundreds of local artists. And she's working on a new gallery collection and has a show in January. I know it would mean a lot to her if you were there."

"I'm not very well versed in that hippy art world she lives in."

"You don't have to get it. But it would be nice to show your support. To take an interest, to try to learn."

"I'm sure Evelyn has told you horrible things about me."

"No, when she talks about you it's with a great sense of sadness and longing for what could be. I don't have kids, and I'm not trying to tell you what to do, but I know I would give anything to have my mother here with me. Everyone thinks they have time until it runs out and all you're left with are regrets. I don't want that for Evelyn and I don't think you do either."

Shereè didn't respond, unlike her daughter she had a well-crafted poker face. If anything I said made an impact, her face didn't reveal it.

"I think I'm gonna go and get some dessert. It was nice talking to you Mrs. Townsend."

~

EVELYN

THE DESSERT TABLE was laden with every sweet treat imaginable: holiday cookies, pastries, three-tiered cakes, and the pies Quincy and I brought.

"What are you gonna get?" I asked, tugging at Quincy's sweater.

"I'm gonna get a little bit of everything. Starting with a slice of pumpkin pie."

"Pumpkin pie?" Evan's deep voice boomed. "We Black over here. We do not eat pumpkin pie."

"I happen to like it."

"Give me your card. Give me your Black card right now," Evan teased.

I didn't understand why Evan had to make a scene. Sure my brother was just joking around but I didn't want Quincy uncomfortable at his first family event. Yes, pumpkin pie was gross and a questionable choice for a Black man in America but I was Team Quincy. And I was gonna ride for him.

Staring at Evan I said loudly, "What are you, the Pie Patrol?"

Quincy chuckled and joined in. "The Dessert Deputy."

"This negro's the Sweets Sheriff." I pointed at Evan.

"The Delectable Detective." Quincy snorted.

"No, no, no he's the Frosting Federalli." I doubled over in laughter.

"The Confection Carabinieri." Quincy wiped a tear from his eye.

"Oh nice one babe. The Pastry Polizei."

Quincy stomped his feet as our uncontrollable laughter floated through the room. "The Fondant Fuzz."

Evan grabbed his plate, shooting us an evil eye. "Fuck you guys," he said.

Our boisterous laughter was the soundtrack to his exit.

After a few rounds of karaoke in which Quincy and I sang "Baby It's Cold Outside," we said our goodbyes. We'd stayed far longer than I intended, but Quincy was such a good sport. Listening to my uncle's stories of yesteryear, recording a Tik Tok video with my baby cousin, and engaging in a heated conversation in the family room with my father and others about the Chicago Bulls' chances at a championship next year. He even coaxed my mother into breaking out a two-step as they danced around the living room to Chaka Khan and Rufus's "Tell Me Something Good."

In the car I reached for his hand giving it a squeeze. I couldn't have asked for a better birthday. He had been the perfect husband listening to all the stories, giving out free legal advice and enduring several questions about his intentions. As we parked in front of our place, I exited the car heading for the house.

"Hold up, we're going for a walk," Quincy said, still standing on the sidewalk.

"What?" I tugged at my scarf.

"I still have to give you your gift, remember?"

My face cracked into a bright smile, so my gift wasn't sex. When he'd said I'd get my gift later in the evening I was almost 100 percent certain it was going to be sex. And truthfully that wouldn't have been a bad gift, I never got tired of the way he made my body feel. Slipping my hand in his, we walked three blocks in the lightly falling snow.

Quincy stopped outside of an industrial-looking building. Inside we accessed a freight elevator riding to the top floor. The elevator stopped with a clink and he pulled back the metal door leading to a small, open space.

"What's this place?"

"Uhm, it's your new art studio."

I belted out a laugh. "Yeah, if I had fifty thousand dollars in expendable income, maybe."

"I picked the top floor because it's got the most light in the day." He walked over to the bank of windows checking out the street below.

Looking around the space, with its exposed-brick walls and large windows, I would kill for a dedicated space like this but this place in this neighborhood had to be way out of my budget. "I don't understand."

"Right now your studio space is so far away. You deserve a place where you can create whenever the mood strikes you. Nice big windows, we could put a fridge in that corner for drinks and lunch or for when you want a quick snack."

"Quincy, I can't afford this. Even if I sold ten paintings,

that money just goes right back into the gallery and to pay Dotty."

"It's already taken care of. I paid six months in advance so no matter what you're covered."

That last sentence hung between us. Highlighting the uncertainty of where we would be in a few months. But it was my birthday and I'd rather focus on what he actually said not what it potentially could mean down the road. If I heard correctly, he'd rented this space ... for me.

"No, you didn't."

"I did." He slid his hands into his pockets.

"I can't accept this."

"Yes, you can."

"Quincy?" He couldn't be serious this was way too much. A place like this would set him back a couple of racks each month. I was expecting a new watch or maybe a nice purse, not real estate.

"You're my wife and this neighborhood is much safer. And the building is secure. Honestly, I got the place for me. When you're working late painting I'll have peace of mind that you're close by. And if I get lonely, I can walk over and visit. It's a win win."

Examining the space, I was already planning where I was going to put my art supply cabinet and canvases.

"I'll pay you back."

"No, you won't 'cause it's a gift."

"A very thoughtful gift." I walked toward him with an exaggerated swing to my hips.

He pulled the keys from his pocket handing them over. "So, did I do good?"

"You did great, baby." Wrapping my arms around his

neck, I kissed his face, trailing kisses down his cheek leading to my favorite spot right behind his ear. A long swoosh of air rushed through his nostrils. After a month and a half I knew all his sensitive spots and the right amount of pressure to apply to get him to respond.

Quincy pushed me away and in the nicest tone he could muster he made a request of the *Why Knot* crew. "Do you think you could give us some time alone?"

To my surprise, the crew complied without objection, packing up their gear before taking the elevator to the lobby. Maybe because it was Thanksgiving and the crew would much rather be with their families instead of filming two horny adults groping one another. Whatever the reason, I was thankful.

Quincy removed his coat and draped it over a wooden desk, the only piece of forgotten furniture left behind in the space. Following his lead, I stripped out of my coat, gloves and hat tossing them in a pile on the dusty floor. The sound of Quincy unbuckling his belt was like a dinner bell calling me home. I stepped out of my panties and before my underwear landed on the pile of accumulated clothing, we were all over each other. Pulling his sweater over his head, I found his lips.

He placed a hand against my stomach guiding me toward the desk. With my ass on the edge of the desk, I reached for him, inserting him slowly I grunted as he filled me up. Wrapping my legs around his waist, I leaned back sliding my hand in between us so I could stimulate my clit as his thrust intensified. I wanted desperately to feel the bare chest of his skin pressed next to mine. The chill in the air stopped me, settling instead for groping his naked ass.

"Fuck me," I rasped in a plea.

Pulling out, Quincy turned me onto my stomach and his next strokes were demanding and urgent. I loved the soft moments when he would caress my face and stare into my eyes while our bodies swirled in sync. But sometimes a woman needed to be fucked. Quincy knew how to deliver, providing exactly what I needed. Collecting my hair in his fist, he punished my pussy, with a deep barrage of thrust that sent my body into overdrive. All I could do was call his name and sing his praises.

"That's it, baby. Just like that. Give it all to me."

My legs shook, initially I thought it was because my toes were barely touching the floor but the shaking was uncontrollable as a fizzy sensation burst in my core before floating through the rest of my body. When my toes uncurled, I dropped to my knees so I could properly thank him for my birthday gift. My tongue circled his erect and veiny member. It was very probable I could get tetanus from a wayward rusty nail but when Quincy let off a low, gratified moan, all that mattered was his pleasure.

Quincy ran the pad of his thumb over the bulge in my right cheek as I throated him. He stared at me with rapt attention while I slurped and licked him to bliss. When his head lulled back and his tight abs started to ripple, I sacrificed my constant need for oxygen to take him all in. I savored every last drop with greedy satisfaction until he staggered backward in a daze.

On the floor, I puffed out a long, triumphant breath. "Best birthday ever."

CHAPTER 16

QUINCY

After Christmas shopping with Evan, who helped me pick out some great gifts and stocking stuffers for my first Christmas with Evelyn, we stopped for a bite to eat.

"What are you getting Shanice for Christmas?" I asked, biting into my turkey club sandwich.

"She wants a ring, but what she's gonna get is the new Gods of War video game."

I offered my brother-in-law a blank stare. "That's not at all similar."

"No, but it's a solid gift. We're both gamers so she'll like it."

"What's Christmas like in the Townsend family? Do you all exchange gifts?"

"We do. Moms and Pops usually come through with the best gifts. So if you had your eye on something pricey you might wanna start dropping hints now." Evan stirred an obscene amount of sugar into his glass of ice tea.

Waving off Evan's remarks, I said, "Oh no I don't expect a gift."

"My mom may not fuck with you just yet but she will still buy you a gift because she loves to floss."

"Truthfully, I don't think your mom is ever gonna fuck with me."

"That's just her way. Evie marrying you didn't sit right with her even though you're kind of a parents' dream son-in-law." He ticked off my good qualities with his fingers. "You're a lawyer, making good money, you own a house, you're respectful."

I understood Sheree's issues had absolutely nothing to do with me. I was just getting hit by the bullets that ricocheted off Evelyn because of my close proximity.

"What happened between Evelyn and your mom? When exactly did they fall off the rails?"

"The shit between Evelyn and my mom runs deep. Evie doesn't always make the best choices and when she was sixteen she started hanging with the wrong crowd. Shit, I was too but no one cared because I was a boy. And then at eighteen she ran off and married that dude."

"Wait what?" *Did Evan just say what I think he said?*

"She eloped with some dude she claimed was the love of her life. Our parents flipped. Evie was supposed to be going to college in the fall but she was yoked with lame ass Darius. Anyway, it didn't work out. Like we couldn't all see that coming and she ended up going off to college a year late."

Evan's delivery was matter of fact, like he was talking about some mundane teenage angst. Evelyn didn't run off and get her tongue pierced; she exchanged vows and made promises to someone else. "Was the marriage annulled or—"

"No, divorced. As you can probably guess my mom was furious. She was more concerned about the family reputation and what everyone would think. Never once did she have a real conversation with Evelyn about why she did it. I think the last straw was when Evie graduated from college and decided not to become an architect. She's always been creative so when she chose an art career over a *stable* profession it was like she turned her back on the family and chose the dark side, like her name was Kylo Ren."

"What happened to her ex-husband?"

"Fuck if I know. Evelyn can tell you her side of the story. I'm just giving you an unbiased account of what went down." Evan cut free a single laugh. "Who am I kidding? I'm always gonna take up for Evelyn, we shared a womb. Evie has always been a rule breaker and I love that about her, but that's the thing that often results in her getting hurt. Like, real talk if y'all don't work she'll be devastated because she really likes you. Probably more than she is willing to admit. But if my sister ain't gonna do nothing else she's gonna fall in love. You think she'd be tired of that shit, it has to be painful."

Driving home, my hands clutched the wheel. Evelyn had never mentioned a previous marriage. This is exactly what you get when you marry a person sight unseen. The truth about who they are slowly leaking out in dribs and drabs. These past seven weeks I'd been holding my breath waiting for the other shoe to drop and here it was crashing to the floor with a loud clunk.

I thought we were experiencing something new together on our wedding day but apparently, she was an old hand at jumping the broom. Sure, it wasn't uncommon for people in their thirties to be divorced or have kids. But finding out my wife had was a bit of a shock. Did she really think this wasn't need-to-know information? She wasn't single when she married me; she was divorced. She was a divorcée. Calling it anything else was misleading. I didn't want a repeat of past disagreements, where I popped off at the mouth and made her cry. But I felt like I deserved some explanation.

I arrived home to find Evelyn on the couch with Totes cuddled up next to her.

"How was shopping? Are any of those bags for me?"

Tossing my keys in the bowl in the entryway, I set my bags in the corner. "Hey, have you ever been married before?"

Evelyn froze, a handful of popcorn halfway to her mouth. "Yes."

I pulled my face into a frown. "Did you tell the show this?" I pointed at the crew that surrounded us.

"Yes."

"How long?"

"What?" Her brows sloped high.

"How long were you married?" I pinched my thumb and index finger together to accent my words.

"Seven months."

"Hmm." I paced the space in front of the fireplace.

"What does that mean?"

"I don't know. Why didn't you tell me?"

"It never came up." She set the bowl of popcorn on the table, and stood which caused Totes to release a soft bark noting his displeasure.

I was trying to put myself in her shoes but it was a tight

fit. A prior marriage wasn't something you neglected to mention. Maybe not in the first week but surely within the first month and a half you would find an opportunity to share that information. Truthfully, I wanted to run. Running had always been easier than sticking around and trying to fix things. I was good at running and I very rarely looked back. But marriage is more of a team sport, so busting out into the one-hundred-meter sprint wasn't an option.

"So our wedding and honeymoon was what ... déjà vu for you?"

"No. I eloped and I never went on a honeymoon."

Disbelief caused my head to shake back and forth. "I gotta say Evelyn, shit like this is why I have trust issues."

What else wasn't she telling me? Did she have a secret love child? Did she have a criminal record? Was her credit score wrecked? Did she like black licorice? I needed answers.

"Nothing has changed, you just know something new."

"Something you should have told me. I shouldn't have heard it from your brother. And quite honestly that's what irks me the most. Not that you have a past or an entire ex-husband but it's the fact that I didn't hear it from you."

Evelyn blinked chuckling nervously. "That's pretty hypocritical from the guy who hasn't even told me his father's in jail."

Shots fucking fired. I took a few steps back. Clearly, she'd been talking to Naomi. I didn't owe her an explanation surrounding the circumstances of my father's incarceration. I'd reached my threshold on surprises for the day. "Not the same, not by a long shot."

Evelyn sucked in her lower lip throwing a glance at the crew like they could offer some assistance.

I was just looking for a "My bad. I should have told you sooner," not all this. "I'm tired. I'm going to bed."

EVELYN

Maybe Quincy could sleep but I could not. Even Totes deserted me for the warmth and comfort of the bed. I had every intention of telling him I'd been married once before, but it never seemed like a good time to bring it up. And truthfully, why should that shit even matter? The production crew asked me if I was OK with marrying someone who was divorced and I said yes. I was certain they'd asked him the same questions and he must have also said yes because we were ultimately matched. So why all the shock and awe when he knew this was a possibility?

His righteous indignation was rich when you factor in the fact there was still so much he hadn't shared with me. How could he be mad at me for withholding this small insignificant fact when I knew practically nothing about his childhood and why he ended up in foster care? There was so much I liked about Quincy but he was judgmental and preferred to jump to conclusions rather than talk things through and I was sick of it.

There was a light knock on the front door. It was well after midnight, who could be stopping by at this hour? This was the time when I should get Quincy, and a large kitchen knife before investigating. I'd watched my fair share of horror movies and I didn't want to be the dumb girl who gets killed because she didn't trust her instincts. Slowly rising from the couch, I stopped in the kitchen grabbing the rolling pin before heading to the door.

In my bare feet I tried my best not to make a sound as I looked through the peephole. It was Otis in the freezing cold and snow in what looked like just his house robe. Snatching the door open, I looked down at his bare feet.

"Mr. Otis what are you doing? You'll catch a cold." Grabbing his arm, I pulled him inside looking around the dark street to make sure there was nothing nefarious going on before locking the door. "Where are your shoes?"

"I'm looking for my Clara." Otis shuffled over the hard-wood floor, his eyes darting around the living space.

"What?"

"Clara, I know she's here and I wanna see her." His voice was loud and irritated.

"Mr. Otis your wife isn't here."

"Clara, honey where are you?" he shouted moving deeper into the space, opening closets and the pantry door in search of his wife.

"Shh, Mr. Otis, please calm down." I grabbed him by the shoulders trying to redirect him.

Shrugging me off he brushed past me. "What you done with my Clara?"

I couldn't tell if he was sleepwalking or just confused. I needed to get Quincy. Leading Otis to the couch I helped him sit. "You know what, you sit right there and I'll go find your Clara."

"Be quick about it," he said wringing his hands.

Still clutching the rolling pin, I rushed to the bedroom

where Quincy was fast asleep. "Quincy," I whispered. "Quincy." This time I shook him.

"What?" His voice was rough and confused.

"Mr. Otis is here."

"What?"

"Mr. Otis is in the living room. He seems a little out of it."

Quincy bolted up, pulling back the covers. "Are you OK?" He quickly assessed me, scanning me up and down. "Why are you holding a rolling pin? Were you baking something?" Wiping the sleep from his eyes, he headed to the living room not waiting for a response.

Otis had left the couch and was peering out the sliding-glass doors that led to the backyard.

"Otis, what's up?" Quincy asked.

"I'm looking for Clara Hawkins. She's a small petite little thing." His hands were balled into tight fists.

"OK well Clara isn't here because she took your son, Junior to his piano lesson. You know she loves to listen to him play." Quincy reached for Otis's hand, leading him back to the couch. "Evelyn, can you get my phone?"

Jogging to the bedroom, I retrieved Quincy's phone from his nightstand. I stopped at the linen closet pulling out a thick, fleece blanket before heading back in the living room. Handing Quincy his phone, I then draped the blanket over Otis's shoulders. Quincy tapped on his phone screen and the sounds of piano keys filled the room playing over the wireless speakers.

"I don't know where he got that talent from, I can't hold a tune," Otis said, his eyes far away. "Clara can sing. She has the most beautiful voice. She sings to Junior at bedtime every night. Maybe that's where he got it."

I watched as Quincy rubbed Mr. Otis's back, still holding his hand tightly. The music seemed to calm him and his body relaxed.

"You should get some rest so when they come home you're ready to greet them. How about we take a quick nap?"

"I don't wanna miss them."

"You won't because the minute they get home I'll wake you up." Quincy reassured him.

Helping him up from the couch, Quincy led Otis to one of the spare bedrooms, tucking him into bed and leaving a dim light on so it wasn't too dark. I couldn't take my eyes off him. This man who pretended he was jaded and people were all horrible disappointments had just been so kind and loving to Otis in his time of need.

"Are you alright?" Quincy asked me.

"Yeah," I said breathlessly, still a bit in awe of him. "Is *he* gonna be alright?"

"Yeah, he just forgets things sometimes. Or like tonight, thinks he's in some memory from the past."

"His family just lets him live alone?"

Quincy placed his hands on my shoulders giving them a rub gently leading me to the kitchen. "He's not alone he has us. And most of the time he's good. It's just sometimes this happens."

"And you take care of him?"

"When I can."

I didn't have the words so I pulled him close, planting a soft gentle kiss on his lips.

Quincy traced my face with his finger running the pad of his thumb over my lips. "Can we talk?"

I nodded as we both took a seat on the couch.

"Listen, I get that we all have a past. But hearing you were married, from Evan of all places, caught me off guard."

With a measured sigh I did my best to explain. "I married my high school sweetheart right after graduation. It didn't take long to figure out it wasn't going to work, so we got divorced. It was a stupid rash decision that further damaged my relationship with my mother and made things harder than they should've been.

"I jump, remember? And most times I don't stop to consider what I'm jumping into and how it will affect those around me. It wasn't a secret. It's just never been a topic we've discussed. How exactly do you just bring it up? Can you pass the Grey Poupon, by the way I've been married before.

"He was my first love and I thought I'd feel that way forever. In retrospect there were red flags I was just way too young and inexperienced to recognize them. You're right I should have told you. And I'm sorry you had to hear it from my loud mouth brother."

"That's fair. I can see that." He scratched at his beard. "I'm sorry for not giving you the opportunity to explain before shutting down earlier."

"It's fine because we're learning what works for us ... together. We need more talking things through and less shutting down and walking away."

He nodded his head in agreement. "So Naomi told you about my dad?"

"Yes."

"What else did she tell you?"

"Just that, that your dad had been to jail. It was really just mentioned briefly."

"My dad is *in* prison, present tense."

"Do you two speak?"

"No, absolutely not I have no words for that man."

I had so many follow-up questions but I didn't want to force him to say more than he was prepared for. "When you're ready to share, I'm ready to listen." I rubbed his cheek.

"Yep." He kissed the palm of my hand.

"Well since we're confessing things ... I once shot a man in Reno, just to watch him die."

Quincy raised an eyebrow. "I too have something to confess. I once got fired from my job on my day off."

"Damn ..." I leaned back, and we both erupted into laughter.

Chapter 17

QUINCY

"So what kinda tree are we going for? Evelyn asked.

"I'm looking for that Charlie Brown Christmas kinda tree." I smiled.

"A struggle tree? No thank you."

I never had a real Christmas tree, Naomi always put up a fake one with the lights already attached, so this outing to the tree farm was exciting for me. We'd stopped at the coffee shop and with warm drinks in hand, were now milling around the tree lot.

"What about this tree with all the fake snow on it?" I asked, eyes growing wide.

"If my baby wants this tree. Then we'll get this tree." Evelyn swallowed hard.

"You hate it?"

"You like it, I love it. This is your first real tree so you get to choose."

"But it's our first tree together and I want you to love it

just as much as I do." I bopped her nose with the tip of my finger.

"Babe, that's sweet." Evelyn tilted her head with a goofy grin.

"You're sweet."

"And we're disgusted." Walt said, while Meryl made gagging sounds next to him.

"Could you two refrain from acting like a couple from a Hallmark Christmas movie for at least the next thirty minutes," Meryl said. "Let's go look at the cute Christmas ornaments." Grabbing Evelyn's hand, Meryl led her away.

"So have you two picked out pet names for one another yet?" Walt teased.

"Shut up."

"No, it's cute to see you two turn into the type of couple we always made fun of. Does she send you text messages with heart eye emojis?"

"Heart eyes, no. Eggplants and tongues, yeah."

"That's much better."

"I don't know what it is about that woman but she makes me wanna wear matching pajamas and sing Christmas carols while drinking hot chocolate and kissing under the mistletoe."

"Probably because you love her." Walt announced matter of factly.

"Shhh." I pulled Walt in the opposite direction of the ladies into a dense patch of artificially colored trees in pinks, purples, and blues. "Could you ixnay with the L word please."

"OK but not saying it doesn't make it any less true."

"You sound like Naomi."

"She's a wise woman. Great minds think alike."

"Listen," I whispered. "I like Evelyn. I like her a lot. I like her more than any other woman I've dated."

"So love ... you basically love her."

If it wasn't Naomi, it was Walt trying to get me to profess my undying love for Evelyn. I was trying to live in the moment and not plot ten steps ahead like I normally did. Being with Evelyn felt easy and I didn't want to complicate things by focusing on what was coming next. Decision day was still a ways off and if we put in the work everything would turn out fine.

"Anyway, did you get the invite to Evelyn's gallery event next month?" I asked changing the subject

"Yeah, already RSVPed."

"Thanks, I appreciate that. I was trying to get her mother to attend but she is one hard nut to crack."

"Why wouldn't she want to support her daughter?"

"I don't know. She's never even been to one of her shows. I told her Evie has a piece at the Art Institute and she was all like why didn't she tell me." I frowned. "I don't know Shereè maybe because she knew you were more interested in holding her accountable than showing her some much-needed support."

"Look at you riding for your wife."

"Damn right I am. Evelyn's a tough cookie but she definitely feels a way about her mom not making the effort. And her stuff is so dope. She's so talented. I just know if her mom saw it she'd feel differently."

"What are you gonna do?"

"I'ma keep trying. There's still a month between then and now."

Evelyn and Meryl stumbled upon us laughing hysterically.

"What's so funny?" Walt asked.

"Nothing just a little girl talk," Meryl said.

"We found mistletoe." Evelyn held up the plant with a shake.

"Like you two need mistletoe to prompt you to start kissing." Walt chuckle.

Evelyn ignored him, placing the mistletoe over her head in hopes that I would kiss her.

How could I resist, leaning in I planted a series of kisses on her lips before kissing her cheek.

Meryl cleared her throat. "See anything you like?"

"Are we still talking about the trees?" Walt asked.

I observed the pair who were sharing a goofy grin. My eyes flashed Walt a no bueno expression. Meryl was off limits. I didn't want Walt fucking around with my wife's best friend. If things got messy it could ruin the entire friend dynamic. What we had worked. Walt and Meryl needed to remain neutral if we were going to maintain the friend structure.

We decided on a seven-foot Frasier Fir, and I may have hopped up and down like a five-year-old with giddy excitement. Making our way back to the car, Evelyn outlined the itinerary for the rest of our day. "OK so we're gonna go home, listen to Christmas music, decorate the tree, and then after we can watch a Christmas movie."

"*Die Hard*," both Walt and I said in unison.

"That's not a Christmas movie," Meryl protested.

"Nope wrong, the writer of the movie confirmed it's a Christmas movie a few years back," Walt countered.

"That sounds suspect." Meryl's face expressed her doubt.

"We will agree to *Die Hard* if you agree to wear clay face masks," Evelyn said.

"Ooo, can we do the turmeric mask? I love how my skin feels after that," I asked, throwing my arm around her.

~

EVELYN

WITH A POMEGRANATE MARTINI IN HAND, Quincy returned to the table setting the glass in front of me.

"So how's everyone doing now that we're halfway through this experiment?" Jace asked.

The *Why Knot* production team set up another get together for us newlywed couples. This time it was cocktails at a popular bar and lounge downtown. Quincy hated these forced meetings but I thought it was nice touching base with people who were going through the same process we were. There was a sense of community in our shared experience. I especially liked Jace and Michelle who I could see us continuing to hangout with after this whole reality show was over.

"It's going well. It's crazy how quickly the time has gone by," I said.

"I know I was just telling Jace it seems like we got married yesterday." Michelle trilled a laugh.

Sarah chimed in. "Time always seems to speed up around the holidays. We both have huge families so navigating Christmas has been difficult. What are you guys doing for Christmas?"

I looked at Quincy. He'd been fairly quiet tonight and I wanted him to participate.

"Ahh, we opted for a low-key Christmas. We're gonna stay home, open presents and cook dinner," he said.

"That sounds romantic. I wish we could do that but my mother would kill me," Michelle said.

"My mom wasn't too happy when I told her we weren't coming to Christmas dinner but we want to make our own traditions." I rubbed Quincy's thigh, allowing my hand to fall to his lap; I gave his member a quick pass of my hand. His eyes lighting up as I stared at him before placing my hand on the table like a good girl.

"Traditions are so important. Sarah and I want to set up some solid traditions for our kids."

I laughed loudly. "Kids? Oh my God no."

"Wait do you guys not want kids," Jace asked.

I pulled my face turning to Quincy, his facial expression announcing he was just as confused as I was. Stammering I said, "I mean … I'm sure someday we'll have kids … but we haven't really talked—"

Sarah's eyebrows hiked up her forehead. "Wait, you two haven't talked about kids? Elliot and I have already picked out baby names."

My breath hitched. Were we supposed to be picking out baby names and deciding our future already?

"Jace and I are house hunting. We hope to close on our dream home at the start of the new year," Michelle added, crossing her fingers.

"Wow, what if it doesn't work out?" Quincy asked.

"The house?" Michelle looked confused.

"The marriage," Quincy said pointedly.

"Of course, it's gonna work. We've already decided to stay together after the ninety days are up," Jace said.

Quincy let loose a loud chuckle before taking a sip of his Moscow Mule.

"That's great." I tried to smooth over the harshness of Quincy's disbelieving laugh. "I think when you know you know and if you two know then that's awesome."

Were Quincy and I the only ones just living in the moment, just going off vibes and energy? Maybe we needed to craft a five-year plan. I didn't even know how many kids Quincy wanted or if he actually wanted kids for that matter. Why weren't we having these conversations? Do you want kids? How do you want to raise those little crumb snatchers? What are your views on traditional gender roles?

"Are you saying you and Quincy don't know yet?" Elliot leaned forward with a smug smile.

"We just bought a Monsteras plant. We're committed," Quincy said, his jaw tightening.

"Yep, we have to water it and make sure it gets sun. And of course, there's the positive affirmations," I added.

"We named him Philbert."

"No we didn't." I shot him a stern look. We had not decided on a name.

"A plant ... that's something," Sarah said, with a smile laced with pity.

When I was in high school I ran track, and right now it felt like I was in a relay race and I was stuck in place while all the other teams blew past me. Unable to move forward until my teammate approached with the baton. It didn't matter that Quincy and I had fun together or that my entire body hummed and sparkled when he was inside of me. Witty conversation and bomb ass sex were not enough to set an entire future on.

My chair squeaked as I stood. "Excuse me. I'm gonna head to the ladies room."

"Wait up I'll go with you," Michelle said.

I didn't stop; I was already maneuvering my way past tables to get to the restrooms. Finding the first available stall, I locked myself inside. *What am I doing?* When I agreed to appear on this show I was convinced that with a little help from the experts I could find the one. I was funny, pretty, and confident and I just needed to find the one guy in all of Chicago who liked that and had common interest. And the experts found him, Quincy was my perfect match and even with all the cards stacked in my favor, I was still messing everything up.

I didn't even know if this man wanted kids. And not once did it even occur to me to ask. Useless facts I knew about Quincy. He hated those Christmas Claymation shows like *Frosty the Snowman*, he said they weird him out. He could recite the alphabet backwards. And his favorite Jackson was Rebbie. REBBIE.

I knew all this but I didn't know if he had a five-year plan. Maybe we had no plan because he didn't see me in his future. Quincy planned for everything but his plans with me always stopped after January fifteenth. Then it was, maybe and we'll see or I'll have to look into that. I was starting to fear Quincy and I were planning for two very different futures.

When I exited the stall, Michelle was waiting. "Are you OK?"

"Is it weird that Quincy and I haven't had any of those long-term conversations?"

"Girl, Quincy is crazy about you. Everyone can see it."

I could feel a throbbing at the base of my skull. "It's not like we don't talk, we talk all the time. Like yesterday we had a two-hour conversation about the Marvel and DC universes."

"That's good, so maybe you two need to dig deeper. Do the work, like Iyanla says." Michelle reapplied her lipstick.

Working soap into my hand, I chewed on my bottom lip.

"Stop doing that," Michelle instructed.

"What?"

"Overthinking, you're overthinking. None of us know what we're doing. We're all just flying blind."

"No, yeah I hear you. I do." I fidgeted with my wedding band. "I just want this to work. If this doesn't work I don't know what I'm gonna do. I'll never hear the end of it from my mother. And my family will just be like 'There's Evelyn always leaping before looking, never thinking anything through. Once again making rash decisions that have real consequences.'"

"I get it. But we're kinda already on this ride. It's too late to get off now."

I was sick and tired of the ride. If it wasn't the merry-go-round where I was constantly moving but made no progress then it was bumper cars where I tried to stay in my lane but somehow still got caught in the middle of a ten-car pileup.

"IT's crazy to hear Elliot and Sarah talk about their future because they're not gonna make it," Quincy said, adding toothpaste to his brush.

"You don't think it's gonna work?"

"No, do you hear the way he talks to her? He's condescending and dismissive and if she doesn't dump him next month she will after the show airs and she sees for herself all the shit she was putting up with. Jace and Michelle will probably be OK, they're just a little clueless."

I wondered if he calculated our odds for a future like he did for everyone else. My hope was for everyone to make it, which I now realized was naive. The odds of all three couples staying together was minuscule. And right now, it appeared the only risky bet was Quincy and me. What if we were the only couple that didn't stay together? That would be humiliating. My chest tightened at the thought.

Quincy dried his toothbrush on his hand towel as I slathered cream on my face.

"Hey?" he asked.

"Hmm?"

"Do you wanna have sex?"

"Yes, always." I giggled, rubbing the cream over my neck before working the remainder into my hands. One thing I could rely on was the sky being blue, Totes McGoats licking my face to wake me up in the morning despite my loud protest, and Quincy wanting to bury himself between my legs.

I walked backward into the bedroom as Quincy advanced.

"You wanna have kids ... someday ... right?" I asked, as he pulling off my tank top.

"Yes."

My body melted as he ran his hand down the center of my chest. "OK good."

Spinning me around, he gently pushed me to the bed before kissing every inch of my back causing my breathing to accelerate as my body squirmed under the warmth of his mouth and tongue.

It felt great but my mind was preoccupied unable to let this issue rest. If I didn't ask follow-up questions now I would obsess and fuck up my chances of orgasm.

Pushing him away, I faced front. I was ready to tick this conversation off my list. "How many do you want?"

"I don't know, two or three," he said, while I nodded. "What about you?"

"Five. I want them all to play instruments, or write stories, or draw. Something creative. And I want to start a garden and plant tomatoes, and squash, and green beans. Ooh, maybe our own collards or lettuce. Like an at home farm to table." I hadn't really given children much thought but now that we were talking, all these images were floating in my head. Maybe if I got them all out we could catch up in some way.

"If we're gonna have five then I'm gonna need to practice." Quincy hooked his fingers through my panties, removing them with ease.

"Lots and lots of practice." I agreed.

Quincy dropped to his knees disappearing between my legs, his hand seeking out the dip in my waist. The conversation was over, I was no longer able to think, all I could do was cry out as his tongue performed figure eights over my bud. I gently applied pressure to his head with my hand letting him know I wanted him to go deeper. My body levitated from the bed when he did. After a few more flicks of his tongue, I fell back with a satisfied smile on my face.

Quincy quickly removed his shorts, lowering himself on top of me. His strokes defied logic, just when I thought I could predict what he was going to do next, he'd surprise me. Short thrust that hit at an angle. Long, intense strokes that made my vision blurry.

I whispered instructions, "Just like that. Right there. Don't stop." But there was no need because this man knew exactly what my body needed.

Sitting on the bed, he adjusted our position so he was behind me, his chest touching my back as he ran the palm of his hand over my nipples. Grabbing my legs, he stretched me wide hooking my limbs behind his. My head fell back and I rewarded him with deep, fuck-me kisses as our bodies moved as one.

Thrust for thrust, shallow breath for shallow breath. When I was intertwined with him like this it was as if time slowed and even though I could barely see straight, I could hear his body speak to me. His heart's frantic beats letting me know he was enjoying this as much as I was. The taste of his lips pressed against mine pouring all his desire and longing inside until I had my fill. The way his hands clutched my thighs as I rode on top of him, his fingers occasionally brushing my bud, sending electrical currents coursing through my flesh.

My body tensed as tingling waves washed over me as Quincy continued to thrust inside. His body shivered underneath mine and he buried his face in my thick hair. I unballed my fist and allowed my toes to uncurl. We had so much more to learn about one another but when it came to my body it was like this man graduated magna cum laude from the University of Evelyn with a doctorate degree.

MY EYES SHOT OPEN, everything around me was still but my blood whined in my ears.

Sweat slicked my face and when I sat up I could feel the cold, clammy wetness pooling around my neck and sliding down my spine. I counted backward from ten hoping to alleviate the building pressure like a heavy slab had been placed on my chest. Any air in my lungs evaporated causing me to wheeze. *Eight, seven, six.* It was as if all the oxygen had been sucked from the room. Jumping from the bed, I stumbled to the bedroom door knocking over a decorative vase.

"Evie? You OK?" Quincy asked, still half asleep.

Careening forward, I compelled myself to place one foot in front of the other trying my damndest to make it to the sliding door. Fatigue flooded my legs and tears pooled in my eyes. I wheezed and gasped in an attempt to capture some air. At the slider my hands fumbled over the latch, slipping when I tried to open it. On the third attempt I was able to rip the door open and throw myself onto the snow-covered grass.

A shrill chime from the security alarm filled the air as I curled into the fetal position, my face wet from the snow against my skin and the tears that were now streaming down my face. The blare of the alarm stopped and the next thing I knew Quincy was next to me. His mouth was moving but I couldn't make out what he was saying. My breath was still a syrup-like sludge clogging my airway. Grabbing my face, Quincy looked in my eyes with fierce determination.

"You need to breathe, baby. Just focus on me and try to breathe."

My whole body tensed as a cramp shot from my calf all the way to my thigh.

"It's a panic attack. We're just gonna breathe through it. I'm gonna countdown from ten."

I shook my head, clawing at my chest. But Quincy never let go, pulling me onto his lap, he cupped my face once again anchoring his gaze to mine.

"Ten, nine, eight."

How was this man so nurturing and calm? I'd seen it with Otis and now with me. He should have gone into the medical profession because he was such a calming force.

"Seven, six, five. That's it, just breathe. We don't have to be where they are as long as we're happy with where *we* are."

It had only been a month and a half but this man knew me. He knew when I was excited, or sad, when I wanted to be alone and when I wanted to cuddle close and have him rub my butt. How he knew I didn't understand, maybe I wasn't as mysterious as I thought. When it came to Quincy I had no doubt that I loved this man. But it didn't make any of this less scary. The other couples seemed to have every-thing figured out. How did the saying go? Comparison is the thief of joy. We were happy and I loved what we had. Our timeline didn't have to look like anyone else's as long as the destination was one we were both happy with.

"Four, Three, Two."

He reached for my hand, placing it over his heart, it pumped against my palm. My lungs jerked back into action, greedily slurping the air. Closing my eyes, I allowed the predictable beats of his heart to regulate my breathing. I relaxed my fists which had been clenched tight, my nails had dug deep into my palms drawing blood.

"One."

My bottom lip trembled; I felt foolish. The last thing I wanted was for Quincy to see me as a bawling mess who let my fears get the better of me.

"Better?" he asked.

I nodded my head too embarrassed to speak.

"Let's get you inside. You're freezing." Quincy scooped me in his arms carrying me back to the warmth of the house. Placing me back in the bed, he held me close not letting go of me for the rest of the night.

The next morning my eyes fluttered open to sounds in the kitchen. My throat was dry and my palms were smeared with dried blood. *Shit.* The shame of the early morning hours slowly seeped into my brain. I vaguely remembered frantic tears, the struggle to breathe, and Quincy's gentle voice talking me through it all until my chest was loose and I was able to gulp down air filling my lungs.

I wanted to burrow myself into this bed and hide there forever. Not so much because of the panic attack, but mostly because of what it represented. My deepest fears and the fact that I didn't trust us. I didn't trust I was enough for him and that when asked to choose he would willingly pick me. I didn't suffer from self-esteem issues. I knew I was a good partner and most men would be happy to have me. But Quincy wasn't most men. He wasn't some dude I met at the gym. He was my husband the stakes were so much higher.

I couldn't camp out in this room all morning. I needed

to face the music. Stepping into my slippers, I made a quick pit stop in the bathroom to clean the cuts on my hands, and calm my nerves. Entering the kitchen, I found Quincy shirtless, cracking eggs into a bowl.

"Hey," I said meekly, my voice still a little raspy from sleep.

"Hey, I'm making cheesy eggs. Do you want some?"

I dipped my head forward standing next to him in the kitchen. "About last night—"

Quincy leaned down guiding my chin upward, he kissed me on the lips. One long, soft, rich kiss followed by a few aftershock pecks. His affable touch let me know it was OK. We were OK, and that words of explanation weren't needed. I wrapped my arms around him running my hands over the taut muscles in his chest and stomach. With my head resting on his back, I listened to his steady heartbeat while he whisked the eggs.

CHAPTER 18

QUINCY

"It smells good in here." I said, tossing my keys in the bowl.

Evelyn's face beamed at the sight of me. "It's angry pasta."

"Ahh and why do tell is the pasta so fucking angry?"

"Probably because all anyone wants to talk about is spaghetti and fettuccine but never penne."

With a quick kiss I gave her the once-over. "Why are you all dressed up?"

"Because Dr. Heather is coming over."

"Is that tonight?" I said, with a frown.

"Yes, that's tonight." Evelyn held the wooden spoon to my mouth, allowing me to have a taste of the sauce.

"Now that's a good pasta." I laid on a thick Italian accent.

"Nope, no we talked about this."

"It's getting better."

"Hmm, It's really not though, baby."

"If I had remembered Dr. Heather was coming through I would have picked up some wine."

"We have wine. I got two bottles. So, if you forgot what are the flowers for?"

"They're for you."

Her eyes grew wide. "Because?"

"Because I can, I should, and you deserve. Because that shit you did this morning made it difficult to focus all day."

Evelyn cleared her throat, a big smile parting her lips.

I could also add, I bought her flowers because I hoped she'd look at me exactly how she was right now.

"Thank you," she whispered caressing my beard.

I leaned into her hand. I'd lived in this house for over two years and only now was it starting to feel like home. We had a routine. When she wasn't working late at the gallery or at her studio she made it home before me. It was so nice to enter the house all warm and toasty with candles lit and R&B classics playing in the background. Sometimes we'd cook, other times we'd order takeout and just spend the rest of the night cracking one another up in between make out sessions. If this was what marriage was like, I was all in.

Standing behind her, I wrapped my arms across her body burying my face into her neck. She smelled like jasmine and her skin was soft against my lips. I wanted desperately to tell her how much I loved her. But that word was so loaded and when said, it shifted expectations.

I opted instead for, "You make me really happy. I love the life we've created together in this short time."

"Ahh, babe that's sweet," Evelyn said, before dumping the al dente penne pasta in the spicy, red sauce.

Babe that's sweet? she could have at least thrown me a

"You make me feel safe and happy and I've never felt this way about anyone else and if the world were to end tomorrow I would die grateful because I got to spend my last days on this God forsaken earth with you." Being vulnerable was a lot of work for me so when I did it, I expected a twelve-gun salute or at the very least an appreciation for the moment. Adding water to a vase, I arranged the flowers and set them on the dining table. The doorbell rang causing Evelyn to move around the kitchen faster.

"You ready?" I asked, plastering a fake smile on my face. At the door I opened it wide. "Dr. Heather, it's so good to see you again." My voice was saccharine sweet.

EVELYN

"Evelyn everything was delicious. You didn't have to cook. But I must admit I'm glad that you did," Dr. Heather Woodland said.

Dr. Heather was one of four experts hired by *Why Knot* to guide the couples through their journey. She was a licensed psychotherapist, specializing in relationships and communication.

"She really is the best cook," Quincy said, clearing the plates from the table.

"Ahh, thank you, both." I beamed. "More wine?"

"Yes, that would be nice." Dr. Heather smiled. "So, I'm interested to hear how the last few weeks have gone for you both. I know it can be overwhelming, meeting someone and then immediately sharing a living space with them."

I nodded in agreement. "It's definitely been challenging at times. Luckily, we lived fairly close to one another so there wasn't a big adjustment regarding the neighborhood."

Returning to the table, Quincy agreed. "Yeah, I think it's mostly figuring out the day-to-day stuff. Like who's a morning person. Fortunately, neither of us are. And then incorporating each other in our routines."

"Have you found it difficult to express your wants and needs?"

"No, I tell Quincy all the time I need more blankets on the bed and he listens." I joked.

"I'm being serious." Dr. Heather set her wine glass down. "I've noticed you two like to joke and have fun. And that is great, but the goal is to get what you need from your partner so you can experience closeness and a sense of security." Her gaze shifted from Quincy then to me. "Let's do a little exercise, shall we? Evelyn, what scares you the most about this process?"

I took a long, thoughtful drink from my glass. A week ago, I feared Quincy and I weren't having the intimate conversations the other couples were having. But now that Dr. Heather presented me with the opportunity to delve deeper my chest felt tight and my throat was dry.

With a glance at Quincy I said, "I guess that ultimately I'm afraid we won't be on the same page."

Offering no reassuring words to my show of vulnerability, Dr. Heather turned to Quincy posing the same question. "What scares you the most about all this?"

"I don't know, if I had to pick something maybe the fact that you found this person who's supposed to be my perfect match and if this doesn't work out then what does that mean? Does that make me unlovable?" He let out a nervous chuckle.

His words caught me by surprise. Was that truly how he felt? For the most part Quincy was always so nonchalant, it was almost like if this worked, he would be fine with it but if it didn't work he'd move on and not spend any time looking back. I didn't want to be a footnote in this man's life. The kooky ex-wife who he married on a whim. I wanted our story to be woven together like an exquisite tapestry. And when our grandkids looked back they could point to this beautiful love story that created generations all because we fell in love and chose love every single day.

"What would this look like if it worked out?" Dr. Heather asked.

"We'd be happy, and growing together and giving the other what they needed." Quincy shrugged.

"So here is the question I pose to you. What do you need from Evelyn?"

"Support, I need to know she has my back."

"You don't think I have your back?"

"That's not what I said."

"You said you need something which would imply that I'm not giving it to you."

I wasn't trying to put him on the spot but since the expert was here, we should use this time to really talk through some of these issues.

Quincy shot me a glance that clearly said he wanted me to do less. "You're supportive and I would like for it to continue. That better?"

I resisted the urge to respond. Quincy was adamant about not wanting us to air our dirty laundry for the world to see. The best way to avoid that was not signing up for a reality show it begin with … but I digress.

"Evelyn, what about you? What do you need from Quincy?"

"Maybe more of this. Conversations that move us forward and allow us to get to know one another better."

"This is good. I have a couple's assignment I want you two to work on. You have twenty-four hours to complete. Because I want to give you some time to think about it. It is very clear you two have chemistry and you enjoy one another's company and that's great. It really is half the battle. What I would like to see is for you two to have deeper conversations and this assignment will help you do that. The assignment is to share three things from your childhood that the other doesn't know."

I could feel Quincy's hand tighten over my thigh. For me this assignment was simple enough; my childhood was pretty vanilla. But from the deer-in-the-headlights look in Quincy's eyes, and the little bit I already knew about foster care and his father's incarceration I could tell this conversation would not be an easy one.

Dr. Heather stood, putting on her coat to leave. "You don't just want to build memories you also want to share them."

QUINCY

AFTER THE CREW went home for the night, I locked up the house and headed to the master bedroom. I found

Evelyn sprawled out on the bed intensely watching a YouTube makeup tutorial.

"Do you want to do that assignment now?" I asked.

"Huh?" She pulled one ear bud out of her ear.

"Do you wanna do the assignment?"

"But the crew went home. You know they have to be here for that shit." Her eyes dropped back to the video.

"Evelyn, I don't wanna share this with anyone else."

She locked her phone, tossing it aside. "OK yeah, let's do it."

Climbing on the bed I looked at her. Head scarf, under eye masks, and zit cream on her cheek she was still the hottest thing smoking.

Smiling, she asked, "So who should go first?"

"You can start."

"OK." She adjusted her position so we were sitting face to face. "My parents divorced when I was five. My real dad moved out and at first, he'd come and get us on the weekends and do cool stuff with us. But eventually he went Houdini on our asses and disappeared."

"That must have been hard, having him around and then nothing."

"Yeah it was. I was a smart kid but that didn't stop me from blaming myself when he stopped coming around. He ended up moving to Texas, remarrying, and having more kids. He created this whole new life, like we were his practice family."

Evelyn's gaze was far away. This was the first time she'd mentioned her real dad. It would appear I wasn't the only one who was holding onto trauma. She may not recognize it as such but I could see the wistful longing for what could have been. For the relationship she could have had with her biological father and the missed opportunities.

Evelyn pointed at me. "You're next."

"Ahh … I went to a charter school for gifted teens when I was in high school."

"OK, Mr. Brainiac."

I chuckled at her colorful tone. "Nothing like that. I had to study my ass off to keep up."

"Don't do that. Don't down play the fact that you're smart. Naomi told me you were the high school valedictorian. And the fact that you went to a gifted school makes it even more impressive."

"Alright, I'll take it. Hype me up then." I laughed.

"Know this. If I don't do nothing else, I'm always gonna toot your horn. You were in the system and you worked really hard to beat the odds and get into U of A and then land a top-notch job. Honestly, I need a six-piece band to sing your praises but a horn will have to do."

I ran my fingers over her smooth bare leg. "Your turn again."

Evelyn rubbed her palms together thinking of a childhood memory to share. Her face lit up, "Here's a good one. And something you can tease Evan about later. I used to model as a kid. Evan and I both did. Like Gap ads, Sears catalog, OshKosh B'gosh."

"Shut up. Where are the pictures? I need to see them."

Evelyn giggled. "No 'cause for real Evan and I were like a big deal in the child modeling industry for a minute. Just stuntin' on other preteens."

"So, you've just always been a star."

She shrugged.

"Why'd you stop?"

"Honestly, 'cause it pissed my mother off. She loved bragging to people about how we were in the latest Target commercial or Macy's ad. When I stopped modeling, she couldn't do that anymore."

"A little petty."

"A lot petty. But it felt good at the time."

"I'm serious about wanting to see pictures."

"I can do that. Your turn."

I took a long breath. Evelyn's expectant face was causing sweat to pebble my forehead. She reached for my hand her expression softening like she knew where this conversation was headed. I always tried my best to steer away from questions about my childhood. When I went off to college and was asked about my family I decided to make up this story about a mom and dad who loved and supported me.

I never mentioned foster care. I never spoke about the shit I endured in some of the foster homes. My hope was to be like everyone else. I'd tell people my mom was a nurse, which was partially true because Naomi was a nurse. My dad was in construction. Siblings? Yeah, sure I had an older brother who'd gone to Stanford and was working at a tech firm.

I lied because it was just easier than the alternative. When people heard the words foster care, they were bound to have questions. Primary of which was what happened to your parents and that was something I wasn't willing to freely share. The last person I told about this was Victoria and her reaction was less than I'd hoped for. She was more concerned about the image. *What if your dad made parole and came looking for you?* That was a literal question she asked after I poured my heart out to her. I checked all her boxes but one and it was something she was never really able to move past.

"You know I was in foster care but you don't know why."

"If you're not ready you don't have to." She cupped the side of my face with her hand, stroking my beard with her thumb.

"I want to. I want you to know. It's important that you know."

She dropped her hand moving closer so her crossed legs touched my knee.

"I lost my mom when I was eight and after she was gone I didn't have any real family to speak of so I ended up in the foster care system. I bounced around a lot. Some of the homes were sketch." My eyes appraised her face, debating how much to reveal. "Some of the foster parents were violent. You know, smacking me around or locking me in a dark closet while I screamed my head off begging them to let me out." My throat lurched with a hard swallow, closing my eyes, I pushed the feelings back down. "I just spent most of my childhood praying to make it to eighteen so I could be free."

"Quincy, I had no idea. I'm so sorry you had to go through that." Evelyn sniffled, tears breaching her lids and rolling down her face. "What happened to your mom? If you don't mind me asking."

"My mom ... she ... she was murdered by my father."

Evelyn's mouth fell open, her eyes splayed wide. "What?"

She didn't expect that, no one ever did. Explaining this

part was always the hardest because I was talking about my mother. When I thought back on my first eight years of life much of it was laced with fear. I remembered peeing on myself at five when my dad hit my mother so hard her nose started to gush blood. I remembered my mom would make me play hide and seek right before my father got home from work so I'd be out of sight just in case he was in a bad mood.

"Yeah, he was abusive and eventually he did exactly what he threatened he'd do for years."

"I'm sorry. I don't know what else to say but I'm so sorry that you had to lose your mother ... and your father in that way."

"It's crazy because I don't remember much about my mom. I used to have a picture of her but I lost it years ago. So when I think about her face it's always weird like it's blurry or out of focus. But I remember the song she would sing to me every night. Every single night, sometimes through her tears she'd sing.

Oh Quincy, my Quincy. My little bamboo.
Quincy, my Quincy. Oh how I love you.
Oh Quincy, my Quincy. No matter how far.
I will always be wherever you are."

Hot tears rolled down my face as I tried frantically to wipe them away. "She sang it better though."

Crawling into my lap, Evelyn wrapped herself around me rubbing my back. *Why was I crying?* I didn't expect to cry but now that the tears were falling I was finding it hard to stop. I clutched Evelyn's waist tightly, my tears chasing one another pooling under my chin.

"I'm sorry." I let out a nervous chuckle. "I don't even know why I'm getting so emotional."

"It's OK."

Mopping away tears with my shoulder, I said, "I'm fine. It's fine. It really is."

"It doesn't have to be fine and you don't have to be OK. With me you can feel however you feel no matter how ugly or scary it may be." She planted a soft kiss on my lips. "Thank you for trusting me with this."

"Thank you for listening and being here. It means a lot. You mean a lot to me."

With Evelyn's arms wrapped tightly around me, I let the anxiety and fear wash away. I'd been in therapy since my midtwenties trying to work through these issues but it was hard to just move past the fear and shame. My greatest worry was about how others would perceive me if they knew. I would never forget the way Victoria recoiled in horror when I shared it with her. I just expected everyone to react in a similar way, but I was wrong. Evelyn was still here and the warmth of her embrace let me know that for her nothing had changed.

CHAPTER 19

QUINCY

"Here you go." I handed Evelyn a cup of wine. When she raised her arm the bells attached to her ugly Christmas sweater jingled.

"How long have you known AJ?" she asked, taking a sip from her cup.

"We all went to high school together. AJ, Walt, and myself. Basically, we've been hanging out ever since."

"And how long has he been hosting this ugly Christmas sweater party?"

"I don't know for like five years now. Any excuse to get drunk and play games so he can talk smack."

My mood was a little bit dark. When we arrived at AJ's house we were greeted by a *Why Knot* camera crew. A few weeks ago, I reached out to my friend letting him know the *Why Knot* crew was going to contact him for authorization to film in his home. I'd instructed AJ to deny them access by declining to sign the necessary authorization forms.

If he didn't sign the crew couldn't film, this was a nice

little loophole I'd used to my advantage. Both Walt and Naomi refused to authorize the *Why Knot* production team in their homes. This refusal allowed me sanctuary. When I visited Walt or Naomi the camera crew was forced to wait outside.

So now I was at a party with the *Why Knot* crew staked out in the corner following my every move. I'd hoped to have a good time and catch up with some friends but now I had to watch what I said and make sure my face didn't make me look pissed off.

A short male approached us while turning and pointing to his back. "Am I a singer?" he asked.

"No," Evelyn chuckled.

Upon entry each guests was given a name tag of a famous person, place or thing. The name tag was placed on your back so you couldn't see it but everyone else could. You had to ask questions to guess what or who you were while also helping others guess who they were."

"OK how about an athlete?" he asked.

"You're not an athlete, however I'm sure you could provide a good workout." Evelyn said.

I frowned flashing Evelyn a leery side eye. She was thirsting after the hunky celebrity on the name tag.

"It's a guy?"

"Yes." Evelyn's face beamed.

"Do I look like him?"

Evelyn cringed.

"You're both Black. But ain't nobody gonna confuse you two ever in life," I said.

The short brother walked away to a group of people and peppered them with similar questions.

"That was a little rude," Evelyn said.

"I hate this game and the forced interaction. Let's just work the room, tell a few jokes and leave. We can be back home and warm and toasty by the fireplace in less than an hour."

"Babe, it's a party I wanna mingle. Plus, I haven't seen AJ since the Halloween party." Her eyebrows mashed into a frown.

I wasn't able to say no to that face and I think she knew it. Just because I was feeling like the Grinch didn't mean I should dampen her fun.

Evelyn scanned the living space of about forty people. Her face lit up when she recognized someone who was at our wedding. "That's Tracy. I'm gonna go say hi."

Evelyn was a social butterfly so she bounded off without a second thought, leaving me alone in the corner of the room. Personally, I preferred simpler events like intimate dinners with my core group of friends. I was what I liked to call a selective extrovert, choosing to engage in only certain situations. Huge parties with a mix of people were not my ideal setting. If I was invited anywhere I was the guy who always asked, "Who all's gonna be there."

Turning my back on the crowd, I scrolled through my phone. For the next half hour Evelyn flitted around the house making new friends and playing drinking games while I reviewed a motion for summary judgment on one of my cases.

"Samuel L. Jackson," A familiar voice called from behind.

"What?" I turned to find Victoria in a red and green sweater with beads all over it.

"Your nametag. You're Samuel L. Jackson." She smiled up at me.

"We need to get these motherfucking snakes off this motherfucking plane." I imitated the actor's voice.

Victoria returned a blank stare.

"From the movie *Snakes on a Plane*," I said, hoping to provide clarity.

"I didn't see that movie."

"That's fair, it's not one of his best." I lied, it was actually one of my favorite movies when I needed a good laugh, *Snakes on a Plane* never failed.

Removing the sticky tag from my back, she affixed it to my chest with a pat. "I cannot believe you're wearing an ugly sweater. I tried to get you to wear one for years."

"Yeah well, Evelyn can be pretty persuasive." And by persuasive I meant she showed me the sweater, kissed me, and then told me to get dressed.

"What's next, matching outfits?"

I bounced my shoulders. "Maybe, I don't know."

"So, things are going well ... with Evelyn?"

"Yeah."

"You never responded to my text asking you to meet me for Christmas cocktails."

I'd seen her text but decided to ignore it. I didn't understand her new found interest in me. Every week or so she'd shoot me a text asking to meet up or she'd want to reminisce about the time we got snowed in, and made love all weekend. Everything she hated about me was now unique and interesting instead of peculiar and annoying.

"It must have slipped my mind. Work has been busy and

Evelyn's working on a new art installation and sometimes she lets me hand her the paint."

Victoria rested her hand on my chest. "You're not trying to avoid me, are you?"

"I'm not. I'm just making time for the things that are important to me."

"There was a time when I was *important* to you." She ran her fingers over the V neck line of her sweater. She sucked at flirting.

"Yeah, and you pissed all over it. So, you can probably understand why I'm not interested in frolicking down memory lane."

Victoria really thought she could coast because she was fine as hell. She was also mean as hell, pretentious as fuck, and arrogant as shit. At one point in my life my world revolved around this woman but every time I'd open up to her, she made me feel small and stupid. And when we fought, she'd throw my words back in my face like a five-pointed ninja star.

"Don't try and blame me for the breakup. You pushed me away, remember? You got scared when I started to talk about marriage and a family. And then you turned around a few years later and married a complete stranger."

It never ceased to amaze me how quickly Victoria could flip the switch. One minute it was let's meet for drinks, the next it was blaming me for every bad part of our relationship.

"Well that stranger feels more like home to me than the person I lived with for over three years." I countered.

"Wow, that was uncalled for." Victoria's eyes splayed wide.

"Why are we talking about this?" I scanned the open concept living space searching for Evelyn. I was so over this Victoria bullshit and beyond ready to go.

"Because I'm trying to understand. Anytime *I* mentioned the word marriage your eyes glazed over, and barely two years after our break up you're sporting a ring on your wedding finger."

There was nothing to understand. Victoria was acting like we had this fairy-tale romance. When I stepped away from the relationship it was very obvious that in the four years we dated we had more bad days than good, more tears than laughter, more misunderstanding than real connection.

I spotted Evelyn coming into the house from the garage talking with her hands to a group of people. I shifted my head hoping to somehow get her attention.

"Quincy, I just want to talk. I'm not happy with how we left things. I guess I'm just asking for clarity." She squeezed my arm before rubbing her hand over my bicep. "One drink. Thirty minutes."

As if from nowhere Evelyn showed up by my side. I guess my version of the bat signal, which consisted of a neck crane and bug eyes in Evelyn's general direction, worked. Her name tag was now on the front of her sweater with the name President Theodore Elmsworth.

"Hi, Victoria how are you? I came to rescue my husband from social interactions." Evelyn joked.

"I'm well thank you."

An awkward silence fell over us as Victoria glared at Evelyn with cagey eyes. If I knew Victoria she was comparing herself trying to figure out why I'd chosen to marry Evelyn and not her. She would find the task a futile one, because I didn't have an explanation for why I'd walked away from a future with Victoria but willingly married someone I'd never met or spoken to before. Maybe I did it because I was afraid of failure and when you marry a stranger there's no expectation it will work. In fact, most people assume it won't. So, if Evelyn and I broke up it would be understandable and not seen as further proof of my inability to maintain a healthy relationship.

Evelyn's eyes pitched toward me. "I'm ready whenever you are."

"I'm ready now." I threw my arm around Evelyn pulling her close, hopefully Victoria received the message.

"It was good seeing you again Victoria. Love the sweater. Hope you have a Merry Christmas."

As we walked down the street to our car, Evelyn asked, "What was that about?"

"That was about the past. And the fact that Victoria is still living in it."

"She seemed pissed."

"That's just V, she walks around with her nose in the air looking for faults."

"She wasn't looking at you like she saw your faults. It was more like she was seeing a missed opportunity."

I stopped, dropping Evelyn's gloved hand. "You know what I don't wanna talk about?"

"What?"

"I don't wanna talk about the creepy Claymation Rudolph movie you forced me to watch last night. And I don't want to talk about my ex who ninety percent of the time treated me like shit."

"OK first, it's clay it can't hurt you."

"It's creepy and the stop action movements are weird." I protested loudly.

Evelyn placed her hand over my mouth. "I'm not interested in talking about your ex-girlfriend any more than you are," she said, dropping her hand.

"Great. Team Parrish." I held out a balled fist waiting for her to greet it with her own.

"Team Townsend hyphen Parrish."

"Nope. Yeah, that's a no. Quincy Townsend Parrish, it just doesn't roll off the tongue." I only half teased.

Evelyn pinned her arms across her chest. "We'll make that decision when we make that decision."

"Fair enough." I leaned in brushing my lips against hers. "We can be Team Townsend Parrish for now." I offered my fist again waiting expectantly.

Evelyn brought her fist to meet mine.

"Boom shakalaka," we said in unison.

As we resumed walking, I could hear the bells attached to the sleeves of her sweater jingle underneath her coat.

"Get these motherfucking snakes off this plane," I called out in my best Sam Jackson impression.

Her face lit up. "You figured it out."

"I did. And I didn't get any help from anybody."

"Liar," she said, pushing me playfully.

EVELYN CAME BOUNDING into the living room dressed in plaid pajamas that matched mine. I watched as she twirled and danced around the room like a kid on ... Christmas. She nearly bumped into the three-person TV crew assigned to us for the day. Waiting for the coffee to brew, I realized I was going to need a large cup of caffeine to meet her energy level. I had hoped the *Why Knot* crew would take a day off and while it wasn't the usual crew of ten plus, their presence was still unwanted.

"Can we open presents now?" She grabbed me in a bear hug fluttering her lashes over my face.

"Wait, we were supposed to get presents?" A look of shock stretched my face.

She pushed me playfully, retrieving the creamer from the fridge.

Coffee mugs in hand, we headed for the couch. We both agreed to keep it simple, deciding to go with the gift giving method of something you need, something you can read, and something you want. Selecting the first gift, I handed it to her. Evelyn's face beamed as she clapped her hands in excitement.

"This is something you need," I said.

Ripping into the wrapping paper with the face of a jolly Black Santa, she found a leather-bound notebook.

"I noticed that your notebook was almost full so I got you a replacement. The same kind you already have because I know you artist types can be very particular."

Evelyn opened the notebook smelling the pages. One thing she never left home without was her notebook. It wasn't uncommon for that notebook to make an appearance when we were out and about. At restaurants, when we went indoor skydiving, or the farmer's market. When her beautiful creative mind was inspired, she would take out that notebook and sketch, or write notes.

I loved to watch her hands move across the paper as the

thoughts swirling in her head took shape. Sometimes we'd be in the middle of a conversation and she'd reach for the note-book because something I'd said sparked an idea she couldn't ignore. I was happy to add artist muse to my long list of talents.

She planted a kiss on my lips before scurrying under the tree to find her first gift for me. The wrapping reminded me of the first present I received from her on our wedding day. Like that gift, this one was expertly wrapped and she'd drawn holly on the tag with my name written in calligraphy. I took my time opening the small box setting the hand-crafted tag on the coffee table before lifting the box lid.

"It's a wallet. So that's why you were asking me all those questions about my wallet?" I smiled, turning the item over in my hands.

"I wanted to make sure you weren't attached to yours before I replaced it."

"I love it."

The satisfied smile on her beautiful face made my heart soar. I didn't need to open another present; Evelyn was the best gift ever.

After giving each other the something-you-can-read gift, mine was a James Baldwin novel and hers was a book of love poems, it was time for the final gift, something you want. Evelyn grabbed them both from under the tree. I suggested she open hers first. It was a flat envelope with Merry Christmas scribbled on the front. Opening the seal she removed several sheets of paper. I leaned in as her eyes scanned the documents.

"I don't understand." Her face was a puzzle.

"I just thought it would be nice to get away and the

Maldives have these insane over the water bungalows. And I know you're always up for an adventure."

Evelyn eyed me cautiously. "You booked this trip for April," she whispered.

"I did." That was purposeful. Our ninety days ended mid-January but I wanted her to know I was in this for the long haul.

"I've never been to the Maldives." She wiped a stray tear from her cheek. "The Maldives in April. It's a date." She blew out a chest full of air. Evelyn wiped her tears on the sleeve of her pajamas. "Sorry, I don't know why I'm crying."

"Hopefully it's happy tears and not because you hate the idea of being stuck with me for over a week in paradise."

"Definitely happy tears." Her eyes looked to the gift she'd given me. "You still need to open your gift."

I'd been too busy worried about how Evelyn would perceive the vacation trip, that my final gift from her lay unopened next to me. Removing the colorful bow and paper, I revealed a slim box. When I opened the box my heart tightened against my rib cage, my hands shaking as I examined a frame.

"What is this?" I asked, my voice shaky.

"I'm a little bit of an internet detective I can find anything and anyone. So I Googled your mom and I found some articles and I learned that she used to volunteer at this church and they had pictures from different events in like an archive." Evelyn tapped on the glass of the frame. "That picture was taken at a clothes drive. The original image was faded and a bit worn but luckily, you're married to a photographer so I was able to restore the image. She had a beautiful smile and you ... that's you on her lap. I'm not sure how old you were but—"

"Six, I was six." I recognized the coat I was wearing.

"I just wanted you to have something to remember her by." Evelyn's eyes pinged over my features trying to gauge my reaction.

Running my fingers over my mother's image, I blinked back tears. How could I have forgotten that face. Evelyn was right; she did have a beautiful smile with big dimples in both cheeks.

"Is this too much? Did I do too much?" Her brow was knitted with worry.

"No. I just need a minute." With frame in hand, I headed for the bathroom.

Shutting the door, I turned on the water in the sink. Sadness strained the tissues of my heart. God, I missed my mother. While I couldn't remember much from my time with her, I did remember feeling immensely loved by her. Even when we were both scared and hurting. The one thing that was constant during that time was her fierce love for me.

Tears welled from deep inside, coursing down my cheeks. Sliding to the floor, my shoulders shook. I spent so many years trying to forget because it was too painful to remember. My stomach curdled and even though all I'd had were a few sips of coffee, the sparse contents threatened to come out. I swallowed the unshed tears that were squeezing my throat. Heat flushed through my body, behind the sadness there was something else ... anger.

In therapy I'd talked about my guilt and how I wished I could've been stronger for my mother, been her protector. I know it's a wild thought to have, I was eight ... and parents are supposed to protect their kids, not the other way around. But for a long time, I was angry at my father, at myself, shit at my mother for not leaving.

With my back against the wall, I wiped my wet face with my shoulder. Focusing on the framed picture I eyed a younger version of myself on my mother's lap as she held me close. My gaze traveled from my face to hers; a face that looked so much like mine. The same lopsided smile that didn't quite reach our eyes. The big ass ears which I clearly inherited from my mother's side of the family. Her delicate hands, unlocked a memory of her lovingly pinching my cheeks before dropping me off at school each morning. I remember hating it because I was afraid I'd get teased. What I would give to feel her soft hands cradle my face today.

I didn't want to forget her and now because of Evelyn I would never have to.

After washing my face and squirting an excessive amount of eye drops into my eyes to help conceal the fact that I'd been crying in the bathroom for the past fifteen minutes, I finally made my way back to the living room. I found Evelyn in the kitchen preparing French toast batter.

When she saw me, her expression was pained. "Quincy, I'm so sorry. The last thing I wanted to do was upset you. I didn't think—"

Crossing the room, I swept her up into my arms kissing her deeply. My cheeks flushed feeling her full lips respond to mine. A mixture of desire and uncertainty quickened the beating of my heart. My hands played with the curls that had fallen from her messy bun. Sometimes words weren't enough I wanted her to feel how much she meant to me. I wanted to etch it into her DNA.

When I pulled away, I croaked out, "I love you, Evie."

Evelyn's mouth fell open and she blinked rapidly trying to process what she'd just heard.

She didn't say she loved me back but it was OK because this time I didn't say the words expecting to hear them repeated. I knew she felt the same, it was in the way she always made me a cup of coffee in the morning, three sugars and lots of cream. The way she bought my favorite snacks from the grocery store without me having to ask. The way her face lit up when I walked into the room like she'd been missing me all day. The look in her eyes when it was late and we were alone and she revealed herself to me, providing me refuge between her legs.

When I said "I love you," this time I wasn't scared because I meant it with every fiber of my body.

EVELYN

Our intimate Christmas dinner consisted of Otis, Naomi, and Meryl. With Quincy acting as my sous chef, we made ham, candied yams, stuffing, and greens. Naomi brought her to-die-for mac and cheese. Meryl was on dessert duty because she was the pastry chef. And Mr. Otis contributed a large pot of gumbo.

"Mr. Otis, you broke your foot off in that gumbo. It was so good." Naomi raved.

"Well, you don't get to be as old as I am and not know how to throw down in the kitchen."

For the last ten minutes Meryl had been giving me the

eye and hooking her head to the side. I was too comfortable and full sitting on Quincy's lap with his hands wrapped around me to move. Meryl wanted a debrief about my Christmas morning and she would not let me or the subject rest until she got it.

"Does anyone want more wine or beer?" Meryl asked, hopping up from the floor. "Evelyn, can you help me please?"

I rolled my eyes but reluctantly stood heading over to the kitchen with my friend.

"What? Do you have some kind of nervous tic?" I joked.

"No, but I do have an itch that only you can scratch. I want details," she whispered.

"We can talk later." I turned, hoping to make my way back to the warmth of Quincy's arms.

Grabbing my wrist, Meryl said, "No now." Shifting her attention, Meryl addressed the room. "Sorry guys I'm gonna steal your hostess for a few minutes. We'll be right back." Meryl hooked her arm through mine and guided me to the master bedroom.

With the door closed Meryl plopped on the bed. "So did he like the picture?"

My friend was always impatient and hated to wait when she suspected juicy gossip was right around the corner. Meryl didn't know about what happened to Quincy's mother. She was my girl, but I didn't feel comfortable sharing Quincy's personal business with her. I told Meryl his mother passed away hence him being placed in foster care but that was all I intended to reveal.

"He liked it," I said.

"Did he cry? I bet he cried."

"He was definitely moved." I'd only been married for a short while but I was quickly realizing I couldn't share everything with Meryl. Some things were reserved for just me and Quincy.

"What did he say?"

"Actually, he told me he loved me ... again." I climbed on the bed crossing my legs.

"Well, he already told you that."

"Yeah, but this time was different."

"How so?"

"First, we were fully clothed. And second it just felt ... real." I shrugged. "I don't know how to explain it but they weren't just words—"

Meryl interjected cutting me off mid sentence. "Anyone with eyes can tell that man is madly, truly, deeply in love with you. I love it, you two confessing your love for each other."

"Woah, pump the brakes. I didn't say it back."

"What?" Meryl coughed out a nervous laugh.

"He told me he loved me and I smiled."

"So let me get this straight. This man has professed his love for you not once but twice and you've essentially left him on read?"

"No, I just didn't know what to say."

"Evie, he kinda gave you the lines. You say it back. Unless that's not how you feel." Meryl's jovial expression was replaced with concern.

"No, I do. I just ..."

I was always the first one to fall, the first one to say I love you. The first one to push all her chips to the center of the table. And in the past, each time I'd crapped out. I was just trying to be cautious. Yes, I'd fallen for Quincy but maybe by holding back I could protect myself from the eventual impact that always happens when one is hurtling through the sky.

Love is very similar to jumping out of a plane. And the love your partner had for you was the metaphorical parachute. My love was earnest and Herculean so my partner always landed safely with two feet on the ground. But the love I freely gave was very rarely returned, causing me to get caught up in trees or end up with scrapes and scratches from the impact.

I'd watched a video once of two matches burning side by side. The first match burned out in a matter of seconds but the second match stayed lit, the flame growing more intense as it traveled down the length of the wooden stick. The second match totally oblivious that it was burning alone, its partner having long ago ceased to glow. That lonely match just kept on burning flicking with light and emanating warmth until it had nothing left to give. I was that second, lonely match.

Sure, Quincy loved me now, but would that flame still burn three weeks from now, six months from now, five years from now. That was the reason I decided to bite my tongue and not say the words back.

Meryl seemed bored with my illogical logic and pivoted to another line of questioning. "What did he get you?" She reached for the hand cream on my bedside table, squeezing some onto her palms before working it into her hands.

I gave her a bashful smile. "A trip to the Maldives."

"I love that you're married to a man with money. You deserve it. God knows you've dated your fair share of starving artists, and starving bank tellers, and starving grave diggers."

"The tickets are for April." I pulled at my bottom lip.

Meryl squealed. "That's well after your ninety days are up. See I knew I liked him. That shows intention. Gotta love a man who isn't giving mixed signals. He loves you and wants to spend the rest of his life with you."

"When did you become all sugar plums and fairies? I'm supposed to be the one with her head in the clouds and you're supposed to be my reliable best friend who yanks my daydreamer ass back to the ground."

"Well not this time. I'm rooting for you two to win. And I like how he makes you smile. And he has a really cute friend."

"Wait, Walt?"I shook my head in disbelief.

"Yeah Walt." Meryl blushed. Her tawny cheeks taking on a rosy glow.

"You're into Walt? Like in a take off all your clothes and ravish me type of way?" *Where the hell had I been? Why was this the first I was hearing about this? Walt?* "Wait, have you seen him naked?"

"No, oh my God." Her eyes grew wide and she had trouble meeting my curious gaze.

I'd known Meryl for close to twelve years and her response was less than convincing.

"WALTER KEMP, ESQUIRE?"

"Yeah, it's bad. When he's around I laugh at his jokes entirely too loud. He's really not even that funny. Plus, you know I have a thing for a man with glasses."

All I could do was stare at my friend in complete shock. Walt was not her type. He went to larping events. This man dressed up and role played as an elven king. He'd proudly shown me his arsenal of fake melee weapons when we went over for game night. Walt was a nerd. Quincy was a member but Walt was the CEO.

Meryl usually went for guys who had tear drop tattoos. I don't even think Walt had a tattoo. But he was funny in a dad-joke kinda way. And the glasses made him look really smart. Now that I was thinking about this, Walt was always staring at her.

"I'm here for this." My eyes gleamed. "Let's make this happen. Then we could have couple's dates and ooh, couple's vacations. Team Meryl and Walt. Team Malt."

"Slow down. I don't think we should pick out couple's names just yet."

"That's fine but when we do, we're going with Malt." I insisted.

"OK Quinlyn." Meryl playfully shot back.

"Wait is that my couple's name?"

"Yep."

"I'm not mad at it," I said. Meryl and I burst into laughter.

Chapter 20

EVELYN

"You never told me your New Year's resolutions," I said, removing my strappy, high-heel shoes.

It was eleven thirty and we'd snuck out of the Townsend New Year's Eve Extravaganza early, preferring to ring in the new year alone at home.

"It would be nice to travel more. If you haven't noticed I'm a bit of a workaholic." Quincy tossed the keys into the bowl, removing his coat. "What about you?"

"I wanna run a marathon," I said, pulling him to the couch.

Quincy's eyebrows raised. "Really?"

"Yeah, something simple like a 3K and then eventually move up to something bigger. I also have so many plans for the gallery. I want a larger space. Our exhibits are always packed and the paint night events are becoming a whole business on its own. Our wait list to book an event is four-months long. If we had more space, we could accommodate larger parties and host more events."

"Well if you need me to draft some contracts or read through any agreements just let me know, boss lady." He twirled my soft curls through his fingers.

"You'd do that for me? I'm not looking for freebies. I can pay you."

"Get the fuck outta here. Just consider me in-house counsel for The Townsend Gallery. I got you whatever you need."

"Ahh thanks babe." I nuzzled my face in his neck. Quincy was always looking out for me. He was right, we were a team.

At the end of another year and the beginning of a new one I was hopeful. More so than previous years. Even though everything was still up in the air, I felt certain this new year would be my year. The gallery was taking off and inspiring me to make big moves. I had my exhibit in less than two weeks. The first in over a year. I was usually a nervous wreck right before a show but this time was different. Maybe because Quincy was an amazing hype man that gassed me up after every paint stroke.

He didn't just see my potential, he saw my genius, bragging about me at every opportunity. After his visit to the art gallery he'd Googled me, something I'd done in the bathroom during our wedding reception, and excitedly reported back to me with all he found like a proud parent. In the past I dated fellow artists and creatives and often they saw me as competition, unwilling to cheer too loudly, or brag in mixed company.

"Dance with me." Quincy extended his arm.

Slipping my hand in his, I watched as he scrolled through his phone searching for the perfect song. When the sultry baritone voice floated through the speakers, Quincy wrapped his arms around me swaying side to side in time with the music. His hand ran down the side of my bare arm before playing with the tassels on my sparkly, silver, form-fitting dress. Hooking my arms around him, I caressed the back of his neck.

I didn't need a crowded party, loud music, or an extended conversation with one of my mother's friends who marveled at how grown I was while reminiscing about the passage of time. All I needed was this man, my husband and the taste of his mouth as it pressed against mine. I wanted to start the new year with our bodies entwined. It's said kissing someone at the stroke of midnight on New Year's is good luck so I could only imagine the luck I'd receive ringing in the year while riding Quincy's dick.

"I need you." I moaned, unable to contain myself any longer. My hands were already unlatching his belt.

He released a whisper of a breath as I slipped my hand in his boxers, transforming the shape of his member in a few jerks. Quincy's hands explored my body, his palms running along my thick thighs before giving my ass a squeeze.

"Take your clothes off," he instructed.

Turning, I let him unzip my dress before shimmying it over my hips, letting it fall to my feet. His eager hands took full advantage of the fact that I wasn't wearing a bra. Rubbing my nipples with his palms until they were pert and stiff under his touch. I reached for his face plunging my tongue into his mouth. When we kissed it felt like an explosion, a mix of excitement and raw passion. I was floating ... no wait, Quincy had lifted me off the ground leading me to the couch.

Setting me down, he kneeled before me and instinctively I assumed the position, opening my legs wide ready to receive everything he had to offer. Quincy hovered over me, running his lips down the center of my body. Stopping briefly to tease my breast before heading down south. I elevated my hips so he could pull off my thong. He kissed my inner thighs, and around my wet center driving me crazy as I waited for the first lick of his tongue on my warm bud.

When he touched down I moaned loudly, wiggling my hips in an attempt to get closer. His mouth kissed and sucked every fold with reckless abandon. He lifted my backside so he could get every last drop. I shuddered as ripples from my core let the rest of my body know that orgasm had been achieved. Quincy backed away removing the rest of his clothes as he watched me try to regain my breath while laughing softly from the happy release.

Lowering himself on top of me, he kissed my neck whispering in my ear. "You are so sexy."

His member slid over my opening before entering. I held my breath adjusting to his penis making a home inside of me. His hand behind my neck, he buried his face in my mass of hair. I planted kisses on his shoulder as the sound of his moans echoed in my ear.

Digging my nails into his back, I whispered, "Deeper please."

Quincy's body froze as he processed my request. Grabbing my waist, he changed our lying position to a sitting one so now I was on top. His head rested on the couch as his eyes danced over my face as I worked my body up and down his shaft. Cupping his face, I kissed his mouth. His fingers tickled my spine causing goose bumps to cover my arms.

"Quincy, you feel so good." With a growl I asked, "Whose is it?"

"Yours," Quincy responded with no hesitation.

"You're damn right it is." I bit his lip causing him to dig his fingers into my thigh.

Sounds of fireworks could be heard in the distance. The pop, bang, and fizz were like the soundtrack to what was occurring in my body. Leaning back I rested my hands on Quincy's knees as I rocked my hips picking up speed. He grabbed hold of my waist, helping me navigate up and down.

"Just like that baby," he instructed me.

His left hand slipped between my legs, his thumb rubbing against my bud caused my body to grow rigid as a series of whirls and kabooms shot through my core like I was an illegal firework. My loud screams helped Quincy cross the finish line, his eyes fluttered closed and his fingers twitched as his grip on my waist loosened.

I collapsed onto his chest and for a long while it was just our strained breathing pattern and the reliable beats of his chest. I absentmindedly rubbed my hand over his beard. It was difficult to keep my eyes open.

"Happy New Year Mrs. Parrish."

My mouth pulled in a lazy smile. "Happy New Year, Quincy. I love you."

Chapter 21

EVELYN

The space inside the Townsend was a buzz with guests in animated conversation as they viewed the pieces on display. I headed to the bar needing a glass of wine to calm my nerves. As an artist you worked in a vacuum creating images you hoped would translate and resonate with others. Before every show there was that tiny voice inside me that doubted every brush stroke, color palette, and even where the art was hanging in the gallery. *What if they don't get my vision or question my artistic choices?* In the art world you were only as good as your last piece. It didn't matter I'd created pieces in the past that critics raved about, all that mattered was right now.

I looked around the space; it was packed with familiar faces and some new ones. But one very important face was missing, Quincy. The event started forty-five minutes ago and he wasn't here and when I called his phone it went straight to voicemail. And all though I wanted to obsess about what it all meant and why my husband was missing out on the most important night of my life, I didn't have time.

"Evelyn?" Dotty's voice snapped me out of my daze. "We have a woman asking about your Solitary piece."

Pasting on a smile I followed Dotty across the gallery. The woman's eyes lit up, eager to hear more about my art. Truthfully, I could talk about my work and the artist process ad nauseam so it was the perfect distraction to the storm that was brewing internally.

"This whole collection is about love. The stages of love. The anticipation. The excitement, the ecstasy, the joy, the fear, the isolation. This piece speaks to that last point. The feeling of being lonely even when you're not alone. The realization that your lover can't fill every gaping hole. That love is not always enough. It's not always the cure."

"What inspired this collection?"

"When I started this collection, I was navigating through a real-life relationship. Everything new and shiny. And over time the collection shows how that relationship evolves. Sometimes in beautiful ways other times in ways less so."

"So how did it turn out? Your relationship ... if you don't mind me asking." The older woman rubbed her hands together flashing me a curious eye.

"My collection ends with a happy ending. Unfortunately, the jury is still out in real life."

The woman cast her eyes to the large canvas once again. "Marvelous work my dear."

"Thank you."

Dotty returned by my side as the critic walked away. "Girl, we have a buyer for the Empathy piece."

"The Empathy piece is twelve thousand dollars," I replied incredulously.

"Yup, just swiped his Amex card two minutes ago it cleared. I'm gonna go place a sold sign on it right now to let the others know they better come out their wallets."

A sale was always music to my ears but my excitement was dampened by my concern and frustration with Quincy's absence. Walking over to Walt and Meryl I asked, "Do you know where Quincy is?"

"No, have you tried calling him?" Walt checked his watch.

"Yes, it's just going to voicemail." I was trying to play it cool but I was almost on the verge of tears.

"I'm sure he's just stuck in traffic. He'll be here Evie. He wouldn't miss this, he knows how important this is to you," Meryl said, squeezing my hand.

I pulled at my lip. "Yeah ... I'm sure you're right. He's gotta be on his way."

Quincy was always punctual. It was one of the qualities I liked the least about him. He wasn't running late. I pushed down my ugly thoughts and decided to work the room. I wasn't going to let him ruin this night for me.

A young lady reached for my hand. "I'm sorry to stop you. I'm just a huge fan of your work and I've been working up the courage to tell you that."

"Thank you so much. That's very nice of you to say."

"I just love this new collection. I'm an art major. I walk past your gallery every day on my way to campus. Sometimes I stop in and dream about buying one of your pieces someday."

"I know the pieces are kind of pricey." Leaning in I whispered, "Little secret I couldn't afford to purchase one of my pieces. Far too steep for my budget."

"I hope you don't think I'm complaining I totally get it. Artists work so hard sometimes for years honing their craft."

"How about a signed print?" I know it's not a canvas but—"

"Are you kidding me. I would die."

I laughed. "OK, well follow me."

After signing the print, I stood off to the side fidgeting with my braided ponytail. Everyone seemed to be having a good time. I liked my showings to feel relaxed, like a family gathering. There was an open bar, appetizers and old school love songs playing over the speakers.

I closed my eyes swaying as Anita Baker sang about that same ole love. Strong arms wrapped around me from behind, swaying along with me. Quincy sang softly in my ear. And just like that all my anxiety washed away as I melted into his arms. I didn't even care that he was late; I was just happy he was there now holding me.

"I'm sorry traffic was a bitch." He bit his lip.

I whirled around. "Not gonna lie I thought you were standing me up."

"Are you kidding me. I wouldn't miss your show. I just had to pick up your mom and Louis."

"What?" I performed a visual sweep of the gallery looking for my parents.

"They said they were coming and I just wanted to make sure your mom didn't back out so I offered to be Morgan Freeman. You know, like *Driving Miss Daisy*." Quincy chuckled.

I knew exactly what he meant but I was still stuck on the fact that my mother was here.

"My parents live an hour away."

"Yeah, that's why I was late. I planned ahead but sorely underestimated the traffic coming back into the city."

"I don't quite understand." My face was a question mark.

"Evelyn, wow. This is nice," my mother said, walking toward us.

"Hi Mom." I blinked owlishly not believing she was actually here.

"Are all these pieces yours?" My mother pointed to a medium-sized piece of a couple kissing.

"Yes." I wrung my hands bracing myself for hurtful words.

"I like this. It's very nice."

My breath was harried in my throat. "Thank you."

"This whole thing is very nice you should be very proud. I'm … proud … of you."

My mother's words were reserved. She hated admitting she was wrong and I understood it took a lot for her to say what she did. For me it was all I needed. I'd waited thirty-three years to hear my mother say she was proud of me. The tears came quickly falling from my face faster than I could brush them away.

"Don't you start with that. You'll ruin your makeup," my mother said.

Throwing my arms around her, I squeezed her into a tight hug. I couldn't remember the last time we genuinely hugged other than forced pleasantries on the holidays. My mother's response wasn't exactly what I was hoping for, her body was rigid and her hands clenched. She gave my back a quick pat before pushing me away.

Clearing my throat, I felt a little silly, getting all emotional. "Excuse me."

As I moved through the space, I forced a smile at the guests who looked in my direction as I passed. In the small storage room, I was able to drop the facade. This event already had me on pins and needles but my mother's presence made everything more stifling.

There was a light rap on the door. "Evelyn, can I come in?" Quincy's voice called from the other side.

Opening the door, I pulled him inside. The space was too small for the camera crew.

"Are you OK?" he asked.

"Yes."

"Did I fuck up bringing your mom here?"

"No, you are perfect. Doing this for me. It was perfect. I always wanted my mom to see my art. To see what I do and why I love it and now because of you she has. She said she was proud of me. I don't know if she actually meant it and I don't even care. Because she said it and she can't take it back."

"I think she meant it. When I took her to the Art Institute to check out your piece she was impressed. I think she's just embarrassed that it took her this long."

"Wait, hold up. You told her about my piece at the museum?"

"Yeah, at Thanksgiving. A few weeks later she called and asked if I could take her so she could see for herself."

"And you did that for her?'

"I did it for you." He brushed my cheek with his thumb.

My lips descended on to his. I wanted to kiss him fifteen minutes ago when his arms encased me and relief washed through my body. He pulled me against him, our lips clinging to each other with a sense of urgency.

There was a knock on the door. "Evie, we have another buyer. He wants to meet you."

"Just a minute," I called back before dropping my voice to a whisper. "Thank you, baby."

"No big deal. I love you. I'd do anything for you." Quincy swallowed hard.

Our eyes locked. I kissed him again hoping that kiss conveyed everything I was too frightened to say.

QUINCY

DOTTY, Walt, and Meryl helped to clean the space at the end of the night. Walking around, we picked up plastic cups and stray plates while Dotty gave the floor a quick pass with the broom.

Walt tossed a stack of plates into the trash bag I was holding. "So you've thrown your hat into the ring for husband of the year?"

"Why do you say that?"

"Bringing Evelyn's mom. You told me her mom has never come to one of these things."

I jerked my shoulders into a shrug. "I just wanted to make her night special."

"Because you love her."

"Could you shut up." I scanned around to make sure no

one was in ear shot. "It's not even like that." Of course I cared deeply about Evelyn. But I wasn't interested in professing my love from the mountain top just yet. If we weren't on the same page if things didn't work out it would be much easier to move on without everyone feeling sorry for me because my love was unrequited.

"Like what? You going out of your way to make your wife happy. No shame in that."

"You're being ridiculous."

"You guys have less than a week left before you have to decide your fate. Have you two talked about it at all?"

"Not in so many words, no." I'm sure Walt must have thought I was a fool.

"Don't you want to make sure you're both in sync regarding your future?"

"I'm not worried about that. We want the same things."

"Which is?"

"You're nosy as hell." I eyed him suspiciously.

I hadn't brought up decision day because the last thing I wanted to hear was doubt in Evelyn's voice. Doubts about me, doubts about our future. You know the saying ignorance is bliss, well that was how I was choosing to exist, in blissful ignorance. I was fairly confident she wanted to stay together but there was always the possibility that wasn't the case.

"I think it's just the lawyer in me. I'm naturally curious."

"Well you'll just have to sit back and wait to find out what happens like everyone else." I patted Walt on the back.

"You and me both apparently." Walt shook his head.

Dotty was the last of the clean-up crew to leave. Evelyn

locked the door behind Dotty releasing a satisfied sigh. "Do you want some wine? We have a whole case left."

"Sure." I walked around the space observing all the sold signs. "This was a good night. How much do you think you earned?"

Evelyn took a swig from a half empty bottle of cabernet before handing it to me. "Eighty-seven thousand and some change."

I choked on the wine as it tumbled down my throat. "You're shitting me, right?"

Evelyn laughed. "It sounds like a lot but after overhead it's far more conservative."

"Still impressive." The wheels in my head were working overtime. If she had an appetite for it, she could make serious dough from prints and branded merchandise. I decided to put a pin in that conversation for now. I could broach it at a later date. Tonight, was all about Evelyn. "You worked hella hard and you deserve all the accolades."

Pulling out my phone, I connected to the wireless speakers. Scrolling through my playlist, I selected a classic, Shalamar's "A Night to Remember." It didn't matter that the *Why Knot* crew was still filming or that in four days we would have to decide whether or not to stay together. Evelyn and I danced around the gallery with reckless abandon singing to one another at the top of our lungs.

THE NEXT FOUR days went by fast, too fast. Tonight, was the last night of the *Why Knot* experience. In the morning we would head to a staged hotel to make our final decision.

That was part of the reason I wanted to keep busy for most of the day. In the morning Evelyn accompanied me to the youth community center where I volunteered. The kids got a kick out of her and peppered me with questions regarding my mystery wife. For lunch we met up with Naomi. When we said our goodbyes, Naomi made a point to tell us she expected to see us both at church that Sunday. I took it as her not so subtle warning telling me not to fuck tomorrow up.

Now back at home we were prepping dinner for a chill night. Both of us avoiding the elephant that was following us around the room. You'd think tonight was just any other Thursday night, but the air felt weighted and thick making it difficult to breathe.

Evelyn came padding out of the bedroom in pajamas and fuzzy slippers. "How can I help?"she asked, rolling up the sleeves of her striped pajama top.

"You could cut the onion and peppers. That would be great."

"We need music. My phone's in the bedroom can we use yours?" she asked.

"Yeah, just pick what you want." I pointed with my elbow.

My hands were covered in seasoning. Evelyn located my phone on the kitchen counter and picked a mellow playlist. The sounds of Sade played over the speakers. Washing her hands, Evelyn grabbed a knife and got to work. These were the moments I appreciated the most. The silent moments when it was just her and me and the crew tucked away in the corner pretending to blend into the Van Courtland blue painted wall. OK, I didn't like that part, but being able to just be in the stillness with Evelyn was something I'd always enjoy.

She was comfortable like my favorite hoodie that kept me snug and warm. Evelyn was chicken pot pie, familiar and cozy like the casserole dish. And I looked forward to diving into her savory goodness every single time. In one day, we would be able to have endless nights just like this one. It's crazy how someone I didn't know three months ago now had a vise grip on my heart. I would walk over hot coals for this woman. If she needed a kidney or a liver I would willingly step up and offer up mine.

Life is a series of choices and I couldn't help but wonder how different my life would be if I hadn't tagged along with AJ to the *Why Knot* casting call. I'd probably be in my kitchen cooking for one, completely oblivious to what life could be. The thought that I could have never found Evelyn sent a shiver down my spine.

"Onions and peppers are chopped." She wrapped her hands around me rubbing my chest before slowly moving her hand downward.

"Evelyn, let's not start something we can't finish." I breathed out as her hand rubbed over me.

"I can finish it."

"Are you not hungry 'cause if you keep pulling shit like this we'll never eat." We literally had sex less than two hours ago. But Evelyn was always ready and willing to go another round. I planned to step in the ring with her again before the night was over but I needed to eat and hydrate first.

Evelyn dropped her hand. "I'll be good, promise." She walked away opening the wine fridge to locate a bottle to accompany tonight's meal. "Are you nervous about tomorrow?"

"No." I added the meat to the hot grill pan.

Pouring us generous glasses of wine Evelyn asked again, "Not even a little bit?"

"No. Why, are you nervous?" I hoped my tone was giving of a nonchalant and not angstful vibe.

She hitched her shoulder upward.

We were under explicit instructions not to discuss or share our final decision with one another. It was a stupid rule because it couldn't be enforced, the crew had to go home at some point. Despite that fact, Evelyn and I had not spent much time discussing this topic. My goal was always to focus on getting to know my wife, not obsessing over whether we would be together in the end. And as the weeks rolled into months, I felt secure in the ultimate outcome.

"Do we really want to spend our last night together talking about this?"

Evelyn's eyes grew wide. "Last night?"

"You know what I mean." The expression on her face told me she didn't know what I meant.

Flipping the meat, I walked to where she stood and placed a hand on her shoulder. "Don't get into your head. We're good. It's all good."

"No ... yeah ... I know. Totally good." Her tone was unconvincing but I didn't want to talk about it any longer so I let it slide.

After dinner and the exit of the *Why Knot* crew. I made good on my promise. With Evelyn's legs wrapped around my waist I buried my face in her chest as she rocked her hips over mine. All that could be heard was the wind blowing outside and the sounds of our panting breath as we worked desperately to please one another. If this woman thought I was leaving her ... this, she was crazy.

My hands massaged her back before landing on her backside, gripping hard I helped her navigate my length. I pulled her close so I was completely hidden inside her love before releasing her to ride me again. With our limbs entangled goosebumps pricked my skin when her erect nipples brushed against my bare chest. I kissed her mouth, before smiling against her lips.

The fact that she had any doubt that I wanted this forever ... that I wanted her forever, was befuddling. This ... her, was all I ever wanted for the rest of my life.

Chapter 22

EVELYN

Lying in bed, I stared up at the wall. Quincy was sound asleep, the ability to sleep anywhere and anytime was his superpower. We could argue and five minutes later he was passed out, while I would remain up all night analyzing our conversation and coming up with counterpoints or better comeback lines. In mere hours we were going to make the most important decision of our lives and Quincy lay next to me completely unbothered.

"Quincy?" I whispered. "Quincy," I repeated a little louder.

"No, it's not hot," he moaned before falling back to sleep.

Exhaling a loud breath, I pulled back the covers, maybe a cup of tea would help. In the kitchen, I added water to the electric kettle and pressing the button waited for it to boil. I was confident I knew what Quincy was going to say today. Of course, he'd want to stay together, why wouldn't he? The past ninety days had gone better than either of us could have ever planned. In spite of all that there was still a sliver of doubt nagging at me and that sliver was keeping me from a restful night's sleep.

As the kettle rolled to a boil, Quincy's phone pinged. It was still on the counter from earlier. Unlike me his phone wasn't attached to his hip. Grabbing a tea cup, I dropped in a tea bag and poured two spoonfuls of sugar into the bottom before adding the hot water. Quincy's phone pinged again. Looking toward the bedroom, I decided to check his phone just to make sure it wasn't an emergency.

Leaning in, I could see a text from Victoria that read:

We need to talk.

Why is Victoria texting Quincy at three in the morning? And what did she think they needed to talk about? Walking back to my cup, I bounced the tea bag up and down in the water. This wasn't my business; I trusted Quincy and he'd never given me cause to question his loyalty. The phone pinged again. I reached for the phone flipping it over. I was gonna drink my tea and go back to bed. Totes McGoats came trotting out of the bedroom pausing to give his body a stretch.

"Can't sleep huh? I know the feeling." I scooped the dog into my arms rubbing his head.

"Totes, why is Victoria texting Quincy?" I waited for a response but since Totes was a dog none came. "OK so question and whatever you say I'ma ride with." I looked at Totes in his big round eyes. "Should I check Quincy's phone?"

Totes let out a big yawn but technically that wasn't a response. I retrieved a treat from the jar, and fed it to him before putting Totes back on the ground. Rounding the counter, I picked up his phone and went to the message app. Why this grown ass man didn't have his phone locked was beyond me. Locating the message thread between him and Victoria, I scrolled.

Today:

Victoria: Are you still up?

Victoria: We need to talk.

Victoria: Please call me first thing in the morning.

January 12

Victoria: Are you gonna stay with her? I tell you I still love you and nothing?

Quincy: I'm married now. I need to see this through. I don't know what you want from me.

Victoria: I want what I've always wanted. To be with you.

Quincy: V, I … Maybe in a few days things will be different.

December 29

Victoria: I still love you, Quincy.

Quincy: I don't really know what you want me to say.

Victoria: So, you don't love me?

Quincy: I'm not saying that. I'll always have love for you.

Victoria: Then you know what you need to do.

Quincy: What is that supposed to mean?

Victoria: You can't stay with her if you're in love with someone else.

Quincy: I don't think we should talk any more.

Victoria: Because of some woman you barely know?

December 25

Victoria: Merry Christmas

Victoria: If I upset you at AJ's party, I'm sorry.

Quincy: Thanks, Merry X-mas. Tell your family I said hello.

December 14

Victoria: I called you. But it went to VM. I was hoping we could talk.

Victoria: Quincy, you know I hate it when you give me the silent treatment. Hit me back.

December 10

Victoria: All this snow we've been getting reminded me of our trip to that cozy cabin. Do you remember when we got snowed in and made love all weekend?

Quincy: What I remember from that trip was you berating me the entire drive back.

Victoria: We had fun.

Quincy: You had fun.

Victoria: Quin you're so dramatic.

December 7

Victoria: How about Christmas Cocktails my treat? We can go to Fetter. I know you love that place.

November 20

Victoria: I know this is completely random but do you remember that one Thanksgiving when my father fell down the stairs and you laughed?

Quincy: I apologized for laughing but it was funny and awkward at the same time.

Victoria: He was sixty he could have broken a hip.

Quincy: I laugh when I'm uncomfortable. You know that better than anyone.

Victoria: I do know you better than anyone. So, are you having Thanksgiving with Naomi?

Quincy: Nope, headed to Evelyn's parents' house.

Victoria: Well hopefully no one falls. Maybe we could meet up for drinks later over the long weekend?

November 8

Victoria: We should meet for happy hour this week.

Quincy: Can't swamped maybe some other time.

November 1

Victoria: Thanks for the Halloween party invite.

Quincy: I didn't invite you but you're welcome.

I wilted onto the floor my shoulders slumping as my chest caved in. Shutting my eyes I could feel the tears pushing against my eyelids. As the first tear escaped I glanced back at Quincy's phone which I still held tightly in my hand. The constant tears impaired my vision. *Why is he texting his ex?*

Dropping the phone, I shoved my face into my knees hoping to muffle the sound of my sobs. I swallowed around the throbbing in my heart. *Was this all just a lie? Why would he say he loved me but continue to entertain his ex?* As I sat balled up on the floor my body grew cold and a heaviness weighed my core.

If he was uncertain or if he'd realized he still loved Victoria he should have told me. But to lie like this for months. We hadn't even been married three weeks before he started talking to his ex again. He never even really tried; he just gave into Victoria because she was safe and familiar. *Think Evelyn, think.* He told me he loved me. He said those words unprompted. But who was I kidding? It wouldn't be the first time a man professed his love and then his actions were the antithesis of the word.

If he wasn't all in then why the plane tickets for April? That wasn't something someone would do if they were planning to file for divorce. It seemed sincere. But this man's a lawyer and they lie for a living. Maybe the tickets were a way for him to say he made an effort even if that wasn't his intent. It's not difficult switching out tickets. Replace my name for Victoria's and you have a nice lover's getaway to solidify their second chance at love.

Quincy was always concerned about controlling the narrative and how we were represented on the show. I thought that was for the cameras but now I had to ask was he also playing a role for me? Pretending to feel a certain way so in the end he wouldn't be villainized and criticized all over social media. If people believed he was trying they couldn't fault him if he decided this relationship wasn't what he wanted.

I was ready to go in there and wake him from his precious sleep giving him every last bit of my wrath. My tears of grief were transforming into white, hot rage. Jumping from the floor, I headed for the bedroom ready to watch him stammer and sweat as he tried to talk his way out of this. But something in my gut stopped me in my tracks. I was too impulsive and I hadn't even fully processed what I'd read.

What if there was a perfectly sane explanation. If I went in there, guns a blazing I could do more damage than I intended. Treading backward, I returned his phone to the kitchen counter where I'd found it. If this was all just a ruse then Quincy deserved a Tony award for best live performance. My thoughts were taken back to his words on our honeymoon ... *I did this as a joke.* He was never serious about the show, the marriage, or me.

$$\sim$$

QUINCY

I ROLLED over looking to pull Evelyn close but when my hand swiped her side of the bed she wasn't there.

"Evelyn?" I called out, looking at the clock.

It was seven in the morning and she wasn't an early riser. Today was Friday, decision day and I'd hoped to wake Evelyn up in the nicest possible way with my head between her thighs.

"Evelyn, babe come back to bed." When there was no response, I rolled out of bed checking the bathroom before heading to the living room.

The space was empty. I checked the other two bedrooms and the backyard, no Evelyn. My phone rang and I rushed to get to it before it stopped ringing. The display read Victoria. *What the fuck does she want?* I let her call ring through to voicemail before calling Evelyn. Her line rang and a ringing sound could be heard from the bedroom. Heading back to the master bedroom I found her phone vibrating still on the charger.

Now I was worried. Scrambling, I changed into some sweatpants and a hoodie before lacing up my sneakers. I scooped up my car keys and headed toward the door, stopping at the sound of keys jingling on the other side. Evelyn opened the door in her painter's overalls, no coat, no purse.

"Where were you?" I asked.

"I went to paint," she said at me.

I pulled her inside, closing the door behind her. "Babe you're freezing. You went to the studio in the middle of the night alone? Evie, I told you if you wake up and feel the urge to paint in the middle of the night I'll go with you."

"I wanted to be alone. I needed to think." Her responses were clipped and her tone was laced with agitation.

I wasn't trying to smother her but I just wanted her to know her safety was paramount to me. "It's not safe to be out at night alone. Don't ever do that again. You scared the crap out of me." I tossed my keys back into the bowl and pulled her deeper inside. "I'll make us some coffee."

"Quincy?" Her voice was raspy.

"Hmm." I looked up from the Keurig, examining her face. She looked exhausted. She should have snuck in a few hours of sleep in between all that creative inspiration because now she would be sluggish for the rest of the day. The majority of which would be spent filming the final episode of *Why Knot*.

"Last night I—"

The doorbell rang interrupting her. Glancing at the microwave clock, I tossed my head back, letting out an aggravated groan. That must be the *Why Knot* crew; I'd hoped they'd be late but as usual they were right on time. I reminded myself today would be the last day I had to have cameras follow me around, or duck my head when the boom mic got too close. In ten hours, our time on *Why Knot* would be over and we could go about living a normal life.

The thought of having Evelyn all to myself excited me. I'd tried hard to ignore the cameras these past few months but it was easier said than done. And the presence of the crew made me bite my tongue when I wanted to speak, shove my hands in my pockets when I wanted to touch her, and walk away when all I wanted was to be closer to her.

Evelyn didn't move at the sound of the bell; she just stood there her face sagged and her eyes were red. On the way to the door I bent, kissing her forehead. "We got this baby. In a few hours this will all be over."

Opening the front door, I stepped aside as the *Why Knot* team came inside with their cases and bags, wasting no time putting up lights and moving furniture.

"Good morning, big day. Are you ready?" Jared, our handler was always a bundle of energy but today he was dialed all the way to a fifteen.

"Morning," I muttered.

Jared had been there since the beginning, for the awkward silences, the fights, and the unquenchable touching. I would miss Jared's twisted smile the least, always telling us what to do and where to go. Asking us to reenact conversations even though none of this was scripted. In our private confessionals he would prod us to say or react in ways that would benefit the show and some unknown storyline they were attempting to create.

"Where's Evelyn I wanted to go over the itinerary for the day?" Jared flipped through sheets of notes.

Where's Evelyn seemed to be the question of the day. I treaded to the bedroom and found her in the closet shuffling through her wardrobe.

Jared brushed past me, his sing-songy voice grating my nerves. "Evelyn darling, good morning." When Evelyn turned to face him, Jared cringed. "Rough night?"

It was a fair assessment, Evelyn, who was usually vivacious and animated, appeared sullen. I knew she could be grouchy when she hadn't gotten enough sleep but this seemed different. When I looked at her she deliberately avoided meeting my eyes. I chalked it up to nerves; she was probably just as anxious as I was for this to all be behind us.

The removal of the cameras would require us to pivot once more, learning how to navigate life on our own terms. Even though I felt comfortable about where we stood and believed we were on the same page regarding how to move forward, there was still a small part of me that had doubts. I loved Evelyn. This I knew for a fact, but when the cameras were gone would our marriage survive? *Would she change? Would I ultimately ruin this relationship like I had all the others?*

"OK I don't wanna keep you because I know you two need to get ready but here's the plan for the day." Jared pulled out his notes referring to them. "We'll leave in under two hours by car. When we get to the hotel you will be separated and your phones confiscated until after filming. You'll be brought back together with the experts present for your final decisions. Evelyn will go first ... yay or nay after which Quincy will follow. After the taping you will come back home together or choose to leave separately depending on the outcome." Jared looked at both our faces, ensuring comprehension.

"Got it. So can we get ready now?" I asked, shooing the crew out of our bedroom. It was obvious Evelyn needed some space to breathe.

"Yes, you have one hour and fifty-two minutes," Jared said, before I closed the door.

With the crew gone, I pulled Evelyn into my arms, kissing her. Evelyn didn't respond. Her body didn't melt into mine as her hands rubbed the back of my neck, she didn't smile against my mouth or release a satisfied moan.

"Are you OK?" I asked, searching her face.

"I guess I'm just tired." She looked up at me. Her eyes appeared clouded and sad.

I smiled hoping to cheer her up. "I forgot to tell you Walt wants to get together tomorrow evening for celebratory drinks. He said he already talked to Meryl and she's down."

"Yeah ... maybe. I don't know." She pushed her hair from her face.

Not the enthusiastic response I was hoping for but I'd have to take it. Maybe after a shower and some coffee her mood would improve. My phone dinged in my pocket, retrieving it I tapped on the screen smiling.

"Who is it?" Evelyn asked.

"It's Naomi, wishing us luck." I turned the phone so she could see the funny picture Naomi had attached.

Evelyn appeared relieved.

Glancing at the time I said, "Do you wanna jump in the shower together?"

"Like I said I'm tired."

"I didn't mean sex." I did but at this point I would take just being close to her. "Just trying to conserve water and make up some lost time."

Evelyn shrugged, shedding clothes as she made her way to the bathroom. With a bright, orange shower cap with a bow on her head she stepped into the shower where I was waiting. I moved to the back so she was facing the hot shower heads. Squeezing some body wash onto her wash cloth, she worked it into a lather before running the soapy cloth over her body. Reaching for the cloth, I soaped up her back.

Wrapping my arms around her, I whispered in her ear, "I love you, Evelyn."

Her body twitched before she whirled around. "Say it again," she whispered.

Cupping her face, I repeated myself. "I love you."

She looked surprised by my words. *What was up with her?* If hearing me say I loved her was shocking, clearly I was doing a poor job of showing it. I made a mental note to be better at that. I didn't want there to be any doubt about how much she meant to me. Evelyn wrapped her arms around me holding me tight; she didn't speak a word and for some reason her embrace felt different. It felt less like excitement for our future and more like grieving the loss of something unknown. I shook the thought from my head. We were fine, it was all gonna be fine.

CHAPTER 23

———

QUINCY

In the car on the way to Loews Hotel in downtown Chicago, I fidgeted with my tie. After our shower Evelyn remained tight-lipped only offering one-word responses to my questions. It was like an episode of *Freaky Friday* in which our bodies had been switched and my mouth was now running one hundred miles per minute while she listened thoughtfully.

Currently I was droning on about my suit choice. Back at the house I'd asked her to help me choose between the navy suit or the gray suit, but Evelyn, preoccupied applying her eyeliner, only offering a non-directive grunt. I'd gone with the gray and was now having second thoughts.

"What if I spill something on myself ... then what? Damnit the navy was the safer choice."

Evelyn's gaze was fixated outside the window as we exited the off ramp and cruised down the city streets.

In an attempt to remove the cloud looming over her

head, I blurted out a joke. "Hopefully our marriage gets renewed for another season." I chuckled.

Evelyn's eyes slammed into mine her gaze humorless.

"It was a joke. *Renewed* for another *season*." I hoped saying the punchline again would illicit a smile. "Because we're on a reality show."

Rolling her eyes, she turned away. No pity laugh. No beard tug. No sarcastic comeback. Just annoyance. *Wait, was she mad at me?*

I reached for her hand but she flinched, pulling it away. "Evelyn, what's going on?"

"Nothing."

"You've been weird all morning."

"I told you I'm tired." Her response was clipped and dry while at the same time filled with emotion.

Claiming her chin I said, "Hey, look at me."

When her eyes met mine they were filled with tears.

"Baby, what's wrong?"

Evelyn's lips trembled and as the first tear fell, she asked, "Why have you been texting your ex this entire time?"

"What?" I blinked rapidly.

The car door opened and Jared was pulling Evelyn from the vehicle. "Chop chop. Busy day. Evelyn, honey you're with me."

"No wait." I attempted to exit the car but because I was still latched the seat belt reeled me back in. Releasing myself I exited the car yelling, "Evelyn!"

It was too late Evelyn was surrounded by the *Why Knot* crew who were whisking her into the hotel and away from me.

"I need to talk to my wife." I pointed in the direction Evelyn had just disappeared.

"You can talk to her at decision time." An unfamiliar male told me.

"No, I can't wait until then. This is important."

It felt like I was being kidnapped as the crew huddled around me corralling me through the revolving doors before leading me to a private room. When I thought the coast was clear, I opened the door but was greeted by security and a smattering of crew milling about just outside. Shutting the door, I reached for my phone. If I couldn't go to her, I'd just call her instead.

The line rang for what felt like an eternity before she finally picked up. "Evelyn, babe—"

"Sorry Evelyn can't come to the phone right now," Jared's voice answered.

"Where's my wife?" I could feel heat creeping up my neck slowly invading my cheeks. I was about to lose my shit and make this the most memorable season of *Why Knot* ever.

"Oh sorry Quincy we took her phone. I'm surprised they haven't taken yours yet. It's part of decision day."

"Is Evelyn in the room with you? Evelyn! Evie!" I shouted hoping she would be able to hear me.

"You have a few hours until we start filming. You can talk to her then." The line disconnected and I stared at my phone in disbelief.

My mind was racing and it felt like I was running on fumes. I'd only had a few spoonfuls of oatmeal this morning. *What did Evelyn ask me in the car? About text messages from Victoria. Had she gone through my phone?* Swiping my screen

I went to the messages, pulling the thread from Victoria up. She'd texted me last night asking me to call her. *Did Evelyn see this message?*

I scrolled further down, reviewing my back and forth with my ex. There was nothing incriminating there. Yes, Victoria said she still loved me but I never once claimed to feel the same way. This couldn't be what had Evelyn all worked up. She had to know that I was all in. I'd bought tickets to the Maldives for crying out loud. Would I do that if I was planning on leaving her?

I slid the phone into my jacket pocket as the door to my holding cell opened and an intern popped in. "I'm gonna need your phone," the intern said, hand extended.

"Ahh ... I already gave it to the other girl." I lied.

"OK, cool." The young intern left asking no further questions. When the door was secure and the footsteps receded, I made my way to the small bathroom, locking myself in.

Scrolling to Walt's number I waited. "Come on pick up, pick up."

"This is Walter Kemp."

I looked at the phone screen, I'd dialed Walt's office number which would explain why he was being so formal. "Walt it's me. I think Evelyn read my text messages with Victoria."

"The text messages that I told you to delete?"

"Yes." I worked my jaw in a circle, I didn't need to be scolded right now.

"Are you sure?"

"She asked me why we were texting one another?"

"That's a good fucking question."

"Walt, it's decision day and I'm in some tiny ass room. They separated us. And Evelyn's mad and she's probably gonna dump me. And then I'm gonna lose the best thing that ever happened to me."

"Slow down," Walt cautioned.

My heart was beating so hard I wondered how it remained in my chest. I needed to sit, sliding down the wall I sat on the cold tile floor.

"What am I going to do?"

"Go find her and explain."

"They're not letting me out of this room. We were separated so the show can ramp up their bullshit decision day drama."

"OK ..." There was a long pause on the other end. "Delete the texts."

"I can't delete the text. If I delete the text now it'll make me look guilty like I'm tampering with evidence. Plus, there's nothing to hide. I wasn't sexting with Victoria. I wasn't making promises. I never said anything inappropriate about Evelyn, or our marriage." I shook a balled fist in the air. "This is so fucked up."

"She has a right to be mad. Evelyn just found out her husband is texting another woman."

"OK, technically. But I never initiated a single conversation."

"And you didn't discourage a single conversation either. And I think you need to ask yourself why."

I knew why, even though Victoria was horrible, at one point she loved me. I could literally count the people who loved me on one hand and I wouldn't even run out of fingers. It was hard to let that go even when the love and care was lacking, self-serving, and conditional.

"I can't lose Evelyn, Walt. I can't lose her." I clasped my hands against my face. "Oh God I think I'm gonna throw up."

"I know this is probably bad timing but you should really lock your phone."

"I don't have anything to hide. If Evelyn wants to check my emails, voice messages, photos, the fucking sudoku app she can."

"If you found messages on her phone, how would you feel?"

"That's not the fucking same," I objected.

"It's the exact fucking same."

"I'd be upset but I'd at least give her the benefit of the doubt."

She'd been weird all morning; the fact that she didn't say anything was pissing me off. Did she trust me so little that she would just automatically assume the worse. If she just talked to me when she came across the messages I could've explained and I wouldn't be sitting on the floor of this bathroom with my stomach in knots.

I huffed out a wisp of air. "Now that I'm thinking about it, why was she even going through my phone? Has she been spying on me this entire time, checking who I called and which pictures I like on social media? If anyone should be mad it's me."

"Whatever you do. Don't say any of that to her."

I was spiraling. How exactly was I going to explain myself? I was tempted to flush my phone down the drain. As if that would fix the problem. Yes, the text messages were ... sketchy. When Victoria texted saying she loved me I didn't take it seriously because this was typical Victoria. She only wanted me when she couldn't have me. When I was single and available it was crickets.

During our breakup her last words were a gleeful announcement that I was damaged and would spend the rest of my life alone. I'd been searching for love and acceptance my entire life. By the time things turned dark with Victoria I was way too invested. Although I walked away several times I never stayed away for long, because I was too scared to open myself up to someone new.

After I finally ended things for good, I started going to therapy and sorting through the issues from my past that were impeding me in the present. Rationally, I knew I deserved a shot at happiness like everyone else but it was still hard to accept. A big part of me still believed that I deserved the facsimile of love Victoria had to offer.

"Quincy, did you hear me?" Walt's voice pulled me from my thoughts.

"What?"

"I said there's nothing you can do until you see her. No use stressing yourself out."

Even though Walt couldn't see me I nodded in agreement. "I guess you're right."

I'd wait because frankly, short of faking a heart attack, I didn't really have any options. For a guy who thrived on being in control, the fact that my fate was in jeopardy was unsettling.

~

EVELYN

"Excuse me. How much longer?" I asked, pacing the floor in the small space I was being housed in.

"We should start filming in about forty minutes," Jared answered before leaving the room.

The nervous butterflies in my stomach threatened to spill from my mouth. *Why did I say anything in the car?* Quincy's face was one of genuine confusion when I asked about the text messages. The entire ride to the hotel I was just trying not to lose my shit or ruin my makeup. Part of me desperately wanted to talk to him and the other part of me was petrified that if we talked it would end with my heart being shredded into a million tiny pieces.

In true Evelyn Townsend fashion, I'd blurted out the accusation with no consideration of the time or place. But in my defense, was there ever an appropriate time or place to confront your husband about his continued relationship with an ex? Victoria told him she still loved him and if he didn't feel the same, he should have shut that shit down.

When I wasn't thinking about the text messages, I was obsessing about the optics. I guess Quincy's reticent nature had rubbed off on me because I genuinely worried how this would be viewed once the show aired. At least in the past all my rash decisions were only witnessed by a handful of people. But this, this would be seen by millions and I could already anticipate the social media chatter. *"How could she be so naive. It was so obvious he wasn't into her. He was just using her for sex. No wonder she's single, she's such a delusional mess."*

And then there was my mother who would throw this

shit in my face for the rest of my life. Shereè Townsend would be on her deathbed and her dying words to me wouldn't be "I love you." It would be "I told you it would never work with Quincy. What did I tell you would happen? And what happened? But you thought you were so grown. Thought you knew better than your mother. I tried to tell you Momma always knows best." After my mother strained to say all that, with tubes in her nose and hooked up to all kinds of machines that beeped and chimed, she would end with, "Erica was my favorite," before breathing her last, labored breath.

It started with the dry heaves, followed by sweat that slid down my back and pooled under my arms. I wiped at my face, smudging my poorly applied makeup. As I headed toward the small bathroom in search of tissue, I bumped into the wall which caused tears to fall from my eyes. The crying wasn't because of the initial pain in my shoulder and arm that was now dulling; it was because everything was all messed up. After falling for months, the visage of the ground below was coming into focus and I knew I wasn't going to be able to dust myself off and walk away from this one.

"Knock knock," Jared said, letting himself in. When he caught sight of me his green eyes grew as big as saucers. "Sweetie, you look a mess. A sweaty, snot nosed mess."

Jared's words made me cry harder.

"Thank God we packed a change of clothes because you cannot go out looking like that. Are you sick? Are you coming down with something?"

"I'm just really nervous."

Jared tsked, glancing toward the door. "Sweetie, you have nothing to worry about. Quincy is so in love with you.

Now some of these other couples should probably worry." He wrinkled his nose. "Please don't repeat that. If you say you heard that shit from me I will deny it." He walked away calling for hair and makeup over the radio.

I took a bit of solace in Jared's words. So, it wasn't just me. The mutual attraction wasn't just all in my head. When I was next to Quincy my body gravitated to his. It was like being sucked into a black hole in which nothing and no one else mattered. In the shower this morning he kissed me but I was too dumbstruck to appreciate it. Fresh tears coasted down my face at the realization that that could be the last kiss we ever shared.

I was between a rock and a hard place. If I chose to stay with him, I'd be a dumb bitch. But leaving him also felt wrong. It couldn't all be a lie, not the way he looked at me. Or the way his breath hitched right before we kissed. This man had shaved my legs and painted my toes with loving adoration. But he'd also carried on texting his ex-girlfriend for the duration of our short marriage. How do I reconcile that? Was Quincy a good lover or just a good liar?

CHAPTER 24

QUINCY

It was like a scene out of a prison movie. Me flanked by *Why Knot* security on the way to my execution. My legs weighted and sluggish with the anticipation of impending doom. Dead husband walking. The last few hours had seen me go from confusion, to apprehension, to anger and back again. But now I'd found a comfortable place to hold all these complicated feelings ... righteous indignation. Evelyn jumped to conclusions like a world class Olympic hurdler. She was always talking about the importance of communication but it would appear she was a hypocrite. Because when communication was most needed, she dropped the ball.

Mind you I didn't plan to say any of that shit to her. Because at the end of the day my actions or lack thereof had brought us to this point. And while I wanted to point fingers at Victoria, Evelyn, and the *Why Knot* production team I was ultimately to blame. Should I have shut down the communication with Victoria months ago? Yes. Could I have said something to Victoria so she knew beyond a shadow of a doubt a reconciliation between us wasn't in the cards? Yes. Even if things didn't work out with Evelyn, Victoria wasn't my rebound. We ended for a reason and most of it was based on the realization we were bad together and didn't know how to make one another happy.

Now Evelyn was a different story. She made me happy, I was walking around the city smiling at strangers. Singing love songs under my breath. When her name flashed across my phone my heart skipped a beat. My heart ... skipped a fucking beat. Because her calling meant she was thinking about me which made me feel better about the fact that I was always thinking about her.

Evelyn Townsend was the real deal and she made me look at love in a new way. It was like I'd been playing the same video game for years only to recently discover there's a whole side mission with its own levels and adventures and items to collect. Evelyn, was that new mission. She changed the game for me. That. Her. This. I didn't want to lose it.

After waiting another fifteen minutes in the hallway while the production assistant whispered to someone on the other end of his ear piece, I was ushered into a room where everyone including Evelyn were waiting. When I saw her my face instinctively lit up. And I could see a whisper of a smile in her countenance. The corners of her lips curled upward slightly and her big brown eyes shined bright. It was only for a second because she quickly caught herself locking her face into stone so I couldn't access her emotions.

This was not how I'd pictured decision day going. I

thought we would be relaxed and jovial as we recapped the past three months and solidified our relationship. Unbuttoning my suit jacket, I took a seat next to her on the couch. My chest was no longer puffed out; the lights and cameras had the effect they always did on me, causing me to retreat into my shell.

I wasn't willing to cause a scene. And I didn't want to be used for ratings fodder. When I was picked to appear on the show I went online and watched a few episodes. One season stood out the most; it involved a Black couple who by the end of the process the show had turned into caricatures. The wife was the stereotypical angry Black woman and the husband was an oversexed lothario who couldn't keep it in his pants. That season was full of red flags and if I hadn't already signed the contract it would've caused me to back out.

I'd always thought people who went on reality shows and then complained about production making them into the villain were full of shit. They can't portray you as the bad guy if you're not providing them with bad-guy material, I'd thought. But now I knew better. These shows often weaved conflict where there was none. A ten-minute argument could be edited in such a way so the viewers would wonder if the couple would even make it to the ninety-day mark. So if I had to sit on this couch and wait my turn to speak then that is what I would do.

"Quincy and Evelyn, it's so good to see you both again," Dr. Heather started. "I know the past ninety days have been filled with so much transition but you made it."

Dr. Heather and the three other experts Dr. Jackie Bhatt, a sex and relationship therapist, Pastor Chance Richards, a religious and marriage counselor, and Dr. Shawn Ward, who was a compatibility expert, all wore bright smiles. It was decision day, the cameras were rolling and they were being paid by the show to recap the past three months and build up the anticipation for the viewers. These experts weren't here for us; they were here for a paycheck. At the end of the day what happened between Evelyn and I was of minor importance.

How the experts managed to blather on when the room was filled with so much tension was beyond me. Evelyn had not looked at me since I'd taken a seat next to her, she just sat head straight, eyes on the experts, fidgeting with her necklace. The necklace I gifted her on our wedding day. I was no better, if I wasn't sneaking glances in her direction, I was tugging at the neckline of my shirt which was strangling me.

After Dr. Shawn delivered his final line, the camera panned back to Pastor Richards. "So now it's time for the all important question. Evelyn ..." The pastor paused for dramatic effect and I'm not gonna lie I wanted to slap the shit out of him. "Do you want to stay married or get divorced?"

My heart was already beating at an erratic pace. But hearing those words caused my heart to rampage behind my rib cage. It was like someone attached jumper cables to my nipples causing my heart rate to rev up. This was most likely my last chance to change her mind.

"Can I say something first?" I asked, looking around the room.

The production assistant chimed in, "Evelyn gets to speak first then you can respond to whatever she has to say after that."

I nodded my head thoughtfully. "OK, I understand

that." Turning to Evelyn I continued ignoring the directive. "I don't know how you can make a decision with all this ambiguity."

Evelyn turned to face me, the pain in her eyes was haunting. "Everything is clear to me."

"I thought the goal was to communicate and talk things through? If you'd just let me explain."

"I don't need your explanations. What could you say to change this?"

Dr. Heather leaned forward in her chair. "What's going on with you two?"

I ignored the doctor. All that mattered was Evelyn. "Listen Victoria isn't even—"

"I don't want to stay together," Evelyn blurted out. "I can't trust him. He doesn't want the same things."

Her words were like a punch to the face leaving me speechless. The room was silent all I could hear was a whirling pulse throbbing in my ears. We jumped and now I was crashing to the ground.

"Quincy?" Dr. Shawn called. "Quincy?"

"Yeah."

"Did you hear what Evelyn said?"

No Shawn I was just sitting here like a dullard, sweat beading my brow and upper lip for shits and giggles.

Looking at Evelyn I said, "That's so fucked up."

Tears fell from her tired eyes. "I thought it could work. I thought we could work but I know now that isn't possible." She wiped frantically at the tears.

I didn't know what to do. Should I beg, and plead, and fight for this? My Adam's apple bobbed as I swallowed hard trying to clear the congestion of emotion welling in my throat.

"You two seemed so happy. Can I ask what happened?" Dr. Jackie said, her faced lined with faux concern.

"We are happy." I managed to croak out.

"Sorry to break the news to you Quincy, but Evelyn doesn't look happy," Pastor Richards said.

The room was silent except for Evelyn's sniffling. Nothing was going to get solved here. The last thing I was going to do was expose my deepest darkest emotions to millions of people. This experiment was over and I was over it. I retreated to my safe place shoving all the hurt back down until all I felt was numb.

"Are we done here? Is this done?" I asked, jumping up from the couch ready to leave.

"Well Quincy we still haven't heard if you want to stay together or not." Dr. Heather's voice was calm as she tried to reason with me.

"That's kinda a moot point don't you think?" I let out a mirthless chuckle.

"No, this time is for the both of you to express how you feel and we want to give you that opportunity," Dr. Heather said.

I pushed out a long breath and in a monotone voice replied, "I wanted to stay together because I love Evelyn but obviously, she doesn't feel the same."

"I never said I didn't love you." She looked up at me with hurt eyes.

"No, but you did say you didn't trust me or believe me after spending three months getting to know me. And then this one little thing—"

"It's not little." Her eyebrows mashed together.

"This one thing. You said we needed to wake up every fucking day and choose us. I did that." My voice cracked. "And today when it counted the most you didn't choose me. And that shit fucking hurts." I jerked my shoulder upward. "I think we're done here."

Making my way to the door, I exited the room. I could hear footsteps behind me from the cameraman as I stormed off. I took hurried steps down the hall stopping in my tracks not sure what to do. Was I expected to just leave without Evelyn by my side?

Dr. Shawn came walking up and he planted a firm round of pats to my back. "Hey brother, just checking up on you. Let's talk. I wanna make sure you're OK."

"I'm great, couldn't be better." I resumed my steady, straight line, walking in one direction before turning around and walking in the opposite direction.

"That was pretty intense in there."

"Is Evelyn coming out? 'Cause I need to talk to her."

"Not really sure that's the best idea, maybe you should calm down first."

I stopped in my tracks staring Dr. Shawn square in the eyes. "I am calm. And if you think you're gonna keep me from talking to my wife you have another thing coming." No sooner had the words left my mouth when two very big security guards appeared out of nowhere. "Really Dr. Shawn?"

Yes, I lightweight threatened him but for the record Dr. Shawn was built like a wrestler. His thighs were wider than the circumference of my entire body. I had no plans to physically assault this man. I wasn't looking to be dumped and admitted to the ER on the same day.

Dr. Shawn gave me a blasé shrug. "We're not trying to get sued because you can't handle rejection."

Like I said I wasn't gonna fight this man all though I really wanted to. Evelyn finally emerged from behind closed doors and I tried to keep my voice affectless so I didn't get tackled by the linebackers *Why Knot* hired as security detail.

"Evelyn can we please talk? I just wanna talk to you. I respect that you're done but I just don't want it to end like this."

I was down bad. At this point I was just clawing to keep some semblance of her in my life. Even if it was a random text saying "Hey I hope you're doing well." I would take a sliver, a crumb, a fragment of a fragment if it meant I didn't lose her completely. Evelyn turned to face me but Dr. Shawn and his muscle blocked my way. For a second it appeared my words worked as she moved in my direction, but Jared, and his bitch ass, grabbed her arm leading her down the hall in the opposite direction all the while whispering God knows what in her ear.

I scrubbed my face letting out a disappointed groan.

"Are we gonna have a problem, Quincy?" Dr. Shawn asked.

I assessed my options, admittedly they were limited. But there is something about desperation that will make you do crazy things. *Fuck it.* I attempted to run around the security performing my best Josh Jacobs impression trying to outrun the defense. I head faked left and then took off in the other direction in my dress shoes. In the five seconds that followed I thought I did it and could see the goal line in the distance but I was sacked hard, slammed to the floor by one of the guards.

Dr. Shawn kneeled inches from my face and said in his reserved voice, "Are we gonna have a problem?"

"No," I grunted while the guard held me face down.

Chapter 25

EVELYN

The car pulled up to the home I shared with Quincy. All I remembered was being loaded into a vehicle by Jared who told me, "Everything was going to be OK," and "This was for the best." *What the hell did that even mean?* Quincy said he wanted to stay together; I heard it. Less than twenty-four hours ago that was exactly what I wanted. So how did we end up here?

The text messages Evelyn. The text messages. But Quincy said he could explain. Don't I owe him that? *You don't owe him shit. You gave him every piece of you and that wasn't enough. You need to cut your losses now before you're too far gone.* Too late. Too fucking late. I am madly in love with this man. *No, you're in love with who you thought he was but apparently that was all a lie.* Or was it?

Inside I was greeted by Totes who had been lounging on the couch but was happy to have some company. I plopped down next to him rubbing his belly. "You're such a good boy. I'm gonna miss you. Yes, I am."

I buried my face in Totes soft coat, sobbing. A heavy feeling crept through me invading every happy memory, tender moment, and loving words Quincy and I shared. The weightiness cast a gloomy haze over everything. Quincy's final words reverberated in my head *When it counted the most you didn't choose me.* Tears tracked down my cheeks. The least I could've done was given him an opportunity to explain. Not that an explanation would absolve him of accountability or afford him my forgiveness.

As Totes McGoates licked my hand in an attempt to console me, it dawned on me that Quincy probably wasn't far behind and he would be home soon. I didn't want to see him. It was best if I cleared out and stayed at Meryl's place for the remainder of the weekend. Standing, I rushed to the bedroom, intent on tossing a few things in a bag and making my great escape. In the bathroom I stopped to smell his cologne; the familiar scent of him made me choke back tears. God I'd miss this man. Replacing the cap on the bottle, I threw it into my bag.

With drawers and cabinets wide open, I tossed items into my oversized backpack, face cream, eye mask, empty box of tampons, there was no time to be choosy. I would sort through all of it later. Flinging open the shower door, I grabbed my loofah, and bottles of shampoo and conditioner. And because I was petty, I opened his body wash, pouring the contents down the drain. I felt like a burglar who was trying to grab as much valuables as she could before fleeing the scene.

I would have to figure out a way to get the rest of my stuff at a later date. Preferably while Quincy was at work so I didn't have to see the disappointment on his face. In all fairness, he wasn't the only one who was disappointed. I was just as disillusioned with the outcome of our marriage as he was. If he was even disappointed. He was probably relieved now he could be with Victoria without me ... his wife, getting in the way.

"You've gotta be shitting me right now." An all too familiar voice called from behind causing me to freeze where I stood. I was too busy listening to the voices in my head and missed the sound of the front door opening and closing.

"What are you doing here?" I asked, trying not to look guilty as I clutched my bag to my chest.

Quincy's eyes pinged around the crime scene that was now his bathroom. "I live here with you, remember?"

Shoving a bottle of chewy vitamins in my backpack I said, "I'll be out of your hair in a few minutes."

"Evelyn? What the fuck?" His eyes were a bit dazed, like he didn't know who he was or how he'd ended up here. *Welcome to the club.* "You embarrassed me back there. Talking about how you can't trust me. And saying, you don't wanna stay together. Since when?"

"That's just how I feel." I tightened my jaw to keep my chin from trembling.

"Bullshit. As far as I'm concerned that shit you said earlier don't fucking count." Quincy removed his suit jacket tossing it onto the bed. "So ... do you wanna ... go get some Mexican or Sushi cause I'm starving."

I released a mirthless laugh. "See, this is part of the problem. You're dismissive and you never take anything seriously."

"I'm not dismissive. I just don't believe a word you said back there. So, if you really don't wanna be with me, you need to say it to my face with your full fucking chest ... right now."

We both knew I couldn't say that so I pivoted to the crux of our issues.

"Why were you texting Victoria?"

"OK, first off *she* was texting me."

"Don't do that."

"What?" He crumpled his face in the way he did when he was annoyed.

"Don't turn this into some joke." I dropped my back-pack on the bedroom floor. I'd just asked him a legitimate question and it deserved a real answer. We were in this situa-tion right now because of those stupid messages. I wasn't a jealous woman but I wasn't gullible either and I didn't like being played. And right now, it felt like Quincy had me confused with a wind instrument. "You begged me to listen to you back at the hotel and now you don't have shit of value to say?"

"OK, wait." He reached for my arm but stopped short instead scratching the back of his neck. "The text messages between Victoria and me are nothing. I am not looking to get back with Victoria. When I said I was over her I meant it. She texted me first. And you are one hundred percent right I should have shut that shit down from the gate."

"Then why didn't you?"

Quincy rolled his broad shoulders shifting his weight from one foot to the other. "Because I'm stupid. That really is the only explanation. I'm married to this amazing woman and once Victoria texted me, I should have blocked and deleted her number. She was never my friend and there is nothing salvageable there."

He retrieved his phone from his pocket and opened up his messages. Turning the screen so I could witness it, he blocked Victoria, deleting her number from his phone.

He stopped before deleting the text message thread between them. "Do you wanna look through this one more time? I can send it to your phone. I just want you to be completely comfortable that the conversation, while inappropriate, was totally innocuous. I didn't make any promises. I never told her I loved her back. That shit was one sided. I did not in any way return her feelings. We never talked on the phone. It was only these messages."

My eyes scanned his phone screen before resting on his face and sizing him up. He seemed sincere or was that just the part inside of me desperately wanting to believe him. Quincy had been nothing but supportive of me these past few months. He gifted me a studio space, put up with my annoying brother and even managed to get my mother to come to one of my shows. If that wasn't love, what was?

"You can delete them," I said, allowing my shoulders and neck to relax a bit. Honestly, those text didn't matter. What mattered were Quincy's next words.

Quincy complied before tossing his phone on the bed. "Evelyn, I love you. I love you deep. My love for you is woven into my DNA. If someone tested my blood right now, they would know I'm A positive and that I love Evelyn Townsend. I've never felt this way about anybody. Honestly, I've never wanted to, but you make me happy and you feel like home to me. And that's something I've only found in one other person, my foster mom. Fucking this up ... us up ... is the last thing I'd ever want to do.

"I don't think you understand, I've purchased stock in

Evelyn Co. that's how much I believe in you and trust you. I'm a majority shareholder because I know investing in you is a no brainer. Investing my hopes, and dreams for the future. Having our kids loved and nurtured by you. How you whisper sweet affirmations in my ear telling me I can do anything and that I'm your everything. You're a sure bet. I'm not scared to share all of myself with you because I know it'll be returned ten times over. I'm fucking crazy about you, Evie. I thought it was kinda obvious the minute you walked down the aisle."

"I really don't know what to think at this point," I said, fidgeting with the skin between my thumb and forefinger.

My chest tingled as my heart thawed. When he said he loved me I wanted to accept it at face value no further questions asked. It was in my nature to forgive. In past relationships, platonic and romantic, I'd ignored glaring red flags in the hopes that things could be salvaged. I was slowly coming to the realization that not everything could be fixed and not everyone deserved a second chance.

Quincy moved closer, his tone taking on the quality of an urgent plea. "What do you need me to do. I'll do anything. Because I cannot lose you. I can't live without you. I don't want to. With you everything makes sense. The air is crisper, the sky is bluer, the warmth of the sun is more intense. It has only been you since the minute I laid eyes on you." He scrubbed his sullen face. "I know I fucked up but please don't leave me. I don't wanna go back to life without you.

"I've spent most of my life really fucking scared. And I don't have many close relationships because I push people away. I always find a way to isolate myself from others. The only reason Walt and I are still friends is because he called me on my bullshit every time."

Quincy fell silent. Tipping his head to the ceiling, he closed his eyes. His chest swelled and his voice quivered around his next words. "Normally in this situation I'd just let you go. Because I don't really believe I deserve to be happy and I'm terrified of hurting you. Maybe ... maybe it's better ... that you leave. Because I just want you to be happy. And if you can't find ... that happiness with me then you deserve to find it with someone else ..." He trailed off, his tone fragile as he tried to fight back the tears pooling on his bottom lids. "I want you to know ... I tried ... I really tried."

My throat was tight as I swallowed back unshed tears. "Quincy, I've never wanted anything or anyone more than I want to be with you. I wish you could see how amazing you are and how much the people around you love and care about you. Baby, you are deserving of love, and joy, and the richness this life has to offer. The way you've shown me devotion in the three short months I've known you is beyond measure.

"When I saw the messages, I got scared because I can't imagine a future without you. I want all of my memories to include you in them. On our honeymoon you said you wanted to try to make this work. And every day since I've done just that. I fucked up. I was frightened and I should have come to you so we could talk it through. But I'm not afraid anymore. I choose you." I cupped his face in my hands. "Do you hear me. I choose you, today and every day. Because I love you, Quincy. Not because of what you have, or what you do for me ... but because of who you are." I pressed my hand to his chest. The predictable beating of his heart grounded me keeping me tethered to him.

Tears rolled down his face as my words sunk in. "I'm sorry," he whispered, while planting kisses across my face. "I'm so sorry."

My bottom lip sagged. "I totally ruined decision day." I sniffled a sob.

"You kind of did, but this is better. Because this isn't about anyone else but you and me. No cameras, no millions of viewers. The matchmakers were right, putting us together but all that other shit we did. We fought for this and we trusted each other."

"Most of the time." I corrected him.

"When it counted the most."

Quincy traced the outline of my face with the pad of his index finger, his gentle touch ran over my eyebrows and down my cheek, finally resting on my chin. His caress was electric, giving my fragile heart a much-needed spark. Quincy pulled me against him and our lips instantly found one another. Parting my mouth, my eyes flutter closed as I flung my arms around his neck. Heat rolled to a boil in my stomach causing my insides to feel all warm and fuzzy like I'd taken several sips of spiked hot chocolate. Just a few moments before I seriously intended to walk away from this man. I knew now just how foolish that thought was.

"I love you, Evelyn Townsend."

"Townsend Parrish," I said, once I finally caught my breath.

"What?" he whispered against my lips.

"It's Evelyn Townsend Parrish and I love you too."

Epilogue

Evelyn

Quincy turned onto Michigan Avenue pulling up to the Langham Hotel, the place where we'd met and married a year ago today.

"So this was the big surprise?" I asked. Quincy had been planning something for our one-year anniversary but it was top secret and he wouldn't share any details. He'd even gotten Evan to keep his lips sealed which was unheard of. I was always able to get Evan to tell me things he had sworn others he wouldn't. I could only assume that Quincy had threatened Evan with severe bodily harm if he told me anything.

"I thought we could return to the scene of the crime."

I raised my eyebrow. "Oh yeah, what crime was that?"

"This was the place where you stole my heart," Quincy said, with a semi-straight face.

"I'm a masterful thief. Fleeing the scene before you even know anything is gone." I joked.

Climbing out of the car, Quincy made his way to the

passenger side, opening my door. I exited the car reposi-tioning the hem of my form-fitting dress. Meryl had helped me pick out the perfect dress for the occasion. I wanted something that would remind Quincy that he was married to a baddie. Domestic bliss also meant getting real. And truth be told he saw me in paint-stained overalls and a head-scarf more than high heels and cleavage-baring outfits. But I made a special effort for tonight and Quincy's wandering hands on the drive over here let me know it was appreciated.

Grabbing my husband's hand, I allowed him to lead me into the hotel. I was transported to this time last year when I walked through these same doors a bundle of nerves but hopeful that I was at the start of my fairy tale. I smirked to myself at how naïve I was just a year ago. Love isn't a fairy tale, it's work and intention but if you want it you have to be willing to roll up your sleeves and put in the emotional labor. Luckily Quincy made my work a joy. I loved this man with my whole being. Not to say that he didn't work my last nerve on occasion but it was all worth it because I got to do this thing called life with him.

"Where are you taking me?"

"Would you relax? All will be revealed in due time."

I pointed toward the opposite direction. "But the restau-rant's that way."

"Who said we were going to the restaurant?" Quincy gently pulled me into an empty elevator pressing the top floor.

I flashed him a naughty smirk. When the doors closed, I leaned close. "What exactly do you have in mind?" My hands moved from his chest and landed on part of his anatomy I was very familiar with.

"Evelyn please don't start. You already made us late getting here because you had the same look you have now back at the house."Quincy warned but he didn't move my hand.

"That wasn't me. I just kissed you; you did all the rest." I was so close that when I blinked my long lashes brushed against his face. Quincy bowed his head planting kisses on my bare shoulder before placing a courtesy kiss on my cheek that let me know that he wasn't gonna take me in the elevator of the Langham Hotel.

The elevator binged, signifying we'd reached our floor. Before the doors opened Quincy said, "I love you."

As the doors slid apart a boisterous "Surprise," rang out into the air.

The yelling caused my heart to jump before my brain processed what was happening. Quincy escorted me off the elevator into a dimly lit room filled with our friends and family.

"Oh my God," I said, breathlessly. Scanning the room, I spotted familiar faces all dressed up with huge smiles. I turned to Quincy in disbelief. "You planned this?"

Quincy gave me a proud smile. "I had a lot of help."

Erica, my baby sister approached first, flinging her arms around me. "Happy anniversary."

Erica was followed by others coming up to hug and congratulate us. I felt a bit overwhelmed by all the love. I'd been emotional all day and being surrounded by the people I loved most in the world was making it difficult to hold it together.

"You were surprised, weren't you?" Meryl asked.

"I had no clue."

"Quincy was so worried you'd figure it out. I told him he could leave a guest list and party plans out on the table and you would see them and never put it together. You are the worst when it comes to figuring things out."

"Gee, thanks." I frowned.

"You know what I mean."

As we moved deeper into the party, Evan appeared with drinks in hand. "Hey Big Bro, this worked out great. She never suspected a thing." Evan handed both Quincy and I a purple-colored mixed drink that I knew was going to be way too strong.

"This was a good surprise." I smiled.

"I helped." Evan informed me like he was a five-year-old child.

"Thank you for helping Quincy pull this off." I set my glass down giving him a tight hug.

My parents were seated at a table with Naomi. When we approached my mother jumped up, giving Quincy and me a hug. Yes, hell had indeed frozen over. I think my mother was more in love with Quincy than I was. OK, that was impossible but he was high on her list. This past year she and I managed to find common ground. We didn't always agree and we weren't always nice to one another but we were trying and that was all I could ask for.

Even after a year Quincy was still surprising me. He claimed he was bad at love but it wasn't true. I'd never felt more loved and adored since marrying him. I asked him to choose me so many months ago and he had followed through. Every day, loving me with intention and care. Love was unpredictable and scary but with Quincy by my side the journey was less frightful.

QUINCY

Life was funny, no matter how much you planned, it was still going to do what it wanted. Fuck you, and your little plans. Life was going to move at its own pace and drop opportunities and people in your lap when you least expected it. I wasn't ready to fall in love with Evelyn but from the minute we exchanged bashful smiles at the altar, I knew I needed to level up. Fortunately, Evelyn was willing to embrace my imperfections instead of viewing them as character defects.

Falling in love with Evelyn was the most unexpected surprise and having her around had made my mundane life worth living out loud. With Evelyn I'd finally taken off the training wheels. I'd always been so afraid of failing or becoming like my father that I never allowed myself to fly because I assumed that the only outcome would be crashing to the ground. But Evelyn was a pro at flying because she never hesitated before the big leap.

"I cannot believe that we are celebrating your one-year anniversary," Walt said.

"Shit, I'm just as surprised as you."

"Look I'm proud of you and Evelyn you make a good match. And millions of people feel the same way."

I cringed.

Our season of *Why Knot* aired in the summer and I tried to avoid the show altogether but my curiosity got the better of me and I took to social media. To my surprise there were millions of people who were team Evelyn and Quincy.

People were rooting for us and hoping we went the distance. And those people were devastated when Evelyn chose not to stay together. Some people blamed me others blamed her but everyone agreed it was a mistake. So at the reunion special, which I tried to get out of attending even though we were contractually obligated, viewers were overjoyed to learn that we'd never broken up.

The show was over but there were still times when people recognized us or asked for my picture like I was a celebrity. It was awkward but I learned that smiling and engaging in a few minutes of chit chat was easier than fighting the impact of the show. Plus, I couldn't be too mad at *Why Knot* because it led me to the love of my life, the future mother of my children, and the best spades player I'd ever been partnered with.

We also gained two new friends in Jace and Michelle. The four of us hung out often bonding over our shared experience. Letting people in was something Evelyn was teaching me. I kept my circle small but it was slowly expanding with the help of my wife. Truthfully, I kind of liked it. We'd lost touch with Elliot and Sarah. The last I heard they were divorcing after initially deciding to stay together on decision day.

I searched the room and found Evelyn where I could typically find her, on the dance floor. Making my way through the crowd where family and friends were cutting a rug, I playfully pushed Evan aside before scooping my wife in my arms.

"Rude. But I'ma let it slide because it's y'alls anniversary," Evan said stalking off.

With Evelyn in my arms smiling up at me all was right

with the world. Her smile did me in every time. And her soft hands that were now rubbing the back of my neck still sent shockwaves down my spine.

Evelyn asked, "So tell me this. Do you have any regrets?"

"The only thing I regret is not meeting you sooner."

"Well you have the rest of our lives to make it up to me." She playfully teased.

"Sounds like a deal." I agreed, sealing it with a kiss.

Thank You. Let's Connect.

Thank you so much for reading Sight Unseen. If you liked the book, please help a sister out and leave a review or tell a friend. Your feedback is important to me and will help other readers decide whether to read my book too.

Feel free to connect with me virtually. I would love to engage with you.

 tiktok.com/@authorkashathompson

 instagram.com/authorkashathompson

 twitter.com/thomkat29

ALSO BY KASHA THOMPSON